Praise for Lilith Saintcrow...

"Darkly compelling, fascinatingly unique. Lilith Saintcrow offers a breathtaking, fantastic ride."

—*NYT bestselling author Gena Showalter*

The Ghost Squad Series

"It has been a long time since I read a book that I was so invested in that I had to force myself to put it down to go to sleep. *Duty* was *such a* good read."

—*Faye, Goodreads reviewer on* <u>Duty</u>

"Short, sharp, FUN. I don't have much to say on this one except I enjoyed it a lot, and look forward to seeing more in this series."

—*Strix, Goodreads Reviewer on* <u>Damage</u>

Sons of Ymre

"Lilith Saintcrow is a master at world building. And her imagination is endless. I can't wait to see what's next."

—*Cheryl B, NetGalley reviewer on Sons of Ymre: Erik*

"From cover to cover, I could not put this book down. So happy to be reading a new and exciting fast paced series from Lillith Saintcrow."

—*Neal Bravin, NetGalley reviewer on* <u>Sons of Ymre: Erik</u>

"In the *Watchers* series, Saintcrow writes stories that are almost always nonstop action from beginning to end. Her women are kick-ass strong, her men ruggedly handsome and dedicated to the women they serve. It isn't a bad combination at all."

—*CJReading*

"I read *Dark Watcher* with growing delight. As chapter followed chapter, I never quite knew what was around the corner."

—*Ebook Reviews*

Books by Lilith Saintcrow

The Watchers

Dark Watcher

Storm Watcher

Fire Watcher

Cloud Watcher

Mindhealer

Finder

The Sons of Ymre

The Sons of Ymre: Erik

The Sons of Ymre: Jake

Ghost Squad

Damage

Duty

Gamble

The Society Series

The Society

Hunter-Healer

Other

The Demon's Librarian

Gamble

Ghost Squad – Book 3

by

Lilith Saintcrow

ImaJinn Books

This is a work of fiction. Names, characters, places and incidents are either the products of the author's imagination or are used fictitiously. Any resemblance to actual persons (living or dead), events or locations is entirely coincidental.

IMAJINN

ImaJinn Books
PO BOX 300921
Memphis, TN 38130
Print ISBN: 978-1-61026-2699

ImaJinn Books is an Imprint of BelleBooks, Inc.

ImaJinn Books was founded by Linda Kichline.

We at ImaJinn Books enjoy hearing from readers. Visit our websites
ImaJinnBooks.com
BelleBooks.com
BellBridgeBooks.com

10 9 8 7 6 5 4 3 2 1

Cover design: Debra Dixon
Interior design: Hank Smith
Photo/Art credits:
Cityscape (manipulated) © Roza | Dreamstime.com
Man (manipulated) © Singaporevideo | Dreamstime.com

:Lghy:01:

Dedication

For my grandfather, a true hero

"Stuck in the Middle With You"
—Stealers Wheel

A Good Place

THE DESERT could be a good place to die.

It wouldn't take much, Tax knew. Dehydration was the number-one contender, growing especially uncomfortable after the hallucinations began. There was third-degree sunburn, but that was chancy. Scorpions and rattlers were distinct possibilities, but provoking them harder to accomplish than it sounded. Given a choice, most critters wanted nothing to do with humanity, and he couldn't blame them.

He could hop off the hood of his SUV and strike out from the rest stop, walking into the dry waste like a sage keeping an appointment with God. A few days in the heat would do it handily—but only if he made no move to save himself when the thirst got to psychosis-inducing levels. And while any member of the Squad was used to ignoring the body's cries for things like food, sleep, or a cessation of brain-numbing fear, Tax wasn't sure he could hold out long enough to get the job done right.

Of course he could just take some of the emergency meds and bow out that way. Poisoning could be relatively gentle, if done correctly. If he didn't care about traumatizing whoever found him, there was more than one weapon available for a quick exit as well.

All it took was a few seconds' worth of willpower.

Still . . . he was expected at Boom's house within a reasonable time-frame. If he was even a few hours late without radio contact his buddy might get nervous, and there would go Tax's smooth shuffle offstage. Plus his mother might have to identify him, and she was getting older. No good son—the kind Mom thought he was—caused his parents that kind of grief.

That was part of the problem, wasn't it? Keeping up the façade was getting goddamn exhausting.

Heavy, colorless sunshine beat down on fraying pavement. The truckers liked this rest stop for naps, to judge by the double rows of shining big rigs in the other lot; this one saw RVs and a smattering of smaller vehicles. He could memorize plate numbers if he wanted to, or get out the gear and make everyone's day a whole lot worse.

They called it *collateral damage* unless you aimed at someone the government wanted alive to pay taxes. Then other terms applied.

Making law enforcement chase him into the desert might be fun, but even John Rambo had a legitimate grievance and Tax didn't, not really. Nightmares, panic attacks, and gruesome stereo-surround flashbacks simply meant he was a cracked plate, a dud bullet, a seized engine.

Not to mention meeting his end in a hail of cop gunfire would be fucking *embarrassing*; the guys would never let him live it down. Assuming they all ended up in hell together, which was very likely and at least he'd have company eventually.

Also assuming the roast beef sandwich he'd bought at the last gas station wasn't full of something bacterial capable of finishing him off. Another embarrassing end, and wouldn't they laugh about that when they got together down below?

Mouthful of food—anemic cheese, wilted lettuce, overprocessed animal protein. Then a hit of tooth-rotting sweet soda, which would dehydrate a traveler more as the mercury climbed and any humidity retreated.

At least it wasn't a diet drink, and the caffeine would keep him awake.

He had to force himself to chew the regulation number of times instead of just tossing the entire thing down the hatch. In the field you ate with silent efficiency, fueling the body so you could evict other poor motherfuckers from theirs. Out here, there were things like manners. Expectations. Civilization, they called it, which just meant the blood, shit, guts, and screams were kept under the rug.

That was a bad thought; they were far more frequent and intrusive lately. Tax hunched even further, the heat like oil against his T-shirt, desert wind ruffling his lengthening hair. He should've been able to smell sagebrush and sand, but all his nose caught was car exhaust and whatever kind of almost-expired onion they put on the damn sandwich.

There was a pleasing simplicity to the view, though. Mountains in the far distance, purple streaks above veils of heat-shimmer. Flats and foothills tawny and olive, slight hills and depressions everywhere despite the illusion of ruler-level sand, spikes of yucca and the dry tortured shapes of small scrub—he'd even seen a tumbleweed earlier, hopping right across the highway as if ol' Wile E. and the meep-meeping Roadrunner were about to show up any moment.

Think about something better. Well, Tax had been useful while stopping off in Oregon to see Klemp. Of course no member of the Squad *needed* backup, perish the thought, but it was always nice to have. And it was good to feel like he'd accomplished what Mom called *some merit*. Klemp wasn't even razzing him about getting his car stolen by a civilian.

Well, not much, anyway.

A vulture sailed high above, turning in lazy circles while scanning for anything snackable. If Tax headed out into the shimmer and dust, he'd have to contend with the birds giving his position away before long. They had a finely tuned sense for when a landlubber below was going to become an entrée, and maybe this one could sense what he was thinking.

"Not today," he muttered into his sandwich, and shifted uneasily. Sitting inside the air-conditioned cave of his car was preferable, but there was only so much of that a man could take while driving all day. At least it was still early in spring; the real heat would come later.

This stop was in a dead zone, too. No bars on his phone; for a few minutes he was blessedly out of pocket. The desert looked good.

Very inviting.

Well, it had been around for thousands of years, it could wait another few weeks. He could see Boom settled, make sure the rest of his squadmates were doing fine. One last checkup, stowing everything neat and tidy the way the Army liked. A fellow got used to order and regimentation after a while; for a high-achieving kid from a military family it was even comforting.

But Mom. How are you going to arrange that? A good son was supposed to hold on for his clan, especially for parents. Doing otherwise was cowardice.

Then again, Tax was just the medic. The rest of the Squad were happy enough causing mayhem; Tax was simply the motherfucker dumb enough to carry around the first-aid kit. Everyone had their little specialty—Dez thought ahead, Klemp told the jokes and got them moving, Boom brought the bang, Grey kept them in contact with each other and the mothership, Jackson was the wildcard.

Arthur Tachmann was simply along for the ride, fucking fatigued from all the spinning and jolting. The holy Army thought his little habit of playing with numbers meant he could keep track of dosages and medical procedure better, so he'd received the training and the losing battle of attempting to keep people alive. *Suck it up and do your job*, that was the name of the game.

He was almost done playing.

The sandwich was finished. He stretched, taking a last long swallow of yellow-green soda. It tasted awful, even if all he cared about was the caffeine.

He looked up, squinting against the glare. Yeah, the vulture was still wheeling in lazy circles, floating unconcerned on thermals and waiting for the next bit of entropy to hit the world.

"Soon, buddy." His own voice surprised him—soft and low, as if they were out on mission and the word only needed to carry from one man to the next. Jungle, tundra, forest, beach, or desert like this, it made no difference. Everything in the damn world was like everything else, and all he had to do was find a handy exit.

Brooding wouldn't accomplish anything. If he pushed, he could be in Vegas tonight and he'd be so busy keeping Boom's pre-wedding nerves corralled he wouldn't have time to sit and stew.

He slid off the hood, landing with a jolt. The mica-starred pavement was simmering, but at least he hadn't burned his ass sitting on scorching metal; he whisked the towel away, draped it over his arm like a maître d', and wondered why it mattered.

Why anything mattered.

It was only habit, he decided. Routine could keep a guy going long after he lost any will to actually live, but even that guardrail crumbled after a while.

He crushed the plastic soda bottle with a sudden, nearly convulsive movement, and stretched again before climbing back in the car.

Festivities

MEG CALLAHAN always preferred to greet the dawn after an all-nighter instead of dragging herself out of bed for the occasion, but adulthood wasn't about preferences. You were lucky if you could squeeze a few nice things in around the edges, but mostly the whole shebang consisted of doing solely what you had to.

It sucked. Still, dragging herself vertical before sunup was better than orphanage, juvie, or any other childhood peril. She was all grown up now, and glad of the fact.

Consequently she kept the music low and took the corners at far, far less than smoking-rubber speed; she cut her headlights before rolling up the driveway's slight hill and stopping soft as a whisper. She even closed the convertible's door quietly instead of with a cheerful bang, though that might've been because it was *her* car, not some teenager's junker.

All fun and games, Eddie always said, *until you're the one paying for dinner.*

The cute little stucco's property value had kept going up, and the rest of the neighborhood followed suit. Meg blew a kiss at the camera attached to the floodlight above the garage—Carl was a big one for security gadgets—and took a deep breath freighted with the smell of mineral-tinged hose water. A few sprinklers were chugging, keeping postage-stamp yards green, but like the more reasonable occupants of this neon-lit valley, the boys had opted for a rock garden with native succulents.

They'd also gone for a small swimming pool in the backyard. *Keeping the hypocrisy behind a fence,* Eddie said, and even though Meg sort of agreed, she still brought her bathing suit over on the regular.

The gate in the fence to the right of the garage had squeaky hinges, but she knew how to ease it open without too much racket. At least the walk along the side of the house wasn't gravel; if she turned an ankle in these heels the result would be supremely inglorious.

There was only a smudge of grey in the east, but the breeze was already full of promise. It would be another beautiful day in good ol'

Lost Wages, and she had plenty to do.

Moving tiptoe in heels while carrying a grocery bag or two was a skill, but she had practice. Letting herself in through the kitchen door was performed as quietly as possible, and she didn't bother turning the lights on yet.

Even in the dimness she could see the clutter; it was hard work finding an empty spot on the counter for her just-purchased supplies. Looked like they'd really tied one on last night, because Eddie wouldn't let the dishes pile up if he could help it.

He'd always been the tidy sort, even before going into the service.

She padded through the dining room and down two carpeted steps into the living, finding her way to the stereo by touch and the slight glow from her phone screen. The stereo's Bluetooth remembered said phone— she'd been the one to show Carl how to set it up, after all—and she spent a few moments thumbing through to find the right playlist.

Oh, yeah. This is gonna be good. Meg checked her timing, hit 'play' before hitting 'connect,' and was in the kitchen again by the time the beat dropped. Marvin Gaye started singing about giving it up, the bass thumping, and though the immediate neighbors might hear a distant rumble they wouldn't complain, since nobody slept with their windows open in this part of town.

She finally flicked the kitchen lights on, blinking owlishly, and stopped short.

The guy near the breakfast bar froze. He wasn't Eddie, and he definitely wasn't Carl. For one thing, he was too tall, too lean, and packed with wiry muscle visible because he was in a tank top and faded camouflage bottoms. A wild thatch of straight black hair stuck up anyhow; he had his right hand behind his back and glared at her as if she'd somehow wandered into the wrong house.

Meg blurted out a squeaky, "Oh, *shit*," lost in the music, and nearly dropped her phone. For a few moments she and the stranger simply stared at each other, and if it hadn't been for the fact that the kitchen was so familiar—she knew where everything was because she'd helped unpack, not to mention dragged Carl to home goods stores for *months*— she might have turned around and ducked back into the hall to reassess the situation.

Now all the cups and dishes stacked in the sink and on the tiled countertop made sense. So did the half-empty blender smelling powerfully of margarita mix, and the half-finished pan of chiles rellenos on the stove.

The boys had hosted a get-together, and this was clearly a refugee from the festivities. "Hey," she called over the music, and lifted her hands, still gripping her phone. "Friendly, okay? Hi."

No reaction. He just stared at her, coal-dark eyes over a proud nose and good cheekbones. He'd have to bulk up if he wanted to do any stage work, but he could probably get some catalog-modeling spots. His lips were compressed, almost bloodless, and his feet were bare.

"Fuuuuuck." A shadow in the hallway turned into a familiar shape, big bear-shouldered Carl scrubbing at his blond head with both palms. He was unshaven, bloodshot, and leaned against the archway's side as he peered into the now brightly lit kitchen. "What the—oh, Meg. God *damn* it, I just got to sleep."

"I can tell." She grinned, turning away from the new arrival—he didn't look happy to be dragged into consciousness by the prince of Motown—and slipping her phone back into her purse. They were locked into her playlist for the morning, and if she knew Eddie, he was going to bitch about it the entire time. "You dumbasses have tuxedo fittings today, but you were up all night with tequila and cheese."

"Not my fault. Eddie's Army buddy just got in yesterday and—" Carl's gaze swung back to where the stranger had been standing, and Meg couldn't help her own double-take.

The new guy was gone, vanished between one beat and the next. Of course the stairs to the apartment over the garage were that way, so he'd probably decided discretion was the better part of valor.

She didn't blame him, especially after a night spent drinking with Ed. "Cute. I like the hair."

"I think he bats for the away team, so have fun." Carl's hearing had clearly adjusted to the throb from the living room speakers. "You gonna make that hangover cure?"

"Coffee first," she chirped back. "Go get cleaned up and roust Eddie, or I'll start playing some death metal."

He knew she would, too.

"Bitch," he said, affectionately, and shuffled back into the hall. Meg shook her head, rolling her sleeves up—this peach linen suit was a good one, she didn't want it splattered—and headed for the coffeemaker.

THIS PARTICULAR playlist was soul-heavy. By the time Aretha was singing about how a man had better think about what he was tryin' to do to her, Meg had Carl's apron on and the bacon in the oven, the coffeemaker was done brewing sludge just the way Eddie liked it, the dishwasher was humming, the pancake batter was standing ready next to the electric griddle, and she was just putting finishing touches on Callahan's Special Hangover Cure, the freshly washed blender whirring as she eyed it critically.

The music's volume fell sharply, meaning Eddie was now downstairs and presumably in a ferocious temper. She was ready when her childhood bestie stamped through the arch from the dining room, glowering hotly from under shower-damp curls. At least he was shaven and his hair was growing out from buzzcut-and-wax.

More than that, though, the marks of sleepless anxiety had vanished from under his hazel eyes, and while he did give the kitchen a once-over plus a glance at the back door, he didn't look guiltily away when she met his gaze.

Progress was being made. She didn't want to drag Ed to therapy at the VA, even if Carl would help.

"Coffee," he growled. It wasn't a question, he could damn well smell it. "Goddammit."

"Talk like that won't get you a dose of Callahan's Cure." She hit the pulse button again and laughed when he flinched at the blender's growl.

"Christ." He drew out the word, a sure sign of defeat, and reeled for the cabinet holding coffee mugs. "Ain't my fault. My buddy from Cali made it in last night, we had to be horse-pitable."

"And now you'll be all bloated for your tux fitting." She pulsed the blender once more, chuckling again when his shoulders hunched. "Shame, shame."

"I could throw you in the pool."

"Then I'd have to raise my rates." Meg decided she'd made her point and got the blender carafe free. The slurry inside was vile greenish, semiliquid, cold, and a closely guarded trade secret; she had three sparkling-clean glasses standing ready. "You're getting a bargain, and don't forget it."

"We're in Vegas, I don't know why we don't just elope." Eddie scratched under his violently cheerful pink and neon green Hawaiian shirt—he'd loved wearing them ever since stealing one from that awful tightass guard in juvie, lo these many years ago. His calves were hairy and exceedingly muscled; the cargo shorts were a crime against fashion but thankfully not comfort.

She pointed at him sternly, and did her best Granny Goose impression from their orphanage days. "I won't hear of it, young man!" *Neither will Carl, frankly. Or his mom.*

"Yeah, yeah." Ed blew across the top of his favorite Teamsters Union mug, clearly wishing the lifegiving caffeine it contained wasn't near-boiling. "So in exchange for the cure, I'm gonna perform a magic trick."

Oh, no, not another trick your buddy taught you in some foreign country. Meg groaned, then had to focus on pouring so each glass received equal amounts. It would be nice to kick her shoes off and feel cold tile against her soles, but if her feet swelled she would have to wear something other than heels today.

She needed all the height she could get; topping out at five-three did not inspire a great deal of respect in most situations.

"No, no," Eddie insisted. With his button nose and baby cheeks, he would probably look boyish until his dying day. "You'll like this one. Remember you were telling me your accountant got, you know . . ."

"Indicted." That was the proper term, and now she needed a new number-cruncher. It was small comfort that the majority of Davy's clients were in the clear—at least, the DA and the cops agreed Meg was, and that was good enough for her. "Thank you ever so much for reminding me."

"Well, now, watch me abracadabra. See, my buddy—hey, Tax."

Meg straightened. The new arrival was back again, this time lingering in the archway leading to the garage and its overhead apartment. He'd thrown a button-up over the tank top and stepped into a pair of loosely laced military boots, which meant he could've been almost local. He was just as bloodshot and scruffy as Carl, too.

All in all, he looked like he was having a simply terrible morning.

Well, she could be nice, since she'd probably shaken him and his hangover out of a nice warm bed. "We've met," she said, airily. "And since it's the first time, I'll give him a cure on the house."

Small Mercies

OF ALL THE things he'd expected to find in Boom's kitchen, a long-legged fairy—a sprite his mother would call a yojeong—with a stacked bob dyed pink at the ends, platinum up-top, plus a peach linen suit both expensive *and* deftly ironed, was not even on the list. She was also nearly lost in Carl's teal *Kiss the Cook* apron, the waist-ties wrapped at least twice around her middle.

Tax had surfaced from hazy still-drunk approximate sleep, laden with uneasy hallucination-dreams full of echoing long-ago screams and blood, to hear stealthy movement and grabbed for the 9mm on the nightstand, creeping downstairs in what had to be a fugue state. He'd almost put a couple rounds into the girl, which was bad. It could even be taken for a sign of combat fatigue, one he'd be ethically bound to report if seen in a buddy.

Fortunately she hadn't noticed, or she probably wouldn't have thrust a glass containing some kind of smoothie and a heavy, washable plastic straw at him.

"Callahan's Patented," she said, brightly. Her lips were peach-glossed too, and smoky eyeliner made a pair of big baby blues even bigger and *more* blue, if that were possible. A pair of silver hoop earrings, seven thread-thin bangles on her left wrist, and a silver nose-ring completed the picture. Her perfume wasn't light or floral. Instead, musk and vanilla mixed, blending with the heavenly smell of coffee that stood a good chance of being strong enough to bother with. "You drink all that, and you'll be ready for the day no matter how much booze you bathed in last night. Bottoms up, baby."

"And devil fu—ah, take the hindmost." Boom grinned from near the coffeemaker, but he also winced when the music changed. Someone started wailing about a sugar-pie-honey-bunch, and Tax had the feeling he'd slipped through some kind of crack in the universe's floor into a *Star Trek* mirror dimension. "Meg, this is my buddy Arthur Tachmann. Tax, this is Miss Callahan, and mind your manners."

Tax had to accept the glass or let it drop and shatter. His throat was dry as the sagebrush hills; the woman had no idea how close she'd come to being ventilated. Civilians, always oblivious. "Thank you, ma'am."

"Oh, my God, it's not even seven in the a.m., and I've been *ma'am'd*." She rolled her eyes, but that megawatt smile didn't diminish. "Drink up, and thank God you're here. Look at what I have to work with—they have tux fittings today, and both of them are going to be all bloated and complain."

Fittings? Oh, for the wedding. Okay. Tax got the idea this lady didn't slow down for anything. "Still can't believe Boom's getting married, the way he snores."

There was gravel caught in his voice and he was sure he looked like he'd just been rolled out of a tequila-soaked grave, but she laughed like he'd made the witticism of the year and swung away.

"*Boom*," she said, and the sarcasm in it was deep and affectionate. "That's not what they called him in high school. Make your offer, Eddie. The cure isn't getting any fresher."

"I was about to tell you." Boom slurped at his mug and made a face. "Behold your new assistant, Meggers."

She turned again, light on the forefoot like a dancer, and gave Tax a critical once-over he was deeply ashamed to meet. "I don't know," she said, as the music shifted yet again. "Can he math?"

What kind of math do you want? If he'd been Klemp or Grey he might have said it, with something approaching a wink even. Both of them knew how to talk to women, or at least they gave a good impression of it.

Even the ol' Lieutenant had apparently managed something in that direction, though Tax would have put good money on their leader being married to the service instead of a flesh-and-blood lady. Klemp said the boss's intended was *a real doll*, just like Footy Lenz would have put it.

Don't think about that. Lenz's blood-spattered face, head lolling; Dez's voice, heavy with finality. *He's gone, Tax. Stop.*

"Can he . . . Jesus Christ, Meg, the guy's a medic." It would be impossible for Boom's grin to get any wider. "Plus, he likes numbers."

Don't help me out here, man. Tax almost winced.

"That could be dangerous in this town." She cocked her head, pink-dyed tips brushing her slim linen-clad shoulder. "You're not gonna go counting cards, are you?"

"No ma'am." Although if he got truly desperate for a way out, provoking some casino security into a bad situation might work. Tax watched, bemused and with his temples throbbing, as this Meg—she had to be Boom's childhood buddy, the one he was constantly talking about getting into trouble with—finished her appraisal.

"That makes twice today I've been *ma'am*'d," she said, heading back for the kitchen island, those peach-gloss lips smiling right along. Genuine amusement sparkled in those baby blues, and god*damn* his head hurt.

He fumbled for the straw and took an experimental sip. Tequila hangovers were never pleasant, but at least he wasn't vomiting.

Small mercies.

Now a woman with a whiskey-rough voice was crooning from the living room stereo about how if you ever needed her, she'd be around. The liquid was cold and vaguely minty. It didn't seem to upset his stomach more, so he took another hit. What the hell was in the stuff? Boom didn't look gleeful and fidgety like he would if his suggestion was some kind of prank. And the pink-haired fairy's expression was downright encouraging.

"So he can be your assistant for a while." Boom shuffled away from the coffeepot, his mug in one hand and the other pleadingly outstretched toward the two glasses full of green slop next to the blender. "He's housebroken and knows how to follow orders."

"Faint praise," Tax mumbled into his drink, and took a longer pull from the straw. No, it wasn't bad at all. But he still couldn't figure out what the drink consisted of.

"And *voila*," Boom continued, "that's the magic trick. Now give me one of those, I'm dying here."

"I dunno, Eddie, he might not want to work for me. He's on vacation, right?" But she scooped up one of the remaining glasses and presented it to him. "Get out of my way. I want pancakes."

"How can you *even*." Boom shuddered, and set to work slurping at his glass of green whatever-it-was.

"Because by the time you finish that you'll be hungry too." She had an electric griddle resting on the stovetop; naturally, Boom would have all the kitchen gadgets. The man had never met a doodad or thingamajig he didn't immediately want to adopt. He was always on the lookout for discarded crap to make into crazy little tchotchkes or simple machines, too. "Yell up at Carl, his cure'll get warm and you know he hates that."

"God, you're so bossy." But Boom made for the hall, coffee in one hand and hangover drink in the other, sucking on the latter because the former was too hot for easy consumption.

Tax took another few gulps. Whatever the concoction was, it soothed the washing machine in his guts and his headache began to seem relatively reasonable instead of a monstrous skull-cracking hippo bite. "Jesus." He sounded baffled even to himself. "What the hell's in this?" *Mind your manners, Tax. She's a lady.*

"Trade secret." She turned her head, tossing the words over one linen-clad shoulder. "So, uh, just because Ed volunteered you doesn't mean you have to do it. I can get a temp for admin and bookkeeping; it's what I was planning on doing anyway."

Oh, Christ. Now he was called upon to be polite. "It's all right, ma'am. I'm here to help Boom out."

"Third time." She shook her head. The platinum looked natural; either that or it was a dye job so beautifully done, it approached classical art. "Never thought I'd be old enough to be *ma'am*'d thrice—before bacon, even. Drink your cure, Mr. Tachmann."

His liver hadn't given up yet, so the rest of him had to make the best of this. "Yes ma—uh, thank you." The throbbing between his temples, beating in time to the music, receded slightly. His tongue felt too big for the rest of him, and caterpillar-furry as well. The smell of bacon should have turned him inside out and sent him reeling for the bathroom, but it was actually faintly appetizing.

He couldn't figure out what was in the drink, so he just stood there, absorbing it as fast as he could and watching her move between the griddle, the coffeemaker, and the blender.

It was a pleasant view.

BIG BLOND CARL looked like a stranded surfer, right down to the streaks in his hair. He hooked an arm casually over Boom's shoulders at the breakfast bar, and it was the first time Tax had seen his buddy actually relaxed.

Normally Boom was a barely repressed set of fidgets poured into uniform, restless fingers just looking for something to fix, fiddle with, wire up, knock down, or blow out. Next to his fiancé, though, the twitches mellowed and he leaned into the other man like a plant with its own personal sunbeam.

"Well," the pink-tipped pixie said, doubtfully. "I really could use an extra pair of hands. But I bet you haven't told him what I do."

Christ, like she thought it mattered? Tax was a scarecrow full of bad wiring and combat stress, just marking time until he could see everyone settled. He kept his smile on, though the pancakes had turned into a bowling ball somewhere in his midsection. Whatever was in that green drink of hers definitely blunted the hangover, but there was no way to erase the amount of Cuervo they'd all taken down. It was a miracle the other two looked so fresh.

"That's part of the trick." Boom beamed, a pacific, almost myopic haze of goodwill that meant he was a hundred percent up to no good. "Better wear a suit, Tax."

"Don't think I packed one." It was a lie, of course—what else did you wear to a wedding? Mom even insisted on sock garters, though he'd never use the damn things. "But you might as well spill. I know that look."

Boom affected injured innocence, wide hazel eyes blinking rapidly. "Me? I'm as pure as the driven—"

"Mr. Tachmann, Eddie seems to feel your masculinity might be threatened if you work as a wedding planner's assistant." Meg—she didn't seem like a Megan or a Margaret either, for all Tax could tell—turned in her chair, digging in her purse. The bag matched her suit almost perfectly, despite being canvas instead of linen. "Right?"

She said it so sweetly the meaning didn't sink in for a moment. Carl laughed, shaking a lock of wavy hair from his forehead, and Boom grinned like a cat full of canary.

Tax, in the middle of a rather healthy gulp of coffee that had just reached drinkable temperature, almost choked. *Now* it all made sense.

As soon as he could talk, he fixed Boom with the ol' eagle eye. "Is this supposed to be some kind of payback for something? I can just as easily take that pickled asparagus home." Mom had sent a little something for each of his buddies, and Tax wasn't above holding a jar or two hostage if necessary.

"Oh, hell no," his buddy said cheerfully. "You're prying those jars from my cold dead fingers, my friend."

"Payback?" The pixie's eyebrows were much darker than her hair, though still blonde, and they rose to a dangerous degree. "Like there's something wrong with my job?"

Oh, shit. Tax decided he should keep his mouth shut, and stared into his mug.

"And now our cute little Callahan has blackmail material for at least two weeks." The end of the sentence held a strangled laugh, and Carl squeezed Boom's shoulders. "Oh man, Eddie, you're never gonna hear the end of this one."

"It's not like I don't have oodles of material anyway." Meg finally found what she was looking for, and produced a shining item from the bag's depths. It was her cell phone, the case decked with what looked like rhinestones. The rest of her was so sleek and professional, it didn't fit—or maybe it did, Tax couldn't decide. "And time's a-wasting, gentlemen. Get cleaned up, we have a fitting to attend."

It was by far the nicest-phrased call to inspection he'd ever had. And at least he'd be busy until the wedding.

After that, Tax figured, everyone was on their own.

Happy Thoughts

ONE OF THESE days she was going to kick Eddie right in the shins again. It used to be one of the best methods for keeping him out of mischief—so far as that particular feat could ever be accomplished—but once he'd left for basic training, the threat lost a lot of its effectiveness. When he came back, he had that faraway look in his eyes, though the rest of him was just the same, so she rarely had the heart to administer a little whupass.

Except verbally, of course.

On the one hand, she really could use some help. On the other, she suspected Eddie was unloading his freshly arrived buddy onto her so he could sneak off and canoodle with Carl. The two of them were like teenagers, but she was glad they'd finally stopped dancing around each other.

Her job description wasn't *matchmaker*, for Chrissake. She was a *planner*, making sure everything went smoothly, keeping vendors and caterers and venue staff on the same page, tactfully giving budget suggestions, balancing on the fine line between *that's a great color on you* and *unfortunately, the cancellation policy can't be changed*. It was a good job, playing to a great many of her strengths, and she was her own damn boss.

But the temptation to dig a toe right into her childhood friend's shin and hiss the old tagline, *behave or I will* make *you*, was well-nigh irresistible.

The buddy—Arthur, what a name—was almost as tall as Carl, definitely strapping, and needed only a pair of steel-rim glasses to get a hot professor look going. He had a perfect tan helped along by genetics, not to mention great cheekbones, and even if his black hair was ruler-straight and clearly softening out of a military high-and-tight, there were no shortage of guys who would be glad to have such a mop. Or women, come to think of it.

Eddie said his buddy's mother was Asian, which tracked. A bit younger and this Arthur guy could've been mistaken for a rising K-pop star, except for the crow's feet and the tightness around his mouth.

He looked, in other words, deeply unhappy. But then again, she supposed the Army didn't give anyone a good time.

However, he was ready to go in less than fifteen minutes, held the front door for her, and folded himself into her blue convertible's passenger side without a wince even though his legs were far too long for the confined space. He didn't touch the lever to push the seat back until flat-out told to, and when she twisted the key and the engine began to purr he folded his hands in his lap like he was afraid to touch anything.

Or as if he was a germaphobe, but he'd been drinking with Eddie. Maybe he thought she had cooties?

Well, a few minutes in the car wouldn't hurt either of them. Meg got her seatbelt carefully situated; the suit was gorgeous, but linen wrinkled if you even looked at it funny. "What kind of music?" That was the most important question.

Carl backed the pickup out of the left half of the garage—there was a just-glimpsed shiny black SUV taking up the other half now, which had to be Arthur's ride.

The grey truck veered delicately around her much smaller vehicle, made it to the street, and Carl set off at a pace guaranteed to drive Eddie near-insane with impatience. God knew Ed took speed limits as a personal affront; once he'd figured out hotwiring in middle school he became an outright menace on the road.

It's a maximum under ideal conditions, Carl would reply, calm and unruffled. *Not a challenge.*

He signaled every lane change, too.

"Huh?" Arthur blinked a couple times. Maybe he was having trouble focusing; it looked like they'd really tied one on last night. Callahan's Cure was great, but it didn't completely get rid of booze fog.

Or the aches.

"What kind of music do you like?" The sky was lighting up, a furnace in the east peering through the haze of a beautiful spring eighty-five-or-so, Fahrenheit not Celsius because this was America goddam-mit. In a little while it would clear up and the mountains would be razor-sharp, except for any lingering smog. "I've got just about everything, and since this is your inaugural voyage and you're helping me out, you'll get a vote. I have to warn you that driver picks the specifics and passenger shuts his pie-hole, and I reserve the right to veto at any time. So. What tune-age does my new friend Arthur prefer?"

"It's just Tax, ma'am." He didn't hunch in the seat, but he did glance up like the roof was far too close for his liking. "And it's your car, play what you like."

"Oh, so you're one of *those*." Meg nodded sagely and reached for her sunglasses. She didn't need them yet, but they could keep her hair back for a while since they were going windows-down for as long as possible.

It would save both her and her passenger from having to make awkward conversation, plus keep the air moving if he was still feeling queasy. And while she drove, she could cogitate on whether or not she really needed to babysit this guy as an 'assistant.'

She loved Eddie, but for God's sake, she had a business to run.

"One of what?" Arthur sounded baffled; he peered past her at the pickup's vanishing brake lights.

"The kind of guy who has to be tortured until a preference falls out." She turned the key; the convertible roused with a soft sweet purr. "And lay off the *ma'am*. I'm Meg."

"Maybe I'm just easy to please, Miss Callahan."

"Then you're gonna have a ball in Vegas, Mr. Tachmann." At least he wasn't nonverbal, or painfully slow on the uptake. So far, even with a hangover, he was keeping up admirably. "All right, driver's choice it is, and don't say I didn't give you a chance."

"No ma'am," he muttered, and dropped his gaze to his lap.

It was a half-second's work to plug in her phone, and she already knew the playlist she wanted—her driving-to-work mix, just the thing to start a day chock-full of fittings, caterers, venue visits, and two phone appointments for final details back at the office.

The first horns blared from the speakers, Cake began singing about a girl with a mind like a diamond, and she popped the car into reverse. She even pulled out rather sedately. Eddie would be in a lather of impatience by now.

Carl, of course, would just shake his head as he obeyed traffic laws. *So she gets there first, Eds. It's not a big deal.*

Meg grinned, twisted the volume knob—not quite to its usual mark, out of deference to her passenger's tender eardrums—and hit the brakes. The convertible sensed what she wanted and was just as eager; when she dropped into drive and touched the gas the world took a deep breath.

Time to make some moves.

AT LEAST ARTHUR didn't grab for the dash. In fact, he didn't comment on her driving at all, which was a nice change; Eddie bitched and moaned *all* the time unless he was the one behind the wheel.

His buddy, however, settled into the seat like it was comfortable, and watched the street signs with every appearance of interest.

And they did make it to Sew Nice Alterations before the grey pick-up hove into sight; she had barely cut the engine when Carl pulled into the spot next to her. "Fabulous," Meg said with deep satisfaction right as the speakers died, halting the Doobie Brothers midway through their estimation of what a fool believed.

She was only moderately annoyed that she couldn't sing along with someone else in the car. Well, she could with Eddie, but he was a special case.

Arthur unfolded gingerly from the convertible, but he still didn't complain. He took in the parking lot, the low brick building with the *CLOSED* sign hanging on the glass door, and glanced at the intersection like he expected a cop car to come screaming after them. Which was just a little insulting, since Meg considered herself a reasonable driver, if a sometimes-loud one.

"Hey, Tax." Eddie bailed out of the truck. "Fall asleep?"

"She's a better driver than Klemp," was Arthur's reply. Apparently the surroundings passed muster, because he swung the car door closed with more gentleness than she'd expected.

"Yeah, but now you've got hearing damage." Eddie was in fine form, even his curls bouncing merrily. He probably felt on top of the world, with both Carl and his Army buddy there to impress.

Meg rolled her eyes, locked the convertible, and by the time she was halfway to the door, her phone had buzzed twice and there was movement behind the glass.

They were expected, the first clients of the day.

"What, like I didn't get that hanging around you?" Arthur made a small scoffing noise, and Meg began to feel quite charitable toward the guy.

"Hey, Marcy." Meg hitched her purse a little higher and made sure her smile for the day was firmly in place. "We're ten minutes early, I know. Can I order you some coffee?"

"This is why you're my favorite." Marcy Nguyen was short, trim, and snub-nosed, smattered with cheerful freckles; she peered at the morning in bemused fashion as she held the door wide. "But nah, I stopped on the way in. Took Anh and Trevor to the airport this morn-ing, so I've been up for hours already."

"That's great." And it was; Meg could feel a warm glow of achievement. Marcy's sister-in-law and her new husband had gone all-out for their vows, the entire ceremony smooth as Skippy despite having to change caterers nearly the day before and a small fire at the venue just prior to the reception. Even the appearance of emergency vehicles hadn't put a dent in festivities. "Alaska, right?"

"You couldn't pay me to go, but I guess Trev wants fishing. On his honeymoon, can you believe it?" Marcy gave a dramatic shudder, holding the door wide. "Anh says they're taking a cruise for their first anniversary though. Oh, Long says hi, by the way, and wants to know if you want tickets." Her husband was an event promoter, and a damn good one too.

"Only if it's to the symphony." Meg stuck a foot in front of the door to keep it open as Marcy bustled away, and half-turned. "Eddie! Carl! Get your asses in here, Marcy doesn't have all day."

"Yes ma'am, drill sergeant ma'am," Eddie called back. Really feeling his oats this morning, and now she regretted leaving his shins alone *and* not extracting a larger price for the cure.

"Jesus, Boom." Arthur probably thought he was *sotto voce*, but the words carried clearly. "I thought she was your friend."

Eddie didn't mean it—sarcasm had always been their mutual love language—but still, Meg couldn't help but feel even more deeply charitable towards the new guy. Carl, of course, was ambling for the door at his own pace, blithely unconcerned. Not much ever ruffled him, and besides he was used to the game.

Thank goodness Eddie didn't ever get snitty in his fiancé's direction, because Meg would have to bring out the big guns. Batting conversational hardballs over the net was a pleasant game, but only when your opponent was well-equipped and liked that sort of thing.

Carl was too much of a sweetheart, so both Meg and Eddie treated him accordingly. And besides, he'd been a real mensch during what they now referred to as the Preston Incident, quietly showing up when she left work each day so even if Press did show up there was social pressure to keep any interaction short and polite as possible.

Those were deeply unpleasant memories, so Meg took a deep breath, banishing them to the place where bad things belonged during the day. Her job was all about providing happiness, divorce statistics notwithstanding. She had to think good thoughts in order to scatter her Tinkerbell dust and bring order out of chaos.

"Keep it up, Eds," she said serenely, waving Carl into the building like a casino greeter with a high roller, "and I'll tell your buddy there all about your favorite scary movie."

"Scary movie?" Arthur looked over Eddie's head, and she could swear there was a twinkle in his dark eyes. "I can't wait to hear this one."

"Fu—ah." Eddie caught sight of Marcy, and changed his tune immediately. "To heck with you both. I'll short-sheet Tax's bed, see if I don't. Hullo, Mrs. Nguyen. How's your husband?"

"He's just fine, Edward." Marcy beamed pacifically in his direction; ever since Eddie had menaced those assholes attempting to extort protection money from the shop, she'd had a soft spot for his antics. "I'll tell him you said hello. Come on in, I've laid everything out in the rooms—yours is the one on the left, Carl, and I can lengthen the kilt a bit more if you want. We have options."

Arthur paused just inside the door. "What do you need me to do?"

Was he taking the job Ed had volunteered him for seriously, or just being polite? Meg's phone buzzed again. "Keep Eddie on track, I've got to see who's blowing up my mentions."

"You got it." Thankfully he didn't salute, though it looked like he wanted to.

Meg suppressed a smile, and unlocked her phone. Her heart thumped when she saw who was texting, and she stepped outside, pressing the call button. *Let it be good news, and not more bullshit.*

"Meg!" Ella Roark's voice came through crystal clear, hitting a pitch more suited to a boy band concert than a Wednesday morning. "Oh, my God, *Meg!* He did it! He did, he did, he did it!"

What the hell? She gazed at the parking lot, the intersection, and the donut shop just visible past the gas station across the way. "Who did what, Ell? Slow down."

"He proposed!" Ella nearly screamed. "Last night. Dinner at Scalise's, and then he went down on one knee and I'm *dying*, Meg! The ring's a real rock, too. It's happening, it's all happening!"

Well, that was good—or at least, the sheer volume of excited squeals made it sound that way. "You mean Ben?" *I hope I have his name right.*

Ella went through guys like a bad restaurant through waitstaff. There was always a line of new applicants, though this Ben guy—if it was him—had lasted far longer than the usual.

"Of course I mean Ben, who did you think? Oh, Meg, I'm so happy. Dad says hi, by the way, and of course we want you to handle the wedding. Say you will."

Huh. On the one hand, there was likely to be a sky-high budget for the nuptials of Gerry Roark's precious daughter. On the other. . . . "Are you sure? I know Aunt Stace has her own event planning business now, so . . ."

"Hell yeah I'm sure. Dad even said you specifically. He wants to see you, so does Tilda. Come over for dinner tonight?"

Meg almost flinched. "I'm booked, baby. Maybe lunch, soonish? Dinner will have to wait until the ceremony's over and I've earned the gigantic fee I'm going to charge."

"That means you'll do it. Yay!" Ell hit a pitch just under 'screaming with glee,' and was officially off to the races. "All right, I'll tell Dad. And don't worry, my brother will behave. Or Dad'll do more than just send him out of state for a few months."

I'm sure that went over real well, too. Still, this would not only give her some liquidity—Gerry naturally believed in paying well for services rendered—but also opened up a whole 'nother client list.

Would she want them, though? It was definitely a good business move, but she wasn't sure if it was an ethical one, given the family's reputation.

Still, this was Vegas. If you waited for a completely clean dollar, you were likely to starve. "How can I say no, Ell-Bell? I'd be happy to. And congratulations, you must be over the moon."

"I couldn't get to sleep last night. Well, that *and* a few other reasons." Good Lord, but Ell sounded downright salacious.

I do not want to know. "No details right now, please, I'm at work. Let me check my schedule, we'll set up an appointment for the prelims. Do you guys have a date yet?"

"Well, you're the expert; I don't know how long these things take. I kind of thought that we could talk about options, really, because I don't want it at a casino. We were thinking Napa Valley, or something like that."

So Meg could add travel costs to the bill. No hardship, California was a nice place to visit. "I'll start looking around. I mean it, Ell—congratulations, I'm so happy for you."

There was at least ten more minutes' worth of breathless details, gushing, and extracting promises that Meg really did mean it, she would handle her friend's wedding to the doctor just out of his residency who had the good sense to propose, of course Meg would take care of everything, the dress would be fit for a princess and the catering would be *fantastic* no matter the venue chosen.

Finally freed, Meg hung up. It was good luck and a great boost to business, but her stomach rolled uneasily as if she'd been the one drinking all night.

It didn't matter. She had work to do, and could brood about handling a wedding for Preston Roark's sister later. Preferably tonight, with a glass of wine.

She took a deep breath, pasted her smile back on, and breezed back through the door.

Contingencies

HE'D HAD FAR worse hangovers, including a few that included being shot at, but Tax had never been driven around in a convertible by a pink-haired fairy while speakers throbbed at near jet-takeoff levels. For all that, she was so careful behind the wheel it was almost restful.

Boom and Carl were given leave as soon as the seamstress finished all her arcane measurements and mutterings; they had plans for the day, which meant Tax was the pixie's problem now. *I'll bring him back in original condition*, Miss Callahan said, air-kissing Boom's cheeks, and the Squad's demo man looked so self-satisfied it was a wonder he didn't bust at the seams.

Tax didn't have time to ponder. And how anyone could think with desert wind scouring the car's seats and music playing so loudly was beyond him; he didn't recognize any of the songs except for a Swedish disco number about changing a mind and taking a chance, which happened to be one of his mother's favorites.

Dad had been more of a Wagner type of guy, but he always listened with headphones, as if it were faintly shameful to like opera—unless he was in the shed out back with his woodworking, cigarette lip-clamped tight in defiance of any fire risk and the good smell of sawdust or the reek of varnish rising in waves. *Ride of the Valkyries* was inextricably linked in young Tax's head with the buzz of a table saw and his father's off-key humming.

Miss Callahan's office was in a four-floor building also holding a medical billing company, a civil engineering firm, and something to do with payrolls; the midmorning heat was just like home, though with even less humidity. The entire place was glass and concrete, relatively new, and her corner office was done in birch and tasteful pastels, smelling faintly of something floral. Pictures of happy couples all dolled up for their big day hung on the wall behind what had to be a receptionist's desk, and the office proper was behind panels of yet more glass.

Tax hoped his job wouldn't include cleaning all that. He hated Windex, let alone ammonia.

"I know Eddie volunteered you," she said, making a beeline for a small cabinet. A pod-based coffeemaker stood proudly next to decorative pottery dishes of shelf-stable creamer and sweeteners. "But you really don't have to—there's the couch if you'd rather take a nap instead, and I can drop you off at his place after lunch. I've got to look over rate sheets and do a few meetings this afternoon, and a guy like you will probably find it super boring."

He was still faintly hungover and a little sour around the stomach, but not bored. At home he would be searching for something to fill the time, at Klemp's he'd stepped right into an operation in progress, and at least he wasn't driving through the desert with only his own increasingly bleak thoughts and 4k hi-def flashbacks for company. This was, all said and done, a real change of pace. "Boom said the guy doing your book-keeping had some legal trouble."

That brought her to a halt—no small achievement, since it didn't look like this girl had any setting other than all engines max—and pulled her around to examine him, a line growing between her perfect, pretty eyebrows. "My accountant's been indicted, yes. I had an admin assistant too, but she went back to Ohio last month and I was just about to get a temp for that when Davy got arrested. So . . ." With her sunglasses pushed up like a headband and those baby blues big and anxious, she looked a lot younger. "You want some more coffee? I can send out for a snack too, if your stomach's calmed down. The cure helps but it doesn't get rid of everything. You like Danishes?"

Slow down, puppy. It was the sort of thing Mom would say, albeit in Korean. Tax's mouth felt a little odd—not like last night's tequila was going to evict something, but as if it wanted to . . . what? Take a distinct upward curve at either corner, maybe. A real smile, instead of a socially acceptable ersatz to keep real feelings hidden.

He hadn't thought of blood, guts, or the peculiar wheeze of a death-rattle for hours.

"I'm all right." He didn't add *ma'am* only with an effort of will, and was almost unjustifiably proud. "What do you have that needs doing? Invoices? Quarterlies? I did a little admin in the Army, and besides, you're the boss. So I'll make the coffee."

"Are you sure?" She pushed the purse higher on her shoulder. There was a faint buzz coming from it again; that rhinestone-appliquéd phone was getting a workout. "You really don't have to. It's not how anyone would want to spend a vacation."

What else do I have to do? Other than wait until the wedding was over and engineer his exit, that was. No flashback or surge of sweating panic all morning either, which was goddamn near a miracle.

"Honestly?" Tax spread his hands. "It sounds like fun."

"Fun?" Clearly doubting, she shifted from one foot to the other. Was she planning on wearing those heels all day?

Tax couldn't imagine; it sounded worse than packing full ruck on a twenty-klick hike. "I'm not getting shot at, nobody's bleeding, and Boom isn't whistling the *Jaws* theme like he's about to blast something into the stratosphere. So, yeah. Fun."

The clouds cleared, the line between her eyebrows went away, and Miss Callahan laughed. She obviously thought he was joking, but really, after the Squad's usual work, pretty much anything civilian qualified as a walk in the park.

He was washed out and combat-fatigued, but this wasn't bad. At all.

"*Boom*," she said, and shook her head. "I'm not surprised that's his nickname, you know. We used to go out in the desert when we were kids, and he always loved blowing stuff up. I could tell you so many stories . . ." The phone buzzed again, and even her rueful grimace was attractive. Boom hadn't mentioned his best friend was so pretty—but then again, around a group of jackals like the Squad, maybe it was for the best. "All right. I'll sign you into the laptop under Francesca's profile and put you on invoices. We'll see if you still think it's fun after that. And of course I'll pay you for your time."

"No ma—I mean, that's not necessary. Boom wouldn't like it, you know, being a friend and all."

"Well . . ." She slipped the purse off her shoulder and dug for her phone again, glancing at its face with the air of a woman resigned to torment. "I pay my people, Mr. Tachmann. One way or another. You don't buy drinks while you're in Vegas and working for me. Fair?"

"Only if you call me Tax, Miss Callahan. Mr. Tachmann's my father." *Jesus, I sound old.* Dad would've laughed, though, his particular smoke-roughened bark of real amusement.

At least his father was safely with the ancestors. He would've taken one look at Tax, known what was going through his boy's head, and probably suggested something like fucking *therapy.*

Every other member of the Squad could hack it. Tax was the exception, but nobody had to know.

"Miss Callahan sounds like a retired burlesque dancer." The megawatt grin was back. "It's Meg, Tax. And given how you can clearly drink your own weight in tequila, you're gonna get the better part of the deal anyway."

He wasn't so sure about that, but at least wading through whatever accounting system she had set up would pass the time. Boom's wedding wasn't until the end of the month; he'd jumped at the chance to come out early.

Whatever he ended up doing, it was best if his mother didn't see. He already felt bad enough about the decision—not that it would alter anything, Mom was better off without the burden of knowing what her son had done, and how many he had failed to save.

"Sounds like a deal." Tax paused, throttling the *ma'am* that wanted to come out, and took a couple steps in her direction, offering his hand. "Meg."

Her fingers were cool and slim, and he took care not to squeeze too hard. A strange sensation slid up his arm from the touch, probably because that perfume of hers was so unusual.

"Right." Her phone buzzed again, and for a moment she looked like Dez, especially when the Squad's leader was doing his best to insulate the rest of them from a higher-up with Clever Ideas About What Soldiers Could Accomplish. "Let's get you set up, then. And be warned, I drink a *lot* of coffee."

HE'D EXPECTED a mess. But not only was Boom's childhood friend fast and professional, she was apparently also ferociously organized. It looked like white dresses and receptions were good business—especially if most of the payments were up front.

Tax tapped on the glass door, and she looked up from the sleek, ruthlessly neat desk, frowning slightly. Her expression was very much like Dez's when there were after-action reports to write and the op had been a real bitch, though she wore it better than their lieutenant.

Of course, she was so winsome she could walk around in sackcloth and it would look good, but that was beside the point. Especially since she was Boom's friend, and a lady too.

"Problems?" The line between her eyebrows was back.

Tax got the idea she expected trouble as a matter of course. "Nope. They're all sent, the software does it for you. There are a couple of outstanding ones, though."

"Let me guess. Sharpton-Tegley and Kriestowicz-Smith." Her pink tips brushed her shoulder as she shook her head, once, like a cat smelling something foul. "Don't worry, those will go to collections."

You want me to do something about that? It couldn't be much different than any other op, really. The Squad's training covered all sorts of contingencies, and menacing a target or two was firmly in the oeuvre.

But no, he was out in civilian-land. "Sorry." Why was he apologizing? "Uh, what else can I do?"

"How good are you at comparing rate sheets?" She leaned back in her ergonomic chair; a slightly higher-grade silver laptop gleamed, set at just the right angle next to a chunky pottery pen-cup. The cup didn't match the rest of her oh-so-modern office, since it was lopsided and was glazed with a combination of violent orange and equally nauseating neon green. The gel pens in it were black, red, and one lone silver number which looked a little more expensive.

"I don't know, but I'll try." He glanced at the window, calculating the drop—not really enough, they didn't build high enough in the desert unless it was downtown. Her file cabinets were pale ashwood barrister numbers, and the tops held neat trays with more color-coded paper. A printer stood on a cabinet on the other side, and all in all her office suited her right down to the ground.

It turned out 'rate sheets' were lists of prices for different wedding venue services, printed on glossy paper with heavily Photoshopped pictures of smiling brides, huge floral displays, tiered cakes, and formal place settings. Inclusive packages and a la carte, just like at a Chinese restaurant—he glanced at the first sheet and had to laugh. "They're overcharging for the Orange Blossom package. It comes out to about ten percent more than all the services separately, not twenty percent off."

Meg blinked twice and absorbed this, handing over another slick, brightly colored brochure attached to a sheaf of small-font printout. Tax scanned the numbers and looked up to find her obviously expectant, her subtly glossed lips parted and those small gold earrings gleaming, baby blues wide and interested.

"Uh." His throat had gone dry again. "The second economy package is the best deal, I guess, but you don't save much with any of them. Five to seven percent, at most. Your best bet is probably a la carte and one of the trio packages if you want to save money, but I don't know what girls like for weddings, so . . ."

"Arthur Tachmann." Her lips curved, her eyes sparkled, and maybe the air-conditioning wasn't working as well as it could in here because all of a sudden the room seemed uncomfortably warm. "Where have you been all my life?"

In the Army, ma'am. But he couldn't call her that again, and besides she was just being . . . what was the word? Kind?

Christ only knew what he would have said, because a flicker of motion outside the glass wall brought him around in a hurry, right hand dropping to his side as if he was open-carrying.

He wasn't, and the flinch wasn't good. He was in *civilian* space, for God's sake, and the laws around here were different than California or Oregon.

The movement was a dark-haired man in a charcoal suit, who had clearly found the desk outside empty. He spotted Meg, grinned with snowy, perfectly capped teeth, and—for good measure—waved like he knew her. The stranger's shoes were buffed to a high gloss but the soles meant he wasn't running anywhere; his tie was subtly patterned, crisply knotted, and clearly his pride and joy.

"Oh, fuck," Meg muttered. Then, a little louder, "Stay here. Keep going over the rate sheets, please."

That didn't sound good. But the lady had given an order, so that's what Tax did, accepting the sheaf of brochures and printouts thrust into his hands.

She skirted the desk, heading for the office door with a determined stride. He tried not to look at her hips moving under peach linen, wondering why in the hell he had the overpowering urge to set the papers down and find some reason to make coffee.

Up the Ante

IT FIGURED—the universe never sent a silver lining without a cloud. Meg let the glass door to her office swing closed and halted, folding her arms. "What do you want?"

"Hi, Meg." Preston Roark looked, as usual, thoroughly tanned and very satisfied with himself. He'd gotten rid of the scruffy stubble and the single stud earring, and there was no hint of bloodshot on him. Which meant he might not have been out until the wee hours partying for once, but that was none of her business. "It's nice to see you."

I can't return that compliment. If it is one, and not a flat-out lie. "What. Do you. Want?"

"That your new secretary? What happened to Fran?"

The pointless urge to explain herself rose; Meg clapped a lid on it and straightened to her full, if inconsiderable, height. Threats wouldn't work, and neither would politeness. So she simply dead-eyed him, letting silence do its work.

It was the most—probably only—effective weapon she had for dealing with him.

Press shifted, a tiny crack in the expensive young businessman veneer. "I was in the area." The smile didn't change, but the gleam far back in his dark eyes said he didn't like her refusal to engage in small talk. "Actually, I heard from Ell, so I thought I'd drop in. Dad's really happy about it."

And you thought you'd come by to see if I was having second thoughts. It was depressingly predictable. Meg's face felt frozen; it was the remote, cheerful mask she used when cornered by a client's relatives who had Ideas and Preferences about what was, after all, not their fucking ceremony. She still said nothing.

"Come on, babe." He tilted his head, and the smile was megawatt-charming, as usual. "It's been six months, we should be past this. Dad keeps asking what happened."

Do not fucking call me 'babe,' you trust-fund jackass. "Maybe you should tell him." A stranger would call her tone *sweet* or maybe even *breathy*, but

Eddie would turn solemn if he heard it, his dark gaze going cold as leftover coffee as he prepared to back her up. "Or maybe I should."

"It was just the one time, Meg. Why are you being like this?"

Like I believe that, especially since you were paying her rent. And none of that covered him lurking when she got off work, or banging on her apartment door at midnight, or blowing up her phone. "One time's too many, Press. Just tell me what you're here for."

"Nothing, really. Just came to see you." He glanced over her shoulder. "Who's that guy?"

None of your fucking business. "Are you planning a wedding, too? What was her name—oh, that's right." Mimicking remembrance, she tapped her index finger against her arm, grateful she was at least in heels. "Kandy, with a K. A bit of a cliché, but then again, this is Vegas. Did you pop the question with champagne and a dozen long-stemmed?"

"Jesus. You know that was nothing." Press's smile fell away so quickly she was surprised it didn't shatter on laminate flooring. "It was George's bachelor party, we got crazy—"

Spare me the details. No amount of verbal pussyfooting would explain why he set the stripper up in Chelle Towers; the building was keycard-access, had its own gym on the third floor, and was generally considered desirably expensive. Meg frankly didn't care that the other woman worked a pole—she'd done it herself, it took dedication and provided a good paycheck. God knew you needed the latter to afford anything in this city, and even if it had been escort work, that was just as honorable as anything else. She didn't even mind the sheer tawdriness of it all; tale as old as time, really.

No, she minded the *lies.* More than that, the insult to her intelligence. It was as if he'd wanted to get caught, and all his attempts to worm his way back into her life afterward veered between ridiculous and . . . yes, scary.

That was the right word. She shouldn't be afraid; he was Ella's brother, for God's sake. Breaking her car window had been an accident, right? Gerry had paid for his son's misbehaving, as usual, and sent him out of state to cool off. Since then, Press had been behaving himself, leaving her alone.

Mostly.

"I'm booked five years in advance." Bright brittle cheerfulness edged each word; Meg's stomach was well and truly rolling now. "So I'm squeezing your sister in as a favor, but I can't take another client at the moment. I could recommend a few other planners, though."

"Will you just talk to me?" He did a pretty good imitation of earnestness, but now she knew how shallow it was.

"We've said everything we needed to, Mr. Roark."

"Don't." Press's nose actually wrinkled. If he was truly ashamed it was no doubt a transitory state, a thin cloud passing over the sun at high noon. "That's *him*, Meg. Not me."

At least your father kept his mistresses decently under wraps. She could say it, she supposed, but if they started trading barbs they'd be here all afternoon.

Worse, he would think she still cared—the thin end of the wedge, Carl would call it, his nose wrinkling as it hardly ever did. Preston Roark was very rarely told *no*, and it showed. The red flags had been there since middle school; she'd been a fool to think she could change anything or anyone.

Especially him.

"Thanks for dropping by, but I've got to get back to work." Her teeth hurt; so did her cheeks. The effort to keep her expression pleasant and her tone soft was nearly as intense as the core workout from a pole invert. Her smile was welded on, and her shoulders were concrete-stiff. "Busy-busy, you know."

"Meg." There it was, the soft tone that had fooled her twice. Preston was obviously going for a third. "Please."

"The elevator's to the right as you go out." If she threatened to call building security he would know he'd gotten to her, so she just freed one hand and gave a tiny, dismissive wave. "Have a nice day."

There was a faint sound—the hinges on the door to her office proper, its bottom edge whispering slightly above the laminate.

"Ms. Callahan?" Eddie's buddy sounded calm, professional, and blessedly normal. "Sorry to interrupt, but I think I've found the problem on these sheets."

Oh, thank God. He was giving her an out. "Great," she chirped. "Our guest was just leaving. Would you make me a cup of coffee? The hazelnut, please, two creamers."

"Coming right up." He moved past her, heading for the coffee counter and glancing at Preston—a short, incurious look, noting and dismissing all at once. Thankfully, Arthur's khakis were pressed and so was his button-up, so he looked relatively professional. Maybe the Army had taught him that one?

The addition of a stranger to the mix—and a male one, at that—obviously destroyed Press's plans. If Francesca had still been here, he might've tried to draw Meg's former secretary into conversation, but today social engineering tipped the balance.

Preston's smile was thin, though perfectly acceptable, and he nodded as if they were finishing a pleasant chat. "Well, I suppose I'll see you around, since you're handling Ell's big event. Looking forward to it."

"Me too," Meg lied, and watched him leave.

A pained silence swallowed her chic, clean, comfortable office; she'd chosen every piece in here, and Carl had helped with the details. Her desk had been Eddie's particular gift. Even miles away doing God-knew-what for the Army, he'd still had time to arrange it with his then-boyfriend, now-fiancé's help.

And Carl had grinned, waving an Allen wrench as he put the damn thing together. *Hang loose, Meg. It'll get sorted out.*

The coffee machine's burbling was loud in the stillness. Normally Francesca would have some classical piano playing, but the hush was tomblike. "Music," Meg muttered, and stalked for the secretary's desk. "Jesus Christ, I need music."

Arthur didn't reply. He just brought her a cup of coffee—hazelnut and two creamers, in the chunky blue pottery mug that just happened to be her favorite. She tapped at the secretary laptop and liquid rill of Schubert began; Meg's shoulders could finally relax.

"Thank you." Fake cheerfulness could cover all sorts of things, and sometimes she wondered if it would etch itself so deeply onto her tongue, she'd be unable to use anything else. "Feel free to have some too. Let's get the rest of those rate cards looked at."

"You're welcome." Quiet and level. Arthur looked like he wanted to add something else, but clearly chose discretion over valor for the second time that morning, heading back to the coffee machine.

All in all the entire encounter had gone reasonably well, even if her knees felt like overcooked noodles and there was an uncomfortable dampness at the small of her back.

She was also deeply, secretly glad Eddie's buddy had been present.

IT WAS NO wonder the man's nickname was 'Tax'; apparently he had a calculator lodged in his grey matter. Just *glancing* at the rate sheets was enough for him to figure out if a package didn't add up, and when she slid the last invoice from Martingdale Gardens across the desk to him, he ran an eye down the columns and immediately announced they'd overcharged her clients by four hundred bucks.

"Three-hundred-ninety-eight, actually," he corrected, squinting slightly. "And twenty cents. Look, right here. The Eternal Love package shouldn't have the extra fee for the higher-grade champagne, and they got the Floral Desire add-on which means the charge for the . . . the 'Orchid Explosion' isn't right. And, uh, the bubble machine." His eyebrows drew together. "There are machines for bubbles?"

"Son of a *bitch*." It took her some time with the calculator on her laptop, but she double-checked and found out he was right, down to the cent. "You're amazing. What did you do in the Army?"

"Medic, ma—uh, just a medic." An easy shrug, broad shoulders under light-blue cotton. He wore his watch with the face on the inside of his wrist, like Eddie when he came back from basic. "I like numbers; it's nothing special."

"I guess Eddie really did earn this morning's cure." Meg's grin now felt entirely natural, and it was a nice change. She leaned back in the ergonomic chair, realizing just how tense her shoulders had been. The sudden relaxation was incredible. "How long are you in town for again?"

"Until the wedding. Speaking of which . . ." Arthur looked perplexed now; he straightened the pile of papers in front of him, getting their edges perfectly settled with finicky care.

Uh-oh. "What?"

"It's none of my business." He shifted in one of the client chairs, dragged companionably close behind the desk. "But how the heck did you talk Boom out of an Elvis-based ceremony?"

"It was Carl who wanted that, actually. He's a big fan of the King. Eddie wanted to come down a canal on a gondola, with a choir singing." Meg blinked. "Wait a second. How did you know?"

"Just wondered." Arthur grinned too. For the first time, all trace of self-consciousness was gone. The change looked good on him, the crow's feet at the edges of his eyes turning into laugh lines. "Do a lot of people want gondolas?"

You have no idea. "I'll tell you, people think being a wedding planner is all about the dream, you know? The fantasy a lot of little girls have about wearing a white dress and walking down the aisle. But it's not." Meg reached for her coffee cup. It was stone-cold, but she took down the dregs in one motion, tossing it far back like vodka. "It's the art of the achievable. Everyone's got a budget, and you get whatever parts of the dream you can."

"I like that." He nodded as if she'd said something profound. "Art of the achievable."

Her phone began to tinkle ABBA's "Dancing Queen"; she reached for it without looking. "What, Eddie? I'm not giving your buddy back, just so you know. He's mine now." A cool drift of air-conditioning ruffled her hair.

"I told you he likes numbers." Eddie was outside, if the background noise was any indication. "Carl called in a favor—dinner at Scalise's tonight? Our treat."

It was a wonderful idea, but she was immediately suspicious. "You're attempting to bribe me with surf-and-turf. No dice."

"Come on, Meggers." It was amazing, his wheedling tone hadn't changed since grade school. Later, Eddie's voice had dropped early, putting him in high demand for prank calls and certain desert singalongs, not to mention fooling social workers or school administrators into thinking both he and Meg were doing just fine, thank you. "It's nothing bad, I promise, and you get a great dinner *plus* my buddy's services out of the deal."

"The buddy who's sitting right here?" Meg's gaze settled on Arthur, hardly seeing him. All her attention was on the tinny voice in her right ear, listening for a clue. "The one I can bet you haven't asked about whatever crazy-ass idea you have this time? I'll say it again, no dice."

"He'll love it and so will you. He gets free chow too." The wheels were audibly whirling inside Ed's skull. "Ask him if he minds."

"One sec." She tilted the phone away slightly. "Arthur, it's Edward. He wants to take us both to dinner tonight, but I have to warn you it's most likely a bribe because he's got some kind of plan he's sweetening us up for. I advise a strong, definitive no."

"Oooh," Eddie crooned, plainly audible though the phone's small speaker, though terribly tinny. "*Arthur*, is it? Double date, Tax. Say yes."

I am going to kill you, Eds. "I will mute you if I have to," she hissed at the phone, then fixed Arthur with a glare. "Say no."

"Uh, he's my buddy, ma—I mean, Ms. Callah—I mean . . ." Tax now looked shell-shocked, a giant change from his easy smile while dealing with Preston or the slightly abstract just-reporting-the-numbers while he compared a rate sheet to an invoice or proposal. And worlds away from the flash of relaxation she'd just seen.

Oh, for Chrissake. "Your buddy appears to have vapor-locked. Put Carl on." She could weasel the details out of an easygoing surfer, for sure.

"No can do." Eddie sounded only a quarter repentant, if that. "Baby's on a liquor run, we're out of margarita mix. Don't be a stick in the mud, Meg. Besides, I'm pretty sure Tax hasn't been out with a pretty girl in a while. You'd be doing a good deed."

That got a reaction. Arthur cocked his head, and a dangerous gleam lit his dark eyes. "Boom?" He pitched it loud enough for the phone to pick up. "Are you saying I'm a *charity date?*"

Oh, Lord. Meg decided to up the ante. "I want to start with that big antipasti platter of theirs," she interrupted, curtly. "You're tipping thirty percent, and I'm having dessert too."

There was no way he'd agree. Not unless the favor was *gigantic*, and there was nothing she could think of warranting a Scalise dinner that Carl had cashed in a gold chip or two for.

"Sold!" Eddie crowed, with disconcerting promptness. "Reservation's at 19:30, but bring Tax by the house before 18:00 so we can spruce up. See you then." And—proving she had just committed a major blunder—he hung up.

For the second time that day, Meg's jaw was suspiciously loose. She lowered the phone and stared at its innocent face, showing her last few calls against a design of pink hibiscus flowers. Looked like a couple voicemails had landed while she'd been going over the paperwork; Eddie was one of the few people who rang through no matter what do-not-disturb settings she had active.

He—and Carl—did the same for her. At least, Eddie did when he wasn't gallivanting all over the globe with the Army. Over the years of her best friend's absence Carl had more than earned his own place in the pantheon of People Whose Calls Callahan Always Took even if he hadn't grown up with her, which made Meg doubly lucky.

People who could make that hallowed list were very, very rare indeed.

"Oh, hell," she said, blankly. "I didn't expect him to agree."

"I'm not a charity date," Arthur muttered, and a giggle boiled up from Meg's middle.

She couldn't help it. The poor guy looked absolutely mystified, though he kept up with conversational hardball middling-well. He wasn't in the same league as Eddie and Meg, of course, but not everyone could play in the Olympics.

She had to clap a lid on the laughter posthaste, so he didn't think she meant it unkindly. "I guess we'd better have salads for lunch," she managed, as soon as she could talk without braying a chuckle or two. "Scalise's is great, and you're going to have to help me make this an *expensive* favor."

"Yes ma'am." He caught himself. "I mean, uh, yes, Meg."

It felt good to laugh again, especially since Arthur's mouth twitched like he got the joke and Meg found herself—for once—in a good mood after a visit from Preston Roark.

Maybe the day wouldn't turn out so badly after all.

Serious Business

THE RESTAURANT was the kind requiring a tie and turned out to be full of red upholstery, candles in glass hurricane lamps, heavy wallpaper doubling as minor soundproofing, and soft strains from a live quartet tucked in its own dedicated, acoustically reasonable space as well.

It made Tax itch all over. "It doesn't matter," he repeated. "I could just get a hotel room."

"The hell you can." Boom looked deeply offended, but he didn't yell. In fact, he managed to keep his vocal volume to a very reasonably level, entirely appropriate to the setting.

It was a goddamn miracle, probably entirely due to his significant other's presence.

Carl glided in front of them, freshly combed and dapper in a tailored navy suit, his long sun-streaked hair pulled back in a ponytail. Even his wingtips shone; he would pass the sharpest inspection with those numbers.

Boom had to go for the formal look of a nicely brought-up hooligan, but he was at least hygienic and presentable, dark curls sworn at and slicked back. "You came all the way out here to help," he continued. "And it works out. She needs it."

I don't think that girl needs any assistance, my good man. He didn't say it, but his expression probably spoke louder than his buddy's beloved C-4. "What, she's in desperate need of basic math and making coffee? Any asshole can do that, for Chrissake. She's got everything else under lock."

"Oh, sure." Uncharacteristic seriousness turned Boom's mouth down at both corners, and he glanced to the right, checking as if they were on patrol in tangled brush. "Just like the Loot, always saying he's fine."

"Captain now," Tax corrected. All of them had gotten a final jump in rank to add to their pensions; penny-pinching was all very well, but even paper-pushers knew you couldn't put guys trained like the Squad out to pasture without giving them good grazing.

If you didn't, it ended up being more expensive in the long run, given what they had been taught to do. Tax could even view his own plans as a cost-cutting measure.

Funny, he hadn't thought about it all afternoon. Nor about blood, contusions, major trauma, or dosages. He hadn't had the obsessive urge to wash his hands, or slop on alcohol-reeking sanitizer either.

"Here we are." The rail-thin, floppy-haired hostess guiding them through the maze gave a bright customer-service smile, indicating a relatively secluded table. Carl stepped aside, letting Boom choose a seat first—wise of him, since any member of the Squad wouldn't want his back to a door.

Or a window.

Heavy tablecloth, thick cloth napkins with brass rings, a flurry of motion to fill the water goblets, a small forest of silverware at every place, nested plates, and Carl giving marching orders for wine and appetizers in a smooth low tone. Meg was apparently on her way—not late by any means, but gentlemen and successful assassins always made arrangements early.

And besides, it took girls longer to get dolled up. Not that she needed much, what with those baby blues and glossy lips. Watching her apply that peach balm was distracting, to say the least.

"I'm worried about her." Boom at least waited until strangers cleared the area before going back into mission-planning mode. "Her last breakup was pretty rocky, and she's been doing the *I'm fine* thing ever since. I know her, she doesn't want me to worry. Then her accountant gets sent to prison and that dumbass secretary—"

"Hey now," Carl interjected, but mildly. "Frannie's perfectly nice."

"Fran thought she'd make it on the Strip and ran back home to corn country when she found out it isn't so easy." Boom's nose wrinkled, and it was rare for him to sound so savagely disparaging instead of just sarcastic. "And a fat lot of good she was during that whole Press thing, too. He fucking stalked her."

"Don't." It was Carl's turn to look like he'd smelled something bad. "If you get going on the subject I'll lose my appetite. At least his father put a muzzle on him and sent him out of town for a few months. More than I expected, frankly."

Huh. Tax settled in his own chair, glancing over his half of the picket. He and Boom were situated to watch each other's backs, and it was good to know that nothing would creep up on either of them. He eyed the table setting, wishing it was an engine, a first-aid kit to sort, or even a stack of paperwork Dez needed help wrangling.

"Anyway." Boom had his eyes on the prize, at least conversationally. "If you're on her I won't have to worry, all right?"

Yeah. From what Tax could see, Meg had all her shit together and her ducks in a row, too. There was very little for him to do in this situation, but at least it wasn't sitting around watching the walls. He'd already helped Klemp and his lady love deal with a clinging ex; if Boom wanted visuals on another for a while it was probably a good idea. The statistics on that sort of thing weren't good, and Tax knew them all. "Where are you going again?"

"Merbelows Hot Springs. Just a little camping, our last fling before the wedding. We had plans to go after, but they had a cancellation. And what else are *you* gonna do, just housesit?"

That wouldn't be bad, Tax thought. Boom had a small pool in the backyard, and the neighbors kept to themselves if that morning was any indication. He could plan his exit at leisure; hell, Tax could even drive around, get the lay of the land, and find a good spot. "You don't have a pet to feed or any houseplants for me to kill."

"We could just go afterward." Carl reached for his water. "But Eddie's right, the cancellation's kind of a gift, and anyway Meg—"

"Shit," Boom said, softly. "Incoming."

Tax twisted in his chair, looking over his shoulder, and for some reason his heart gave a funny little hop as if a mortar had fired in the distance, signaling the start to yet another session of murderous chaos.

Meg glided between tables both empty and full, her pale head held high. Her hair was twisted up, the pink tips barely showing, tendrils softening the severity of the style. Glittering silver earrings swung as she saw Boom and smiled, lifting one hand in a tentative wave. The dress was silver as well, hit just above the knee, and hugged her curves like it enjoyed every inch—and who wouldn't? Spaghetti straps lay lovingly against her shoulders. A tiny beaded clutch in her other hand, a small silver cross nestling just under the notch between her collarbones, and thread-thin silver bracelets on her left wrist completed the outfit, along with a pair of diamanté heels that looked a bit like glass slippers.

She made a helluva Cinderella, and watching her approach was like hearing Bach after a long time in the wilderness. The world took a deep breath, and something unknotted inside him.

Weird, but then again, he'd been driving long-distance for a few days, pretty much bathed in tequila last night, spent hours looking at wedding brochures, and was now in a Vegas restaurant that probably got its start with bootlegger cash, judging by the age of the building.

Besides, these were his last few weeks before he turned off the lights and stepped away, right? He could go with the flow. The lack of flashbacks or panic attacks today was probably just a function of sheer exhaustion.

Then, all of a sudden, she was *right there*, and he had to hurry to rise because both Boom and Carl had. Tax was the only one who hit the table with his knee on the way up, rippling the water in every goblet, but thankfully nobody seemed to notice.

"Evening, gents." The smile lit her up like a marquee. Her eyes downright sparkled, and instead of businesslike lip gloss, she wore wicked red lipstick and heavy kohl eyeliner. "I'm not late, am I?"

"Right on time." Boom offered his cheek for an air-kiss, and attended to her chair like a good little officer candidate. "And your antipasti's on the way, my fair lady. Where did you score that frock? It's divine."

"Salvation Army, but Marcy had some ideas on how to alter it." She beamed in Carl's direction; watching her sink onto red velvet upholstery was a treat.

Tax realized he was the only one still standing and hurried to drop back into his own seat, thankfully not bumping the table again. His knee throbbed, but he didn't feel it; she'd turned those big baby blues in his direction.

"There he is, my knight in shining. Eddie, your buddy saved my clients oodles of cash today and gave me ammunition for negotiating with at least five separate venues as well. Are you hiding any more like him back in the Army?"

"Christ, I hope not. One gives us enough trouble." Boom's grin was infectious. The wine arrived, menus were consulted, and Tax could sit back, listening to the conversation. Carl regarded him steadily over the table—looked like surfer boy was content to let the two social butterflies do their thing. Or maybe he just anticipated the fireworks when Boom finally laid out his proposal.

It was going to be an interesting dinner.

"YOU'RE GOING to Merbelows?" Her eyebrows arched, her wineglass's stem held in delicate fingertips, Meg pinned her childhood friend with a very amused, very blue stare. "Eddie, you utter sleaze."

"They had a cancellation." Boom had his puppy-dog stare on, full power. "It works out—Tax watches our place, we get to go on our honeymoon early, and you get an assistant who can do long division while standing on his head. It's a win for everyone."

Meg was clearly underimpressed with his enumeration of benefits.

"You're unloading your friend—who came out early to help you, no less—onto me so you and Carl can glamp and canoodle at the hot springs." She shook her head, and took a tiny sip of vinho verde. "Very disappointing, Edward."

The vast, aesthetically arranged antipasti platter was being thoroughly plundered and so was the wine selection. Tax stuck to water, since someone had to be the adult. Fatigue sank dull iron claws into his neck, but any member of the Squad could set that aside.

"We won't canoodle." Boom lifted three fingers. "Scout's honor."

Carl stirred, his eyebrows raising. "You told me you were never a Boy Scout."

"I got all the badges though, twenty-five cents apiece." The Squad's demo man glanced over Tax's shoulder, checking the restaurant's interior. Even while doing his best to charm and bamboozle, he didn't forget his job. "Seriously, though, Meg, it's the chance of a lifetime so I'm prepared to sweeten the deal. Name your price."

"Hm." The lady leaned back in her chair, and—why, God only knew—turned her attention to Tax. "What do you think, Arthur? You came out here for vacation, didn't you?"

I came out here to get everything tied off before a permanent AWOL, ma'am. But he couldn't say that; everything depended on his buddies as well as everyone else thinking he'd met with an accident. "I believe my orders were to help with wedding arrangements."

"Aha." Boom poured Carl another measure of wine. "But the orders didn't say which wedding, now do they? You could help at least fifty of them along while we're gone."

"Two, Edward. Not the ceremonies yet, but venue checks, tastings, at least one last-minute dress fitting, and that's not even counting the meetings I have to have with half a dozen assorted professionals who want my recommendation. Not including the ones with prospective clients." The correction was instant, the list delivered nearly all in one breath. "And I didn't ask you, so let your friend talk, for Chrissake."

Boom subsided, but the twinkle in his eye said he wasn't even close to chastened.

To be fair, Tax's remit was to help his buddy, and if Ed Baumgartner wanted to slip away for a week or so it fell to the team medic to hold down the fort. Which included covering during any inspections and keeping the CO happy.

Though if any of their commanding officers had looked like this, the entire Squad might still be in the Army. She tilted her head, those baby blues fixed on him once more, and Tax was wishing he was able to get a hit of the booze.

"It sounds interesting," he heard himself say. "I've always wondered about weddings."

Carl hid a smile behind his wineglass's rim. Boom's mouth compressed; he was trying like hell not to laugh in style and volume reminiscent of a foghorn.

But Meg was studying Tax anxiously, and for a moment she looked a lot younger. Maybe it was the wine's gentle haze on her, or those soft, practically bare shoulders. Beneath the veneer of quick, bantering professionalism was . . . something else.

"It's serious business." She sounded like she meant it, too. "People spend a lot of money on weddings, and it's important to them. If you come in cracking jokes and thinking you're better than they are, it shows."

Well, Tax didn't have Boom's sense of humor, or Klemp's. In fact, he wasn't finding a whole lot funny these days, though he did a good impression of amusement when he had to. "I'm a medic, Meg. I'm used to serious situations."

Like Klemp, pulse-bleeding from a hole torn in his artery. Or Jackson that one time in Guatemala, the knife still stuck in his back. Or poor, unlucky Footy Lenz.

Christ. Don't think about that. He was so goddamn tired of trying not to.

"Never loses his cool," Boom piped up. "Count on it. There was this one time—"

"Boom, for God's sake." What Tax wanted to say was *shut the fuck up, especially if it's classified.* "I'd love to help out," he continued, a little more loudly than necessary. "Really."

She searched his expression, and it was like being under one of Vincent Desmerais's inspections. Dez could paralyze a guilty soldier with a searching look and a half-drawled *well, what are we gonna do about this now?* It was probably one of the main reasons why he'd assumed command of their little outfit.

If you were gonna follow a man into hell, he had to be able to detect bullshit *and* express nearly parental displeasure in a way that forced even the most recalcitrant jackass to feel a little shame.

"Well then." A slight smile tilted up the corners of her mouth; Tax stared, helplessly, as she turned back to Boom. That lipstick was a few shades away from crimson, and it looked downright amazing on her. "I suppose I can be bought, if you're serious. I think our entrees are about to arrive, and both Arthur and I deserve dessert too. You're tipping thirty percent, don't forget. And after you're a married man, Eddie, you're going to owe me six months' worth of tango lessons. I always wanted to learn."

Boom groaned, sagging in his chair. "I should have known. Come on, Meg. Six months?"

"Half a year. Arthur?" Mischief damn near sparkled in the air around Meg, and she brushed at a tendril of pale, pink-tipped hair falling in her face. "What's three hundred and sixty-five divided by two?"

"One hundred eighty-two point five," he supplied, automatically. Good God, he was only drinking water, but he felt lightheaded. Maybe it was lack of sleep and only having a chicken Caesar salad for lunch—although any soldier could go for miles on empty. Was he turning into a numbnuts civilian already?

Nope. For better or for worse, he was a soldier. And now he was broken.

"One hundred eighty-two and a half days," she repeated. "You'll go to all the lessons with me, Eddie, and you won't bitch, moan, or complain. In fact, you'll act like you're having a great time. Deal?"

The arrival of the main course interrupted their bargaining, but by halfway through the leisurely dinner—the steak was good here, and the wine switched to red in honor of it—his buddy had given a solemn pinkie promise. Six months' worth of being Meg's partner for tango lessons didn't sound awful to Tax, but Boom acted like it was pulling teeth.

Doesn't matter. By then I'll be gone. Tax concentrated on mannerly instead of efficient eating, listening to the two of them bicker good-naturedly. Carl threw in a word every once in a while, and all in all it was . . . pleasant.

Dessert took almost as long, because the lady wanted to sample a few different things. Boom shared her gastronomic adventure, Carl had plain cheesecake—*like always*, Boom said, with a despairing sigh—and Tax went for a gelato something-or-another. He noticed Meg didn't share the strawberry shortcake, and despite the lateness of the hour she took down a few shots of espresso.

"Of course it won't keep me awake," she said, cheerfully, and when they all spilled out into a soft, dry desert night, a surprisingly chilly wind from the mountains should have made her shiver. Tax would've offered his suit jacket, but her rideshare was already pulling up in a silver Nissan and the lady was sternly admonished to text as soon as she got home.

Driving a slightly sloshed Boom and a serenely smiling Carl back to base was damn near enjoyable, especially with the windows down, and when Tax fell into his bed for the next few weeks in the room above the garage, he thought about her voice saying *a knight in shining*, but then he was out like a light almost as soon as his head touched the pillow.

There were, for once, no nightmares.

Impermeable Barrier

FOUR DAYS AFTER that very nice dinner, Meg waved goodbye as the pickup backed sedately out of Edward and Carl's driveway. The truck made a passable facsimile of halting before gliding past the stop sign at the end of the street—Carl must've been excited, it wasn't like him to California-roll.

Tax loomed behind her right shoulder. He didn't mean to, he was just so *tall*; he cradled a stainless-steel travel cup full of coffee black as sin and strong enough to eat a spoon. He and Eddie both preferred it that way, or the Army had put them in the habit.

"There they go," he muttered, and took a slurp. "Only half an hour late."

"I used to set Eddie's clock ahead on test days when we were in high school." Far enough in the past she could laugh about it now—waking up in a different room each morning, scrambling to keep each other fed and safe. "He never could get up on time until he went into the Army."

"Yeah, they'll teach you to do that." Morning gravel lingered in the words.

Carl still had a smoker's hack though he only sneaked a coffin-nail every once in a while, but Arthur sounded like talking hurt until noon. At least he was polite.

Well, that's that. She had a busy day, and parts of it were likely to be unpleasant. "Okay. It's Wednesday, which means I have pole class first thing, then I've got to go in for a few client calls. There's some filing and other stuff to do, but after that you can take the afternoon off."

"Time off?" Mock-dubiousness tinged the words. "Is that legal?"

"Today it's an absolute requirement. Are you sure you don't want to meet me at the office?"

"And miss out on something called pole class?" Fortunately, he didn't sound salacious at all, but honestly interested.

She had to laugh. "Just remember the rules."

Traffic was no problem since she knew the back way to Pleasant

Hill; Tax hadn't complained once about either her driving or the music. Spring was heating up, so it was her patented ready-to-rock playlist, with a heavy dose of 80s hair bands—Poison, the Crüe, Slaughter, Axl and Slash. But, since any good list needed tension and leavening, there was also plenty of contiguous pop and quite a bit of Meatloaf, not to mention some New Wave to provide angst and synthesizers.

The wood-floored, cavernous studio was comfortingly familiar, the air-conditioning earning its paycheck even this early in the season. Tax took one look at the forest of static poles filling a third of the main room and his eyebrows went up a little, but he settled in the mommy fishbowl—where parents lingered to watch their kids stumble-stagger through barre and floorwork—with his coffee, a Serious Look, and a reiteration of deadly serious instructions.

No whistling, no banging on the window, no jokes about dollar bills. Do not embarrass me or Eddie will help bury you out in the desert.

All she got was a nod and a mumble, like he'd wanted to say *yes ma'am* and stopped himself just in time. He settled on one of the couches with his legs stretched out, coffee on a rickety magazine-strewn table at his elbow and his smartphone held up like a shield.

The class for current and former professionals was usually either deserted or every single pole taken; today it leaned heavily toward the latter and Shannon the leggy, teased-hair instructor was already warming up, fuzzy disco throbbing through recessed speakers.

"Meg!" Redheaded Penny had saved her a spot near one of the best mirrors. "Over here!"

It was good to stretch out, good to warm up, and by the time they were halfway into the first sequence she was beginning to feel almost awake. Pole class was her time to think, to plan, and to move without worrying, plus it was great for core strength. It was the one thing she did purely and solely for herself, thrice a week.

The music shifted to trap-and-bass instead of disco or the shop-worn beats any professional got sick of inside a week of serious stage-work, and even the air-conditioning couldn't hold back the sweat of twenty women as they climbed, leaned, kept their centers tight, felt the burn in thighs and glutes, and stretched their arms.

Cooldown was old-school deep-dive R&B, like every other class with Shannon, who always kicked your ass but made sure you didn't leave without a good stretch and even a bit of yoga. Pleasant Hill's showers were capacious, the water hot, but Meg didn't take long and Wednesdays were low-makeup anyway. She could even bring her big tan leather purse instead of a bag color-coded to her outfit.

Her life had a schedule now, instead of the frantic scrabble for survival in her early years, and she was pleased to keep it. Unfortunately, today was out of the ordinary, and not just because she had cargo.

Arthur was still in the waiting room, but the dance magazines on every table had been stacked neatly and the tissue boxes placed precisely near every lamp. It was vanishingly unlikely that Molly the receptionist had popped in to take care of that, unless she'd been curious about a guy waiting for the pre-opening class to finish; the desk was still empty when they passed on their way out.

Shannon was at the door, unlocking and flipping the open sign. She waved benevolently as students trooped out and petite, brunette Molly hurried in from the parking lot, her purse slipping from one shoulder and her eyeshadow askew.

Looked like she'd had a rough night, but then again, this was Vegas.

And Tax *still* didn't say anything, though—like Eddie when he got back from basic training—he wanted to open her car door. She'd broken Ed of that particular habit, but this guy probably wasn't going to be around long enough to teach.

IT WAS PLEASANT to work with the glass door between the inner and outer office propped open. Client calls went well, with only the usual hassles—newly discovered guest allergies necessitating catering changes, schedule conflicts discovered, future mothers-in-law with bright ideas the brides wanted to either get a price tag for or needed help tactfully deflecting, relatives in a budget pinch needing hotel space priced accordingly, grooms uneasy at the mounting costs or brides determined to get every last penny's worth. Each problem demanded sympathy, practicality, and sometimes a promise to smooth things over before administering a carefully calibrated dose of asskicking, though she made it a policy to never accept feedback from anyone except the about-to-be-wedded couple.

It got messy if you let *anyone* past that wall. An impermeable barrier was good policy for all sorts of things.

Work went so well, in fact, that they were both done early. Then it was back to Eddie's to drop off her hardworking temporary employee. She even punched the stereo knob to turn her midday rap playlist off completely as they idled in the driveway. "You're a lifesaver." She kept her foot on the brake, and wished she had the rest of the day to herself as well. "I'll pick you up tomorrow at eight—it's venue tours with a couple clients, so we'll be out and about all day. I'll need you to look over amended rate sheets at each place."

"Sounds like fun." He collected his travel mug, and hesitated. "You sure you don't need me?"

Maybe he got bored easily. Some people couldn't relax if they weren't *doing*, and she should know. "I've got a lunch date with a special client. The family doesn't like strangers, so it's best if I go alone."

"Oh. Okay." He still didn't move. "You've got my number, right?"

"I do." *Clearly, since we were just texting yesterday because Carl was freaking out over not having enough sunscreen.* Still, she had to grin; he had an eye for details, another quality she appreciated. No wonder Eddie spoke so highly of his buddies. "There's no cell reception out at the hot springs anyway, so if something goes wrong or you can't find something in the house, just text me. You shouldn't need any passwords for cable or streaming since their box is all set up, you're already on their Wi-Fi, and you know where the liquor cabinet is. Just don't drown yourself in the pool, all right? I promised Eddie I'd look after you."

"Yeah. Sounds great." He reached for the handle. "Same goes, all right? I promised him too."

She restrained an eyeroll only through massive force of will. "Don't worry about me, Arthur, I'm a local. Go sit in the pool and try to unwind. Do some long division for fun or something."

He didn't even crack a smile, but at least he didn't make one of those uncomfortable twitches like he wanted to salute, either. Meg watched to make sure he could get in—he had the spare key that was usually tucked under a particular rock in the backyard—and was surprised by a deep sigh.

Really not looking forward to this. She turned the stereo back on and picked up her phone, deciding the situation called for battle music.

By the time she hit the stop sign at the end of the street, Lizzo was singing about being good as hell. The rest of the mix was Sia, Halsey, Carole King, Joan Jett, the immortal Siouxsie, Callas and Caballé among others—no boys, just girl-power ballads all the way.

Play Along

THE MORNING'S dishes were put away, his hands stinging with repeated washing and sanitizer, his temporary quarters were so shipshape a half-dollar could bounce off the neatly made bed, there was no trace of his presence other than a toothbrush in the porcelain holder of the attached half-bath, and the television had every channel known to man as well as all the streaming services God could ever ask humanity for.

Tax had even found the arsenal—at least, the bits of it a fellow Squad member could dig up. Naturally Boom would have a few little surprises elsewhere, but it would be rude to rummage around for those.

It was enough to know he had options, as well as the kit he'd brought with him. Tax roamed the tiny guest quarters over the garage, the living room, the kitchen and dining room. Housesitting was like being on a stage set; breathing in the odors of someone else's habitation gave a weird sense of being on an alien spaceship.

At least there were no cameras inside. Boom knew better than *that*, and had talked Carl into confining their security footage to outdoors.

Wonder what she's doing. Lunch with a special client, she said, but that calm professional mask slipped for half a second and her glossy lips turned down a fraction. Subtle, but then any glimpse behind the wall was like that.

Oh, she put up a good front. Quick as a whip with verbal self-defense; she handled Boom's wisecracks effortlessly and probably could even give Klemp a run for his trash-talking money. Listening to her on the phone was a joy, because she could shift from Zen calm to bright cheery *go ahead and fuck with me, son, you'll regret it* on a dime, with no discernible hitch in between. Smoothing ruffled bridal feathers to politely reading an overcharging venue the riot act with level logic and disdain even the crustiest up-chain commander would have to give way before—was there anything the girl couldn't do?

And then there was 'pole class.' Any member of the Squad might have a moment of aesthetic appreciation while watching twenty women and an instructor climb, lean, spin, invert, and . . . good God, he was almost sweating just thinking about it, because he'd barely seen any of the others. One platinum-haired pixie in shorts and a battered sleeveless sweatshirt drew the gaze like a magnet, and while she was contorting in ways that required serious core strength she forgot to keep that ironclad little smile. He could see behind that polished, cheerful veneer.

It was a shame, really. Even if he hadn't had a panic attack for a few days and the nightmares were in temporary abeyance, he still had one foot out the door so it wasn't fair to even think about . . . whatever it was he was considering.

So Tax settled on the big cream-colored wraparound couch—good thing Boom didn't have any pets—and flicked through channels. Nothing was worth more than a few moments of abstract attention. Occasionally he'd happen onto an action scene or war documentary, staring dully as his brain raced through treatment protocols and likely triage. One channel featured surgeries, and he made himself sit and watch for the required time just to be sure he now felt nothing at the sight of another person's insides.

Then the memory of hot blood against his fingers intruded, his heart sped up, and the telltale black blots bloomed at the edge of his vision. A finger-flick changed the channel; he had to think about something else.

What's she having for lunch? He wasn't hungry, and it didn't matter anyway. Why should he fuel this particular body? There might be another one waiting if reincarnation was real, but that might be its own particular kind of hell.

On the other hand, Boom would be worried if there was a single wrong note. Tax had to lean in, consume just enough to play the part, and it was two weeks to the wedding.

Christ, I'm not gonna make it. But he had to.

He left the TV on but the volume a low formless mutter, wandered into the kitchen, and checked his phone. It was a Wednesday, Mom was playing pinochle with her card club but she'd texted a couple times. She wasn't worried, it was all habitual, normal. Later, she'd say there was no warning.

He had to make it look like an accident. Which required a little more planning, but it would also absolve his buddies and his mother of any bad feelings. The only trouble was doing it in such a way Dez or Jackson wouldn't catch on.

You had to get up pretty early in the morning to get one over on

Desmarais, and the Squad's resident wildcard had a weird variety of constantly operating low-grade bullshit detector plus all the restless curiosity of a coked-up raccoon. Neither of them would stop digging if there was even a hair out of place.

Tax thought about it while making a ham sandwich, cut precisely on the diagonal, and rustling up a single-serving bag of plain potato chips. Boom liked Doritos and Carl was fond of corn chips, but the rejects from the assorted packs were just fine by Tax. A crunch and a little salt, what more could anyone want?

Well, there were things a man *could* wish for. Was she at a table in a nice restaurant, laughing at a client's feeble joke? No, any male client she met was likely to be engaged.

But what if a groom-to-be brought backup? That could happen.

She drove like a law-abiding, considerate bat out of hell, and usually with bass thumping all through that blue convertible. There didn't seem to be a single genre of music she didn't like, but she wasn't an indiscriminate listener. Someone could spend a few years figuring out her favorites, why she played certain things at certain times, and still be hopelessly puzzled when she pulled out a new beat.

Tax went back to mindless flipping through channels after the lunch dishes were washed, dried, and carefully put away. The pool looked nice, but the air-conditioning was better. It was the most peace and quiet he'd had in a very long time, and the mounting discomfort was going to get outright painful before long.

He kept waiting for a shoe to drop. A bullet to whiz past, a mortar to thump, a sudden burst of quietly lethal violence, the snap of a tripwire, something. Anything to break the tension, even if it ended with writhing-wet intestines spilling over his hands and the light dimming in a soldier's eyes.

You're really fucked up, Tachmann.

The thick dusty sunshine glaring outside took on a richer cast as afternoon began to die away. It was drier than California light, and sharper. He and Boom were desert creatures; ovens were just fine by them, but only if the humidity was middle-to-low. Jungles sucked ass.

He slipped into a doze. Was she heading out for dinner, nodding along to a throbbing bass line? Getting dressed up for a date, glad she'd gotten a reprieve from babysitting Boom's buddy? The television was a colorful smear, and he could have been in a ready room waiting for jumpoff except Carl had scented candles scattered around, so it smelled better than any Army base could.

He could dream, couldn't he? That was free. . . .

BZZZZT. Pause. *Bzzzt*.

Tax jerked into full wakefulness, reaching for a gun that wasn't close at hand since he was a guest, goddammit. His phone slipped off the edge of the cushion; he lunged for it and missed, got the toe of his boot underneath the falling rectangle and popped it back up, neatest trick of the week. Caught it and stared, blinking at the screen for a moment before realizing what he was seeing, letters making a name.

Meg Callahan. No picture, but at least he'd put her in contacts. It was buzzing because he hated hearing a phone ring; even the haptics were enough sound for someone to find you in a darkened room.

It vibrated one final time, and he realized it was about to go to voicemail. He jabbed at the phone's face, swiping frantically, and managed to get the damn thing both to answer the call and to his ear upside-down. "Hello?" *Shit*. He righted it, rubbing at his eyes with his free hand. He'd slept hard enough to get grainy, and no dreams.

At first he thought it was a wrong number, or a butt-dial. There was the formless almost-static of outside air, a mutter of traffic . . . but no music.

"Hello?" he repeated, stupidly. *Not reading you, Base. Come in, repeat, come in.*

Another sound, one he couldn't quite identify at first. His body knew, though, and his guts turned cold, skin tightening as adrenaline hit the bloodstream and the feeling of *oh boy here we go* slid soft fingers down his back, dread plus high hard brassy excitement tipping their gently scratching claws.

"Meg?" Nice and even, the same tone he'd use with a terrified civilian package they had to retrieve from enemy territory. He hated calm-them-down duty, but he was the medic; he and Klemp were usually in charge of keeping the rabbits from going into shock or doing something stupid. Surprisingly, Boom was best at it, but he usually had other duties.

The sound came again—a small sob, with a sharp inhale at the end. "Arthur?" she whispered.

"That's me." He should've been already moving, gathering kit and his car keys; a woman didn't sound like this unless shit had, in proper military parlance, gone *fuckin' fubar*. But he was frozen, perched on Boom's ghost-pale couch like a bump on a log. "Where you at, Meg?"

"Arthur," she repeated, and her breathy, broken little tone didn't just ring the alarms. It hit every panic button in existence, and he was at DEFCON Two only because he didn't have a location to go straight to One on. "I'm sorry, I . . . I'm so sorry."

What the hell for? "Where are you, Meg? Take a deep breath and tell me where you're at."

"I'm so sorry." Still whispering—was she hurt? Bleeding? No way to tell. "They shot my car."

Step Lively

IN ANY OTHER city the big stone mansion with its red-tiled roof, carriage and poolhouses, ten-car garage, rolling green lawn, and overwatered garden would be garish. Still, in Vegas a quiet sort of garishness—all things considered—passed within kissing distance of class. The long driveway had just been unnecessarily but thoroughly resealed, black as pitch and shiny enough to give a tired driver migraines; the mini hedge-maze just to the right of the main house was a little taller since she'd been out here last, despite being clipped into shape every week.

The front door was for salesmen and party guests; Meg used the side entrance from the garage leading into a tiled utility room and was greeted by a lean, lantern-jawed man, dapper as usual in a navy suit, a silver tie clip glittering against blue silk, and wingtips polished to a mirror gloss. "Lovely as always, Meg. The hair's a nice touch."

"Hi, Barton." She offered her cheek for an air-kiss, getting a good whiff of his aftershave—expensive but not overwhelming, to match the rest of him. "Where's Matilda?" The housekeeper was usually eager to see the family's almost-adopted child, the only one of Ella's high school friends to stand the test of time.

"Day off. Her granddaughter's quinceañera, I think." Rob Barton's eyes were the exact color of cold leftover coffee, like Eddie's when he got into That Mood. *Roark's right hand*, they called him, or *that goddamn Ivy League bastard*, but the latter never where he—or Gerry—could hear.

He handled the legal side of the Roark businesses, which over the past twenty years or so had come to outweigh the other more and more. Still, the family name commanded respect, and in some cases outright fear.

It wasn't smart to know more about that, so Meg pretended she didn't. You heard all sorts of things in this town, and some of them were even true. Fortunately no crusading journalist or tin-star lawman had decided to go after a man who was, after all, taking his family *out* of the shadows, and everyone in the gloom of the underside figured it was safest to leave Gerry alone.

Though there were still whispered tales about his younger days. You did not fuck with Gerrald Roark, no sir.

"Good Lord, Tammy's fifteen?" Meg had to stop and think. "Wait, no, or is it Alma?" *I'm too young to say 'how time flies.'*

"The younger one." Barton paused, half-turning and indicating the hallway with a slight, urbane motion. "She likes whales, I think?" It was the type of detail he was good at.

"That'd be Alma, yeah. Tilda must be over the moon." Meg fell into step beside him, her kitten heels tapping but his shoes silent. Air-conditioned quiet enfolded her, along with the scent of a house too big for its occupants yet nonetheless cleaned relentlessly daily. "So, you've checked out this guy Ella's getting hitched to, right? Ben?"

"Thoroughly. And yes, Benjamin McMurtry. Thirty-two, good record, he's done with his residency and he has no debts other than school loans." Barton glanced down at her; his leanness made him look shorter than Gerry, or maybe it was just charisma which made the older man seem larger than life. "Quite a relief."

You said it, I didn't. "Especially that last bit. Aunt Stace isn't going to be upset, is she?" That was important; Stacey had married into the Flanagans, but she would always be Gerry's only sister and pissing her off was not in Meg's best interest.

"Of course not." A ghost of amusement lingered in Barton's tone. "She's very busy—Levi's second child is due in August—so she suggested to Gerry that you handle the planning."

That was a deep relief. Meg hesitated, not sure how to broach the next subject.

Of course, since he was Rob, he anticipated. It was what he was good at. "It will just be us, Gerry, and Ella today. Preston had another appointment."

More relief, almost making her knees wobbly. Or maybe that was just the morning's workout lingering in her limbs. "Ah. I see." She sniffed, cautiously, as they took a hard right; the kitchen was just ahead. "Is that . . .?"

"There she is," a rich round tenor crowed. "Finally! Was beginning to think you'd never visit your auld da again, Miss Callahan. Come over and give us a kiss."

Copper-bottomed pans hanging from the ceiling, the appliances commercial-grade and the two stainless-steel refrigerators burnished to glowing—the rustic kitchen was blessedly familiar, especially the bar of sunlight falling through the bay window glowing in Matilda's carefully tended herbs. Gerry Roark was at the smaller range, a snow-white towel flung over his shoulder; fragrant steam puffed from the skillet in front of him.

"Fajitas." She hurried to obey, peeking at the stove; the table in the breakfast nook was set for four and there were three capacious terracotta holders, probably packed with Matilda's signature tortillas in both flour and maize. "How did you know?"

"Your favorite, kiddo." He offered one shaven cheek for a decorous peck and grinned, his veneers as polished as ever. "And don't worry about Stacey, she told me I'd better have you handle the wedding because she can't, along with, I quote, *little Meg will make sure it's done right.*"

"I do my best." Of course he'd predicted her unease; he wouldn't have lasted long on the underside if he lacked that sort of skill. Then again, Meg did her best to live an uneventful and predictable life.

Staying inside the lines was boring, but it was also safe.

She would have firmly friendzoned Press all their lives if Gerry hadn't already been moving away from what the family called *real business.* All the long-stemmed roses and champagne dates in the world couldn't make up for marrying into that kind of mess.

"Meg!" A shriek from another hallway was Ella, who burst into the kitchen on a cloud of perfume. Her sundress was covered with bright red cherries; her long sheaf of entirely natural strawberry-blonde hair swayed heavily. "And just in time. Want a drink?"

"Coffee, Ell, I've gotta drive later." Meg stole a bit of sliced bell pepper, grinning as Gerry mock-menaced her with the spatula. Rob headed for the fridge, probably for sweet tea; it was amazing his teeth were in such good condition, but no doubt he flossed more than once daily and counted every toothbrush stroke.

For a short while Meg could be fourteen again, a stray teenager scared to death of taking up space, staying too long, or even breathing too deeply. Eddie understood what it was to be a forgotten kid, and ever since the orphanage, they'd done their best to look out for each other.

But the Roarks never made her feel anything less than completely accepted since the moment Ell brought her home and announced *Dad, this is my best friend Meg.* Even Mrs. Roark—divorced now and retired to Palm Springs with a hefty alimony Gerry never openly complained about paying—had been kind enough in a distant, alcoholic-hazy way.

"Be a love and get the sour cream, will you?" Gerry returned his attention to the skillet, fierce concentration settling over his tanned, beaky face. His hair was still dark and vigorous, but receding swiftly. "And Ell, my dear, make enough coffee for me and Rob too. Seven minutes to lunch, everyone, step lively."

"AUGH, NO, I can't." Meg waved away the tortilla container. "Thanks, though. And if you believe it, the mother-in-law next starts screaming about the price of the scented candles, and her son's trying to get her to calm down—"

Gerry leaned back in his chair, his hard little middle-aged potbelly shaking as he laughed. Even Barton was smiling as he poured coffee from the stainless-steel carafe, settling back into his chair with a satisfied sigh. Ella was half out of her own seat, leaning on Meg's shoulder, giggling soundlessly.

Meg shook her head. "It ended with the other three parents dragging the lady out, the bride in tears, and the poor groom looking like a confused sheepdog because his ponytail holder had snapped. The guests either had secondhand embarrassment or were trying like hell not to laugh. Then the photographer leans over . . ." She had to pause, take a gulp of ice water, and suppress her own chuckles. "And he says to me, *Should I get a few shots of the candles?*"

"Oh, Christ Jesus," Gerry moaned. "Noooo."

Rob laughed outright, covering his mouth as if he couldn't quite believe he had permission to chortle. Ella shuddered with merriment, her knee bumping a table leg and making the silverware rattle.

"Weddings are crazy," Meg finished, triumphantly. "So believe me, Ell, if I can handle *that*, yours is gonna be no problem at all."

Ella sagged, hiccupping with giggles. Barton coughed, wiping at his eyes; for a moment they were a bit warmer than usual. Gerry shook his head, dabbing at his mouth with a sky-blue linen napkin.

It would take the hilarity a little while to die down, so she carefully pushed her chair back. Ella swayed, returning to her own seat while still giggling chipmunk-quick; Meg grabbed her purse from the back of her own chair with a flourish. "And now I have to visit the restroom," she announced, "so you'll all have to amuse yourselves for a minute."

Always leave them wanting more was a necessity in Vegas, and besides, she had to check her phone and put a bit of lip gloss on. It was a low-makeup day, true, but she still felt a little too schlubby for public consumption.

The good smell of seared steak, grilled onions, and bell pepper followed her down the hall; the bathroom was another old friend.

Scented soaps and potpourri changed at regular intervals—Tilda had very definite ideas about that sort of thing—and the pale green towels were new, but still, it was comforting to know exactly what was under the sink and that when she returned to the table Gerry would ask her a few questions about wedding prep, showing his interest even if he was mystified by the arcana of 'woman stuff.' Barton would listen, leaning back and sipping a fresh cup of java; Ell would fidget through the boring discussion until she could kidnap Meg for a good gossip session in her bedroom or the upstairs lounge, both she and Gerry overriding Meg's offers to do the dishes since Tilda was gone.

She'd still do them before she left, as a silent thank-you to the housekeeper who had taught her more about etiquette than any expensive finishing school could ever dream. Meg would have to send a present for Alma, something suitably small and tasteful, probably whale-related.

She took her time, washing her hands, applying eyeliner, enjoying the quiet. Gerry rarely had music playing downstairs, preferring an almost funereal hush. Ell would turn the TV on as soon as they settled in a room—the channel didn't matter, just a bright picture and the breathless sense of exciting things happening somewhere, anywhere.

A final once-over, and Meg was ready for the afternoon. She headed down the hall at a brisk clip, thinking maybe she could in fact handle another fajita—Gerry regarded the proper cooking of steak close to a religion—and was almost to the kitchen when two coughing *pop* sounds barreled past her.

Maybe Gerry was breaking out some champagne? If Matilda had left some strawberry shortcake in the fridge to celebrate with, maybe—

Meg stepped into the kitchen, a greeting dying on her lips, and stared.

The pans on the stove were normal, and so were the prep bowls piled in the sink. A plastic spray bottle stood next to the skillet, labeled *Agua* in Tilda's careful copperplate script—you couldn't cook without steam, she averred—and the towels hanging over the bar on the oven door were cheerfully mussed. Thick yellow sunshine poured itself on the herbs in the bay window, a golden stripe almost reaching the breakfast nook.

The table was cluttered with dishes, but the blue pottery sour cream container was on its side. One of the tortilla holders had fallen and shattered, terracotta slivers and two maize discs scattered on the floor. A good smell of fresh coffee mixed with an acrid stink, and for a moment she thought Gerry might've had a heart attack and fallen, because his chair was on its side and he lay on the floor with a hand pressed to his chest, one of his house slippers kicked free and the foot it belonged to twitching madly in a plain black cotton sock.

Ell was leaning over her chair arm again, but to the opposite side. Her big hazel eyes were wide and thoughtful, her mouth open slightly as if in surprise. There was a small, tidy hole in her forehead, over her right eyebrow. Her hands dangled to either side, pink-lacquered nails gleaming as if still wet.

"Meg," Barton croaked, harshly.

Meg flinched, staring, her head slightly tilted.

There was a stranger in the breakfast nook, a stocky man in a dark tracksuit and grey hoodie. For a vertiginous instant she thought he was hugging Rob, but then she saw an ugly metal muzzle with a dark hole at its end, and Barton made a hoarse sound of effort.

It had to be a practical joke. Any second now Gerry would leap to his feet. *Fooled ya, Meg! Come over, give us a kiss.* Or Ell would start to laugh, unable to contain herself, like during the eighth-grade drama club's very serious rendition of Peter Pan's 'clap for Tinkerbell' scene, when she'd gone into hysterical giggles opening night, right on the stage.

Now Meg could see that Gerry had a hole in his face too, but it was bigger, half his cheek gone and whitish flecks amid the mess. Teeth, she realized.

Bits of his *teeth*.

"Meg," Barton rasped again. "Run."

The man in the hoodie gave her a brief, disinterested glance. He looked normal except for the gun, pointed straight at her because Rob had him by the wrist. The stranger was wearing yellow latex gloves, and a bit of reddish hair peeked out from under the hoodie. He had freckles, she saw with a strange, swimming sense of horror, and wondered why that should seem so awful. Maybe it was his eyes—clear and greenish, but terribly empty.

"Meg, goddammit." Barton shoved at his opponent. The gun twitched, made a loud popping noise, and something in the kitchen shattered. A curl of smoke rose from the round black mouth. "Son-of a*bitch*—"

She could count on one hand the times she'd heard Rob Barton curse. He never sounded irritated, let alone angry, even when Press had that second DUI and. . . .

Another flurry of shoving; the two men hugged again, almost indecently close. Meg's hand flew to her mouth, clapping hard over a fresh application of Strawberry Do lip gloss. Her heartbeat, thick and cottony, pounded in her ears.

The gun was now clasped between the two straining figures. Barton's gaze met hers, surprised and thoughtful as Ella's. His lips moved, and she knew what he was saying even if she couldn't hear it over the roaring in her ears.

Meg. Fucking run.

Meg backed up. Her hip hit a copper drawer pull, but she didn't feel it. Rob stiffened, his mouth opening slightly like he'd just had a helluva good idea and couldn't wait to share.

Oh, God. Meg staggered back, slipping on beautiful cherrywood laminate, and ran.

SHE TRIPPED ON the steps to the garage and fell heavily, almost losing the tan leather purse, her hair knocked free and falling in her face. Scrabbled to hands and knees, ramming her shoulder against the bumper of Ell's little red Miata—this year's model, because nothing was too good for Gerry's little girl—and lunged upright, staggering drunkenly toward her own car, pulled in right next to it. The opener for this bay lived in her glove box, presented to her with the keys to a used green Honda sedan the day she graduated high school.

And no arguing, Meg, Gerry had said sternly. *You can't ride the bus in this damn town. It's too dangerous.* Eddie had been both pleased she'd acquired wheels and deeply distrustful of such a huge gift from a man like Roark. . . .

Someone was making a thin, whistling little noise, interspersed with sobbing gasps. It was her, Meg realized. She was doing it.

A nightmare. It had to be a bad dream. She'd wake up in her own bed, an entire day of work, arranging events, and smoothing the waters in front of her. Meg pawed at the blue convertible's driver-side door, managing to swing it open with more luck than anything else, and collapsed into the seat, her chest heaving.

"No," someone was whimpering. "No, no, nononono *Ellllllaaaaaa . . .*"
Stop it.

She jumped guiltily, pale hair falling into her face as she peered wildly in every possible direction. The voice was Barton's, a low commanding tone she'd only heard once or twice when Gerry sent him to collect Preston on the rare occasions Roark Senior decided the young man had Gone Too Far. Why she should hear it now was beyond her, but there was no time for that, because it spoke again.

Get your key in the ignition, Meg. Do it now.

She had to dump her purse's contents over the passenger seat; her phone went skittering into the footwell. She jammed the key home, twisted it, and the engine sprang to life. Then she reached blindly for the garage door opener, left on the dash; she had to jab at the button twice before a widening streak of sunshine showed on the wall in front of her. There were tools and other things hanging on the far right-hand wall's pegboard sheets, but all she could see through the windshield was blank white paint since she hadn't backed in.

Put the car in reverse. Hurry.

Meg obeyed. Her vision blurred, a hot film of tears stretch-warping the world. The convertible jolted into motion just as a shadow filled the door to the utility room.

It was the man in the hoodie, the gun in his hand pointed at her convertible. His mouth moved as if he was cussing, too, but she caught only a glimpse as her car lurched drunkenly out onto a wide black plain of pavement. She cut the wheel with a vengeance, hit the brakes so hard the tires squealed, and frantically clawed the steering in the other direction while fumbling for the gearshift again. No music, just the muffled thumping in her ears and the ratcheting sound of her breath—the car dropped into neutral, and she sobbed again before getting it firmly seated in drive.

"OhGod." A low terrified moan. "OhGodplease, *please*, Ella . . ."

Step lively now, Gerry whispered. But he couldn't be talking, because half his face was gone.

There were two SUVs that didn't belong in front of the mansion, a pale-blue one near the front door and the other, big and black as sin with privacy tinted windows, slanted with its nose pointed at the driveway. The doors on the former were swinging open, and there were two more men in hoodies hopping out into the sunshine.

Meg stamped on the gas. Tires chirped and her precious blue baby gulped fuel, probably not believing she was being so abrupt. There was a popping sound and a shivering—later, she could swear she felt something brush past her ear, a ragged circular fissure blooming in the back window, thank God she had the top up but. . . .

The windshield shivered, cracks spreading like a bad special effect from a suddenly blooming hole, and she realized the guys near the driveway had guns too.

Big ones, and about to be pointed right at her.

Drive, Meg. This time it wasn't Barton's voice but Ella's, deadly serious as she hardly ever was. *Drive fast, right now. Come on, bitch, let's go.*

The gas pedal hit the floor. Meg clutched the wheel, and she screamed as the passenger window disintegrated. Then she was past, veering down the driveway, hoping like hell the gates at the bottom of the slight hill were open.

And also praying desperately she wouldn't lose a tire.

A Bit of Business

IT'S A RESTAURANT, she'd whispered into the phone. *Across from the gas station. I'm so sorry. Please hurry.*

The city was unfamiliar, but no more so than any other the Squad had navigated. GPS was a lifesaver—when you didn't have to worry about your device being tracked, that was, and if he had her location someone else might too.

He was trained to think that way. It didn't necessarily mean she was in that kind of trouble.

Did it?

The urge to smash the pedal down and career through traffic like Klemp given the go-sign for a quick retreat had its teeth in Tax's guts, but he ignored it. Getting more details out of her over the phone was a distraction, and in any case, she sounded about ready to collapse—*stay put*, he'd said, and now he was hoping it was the right advice.

It was probably nothing. A simple car accident, a shaken-up girl blindly grasping for reassurance—but why would she call *him*? Sure, Boom was out of pocket, but she had to have other people she could count on. Probably a whole battalion; she was just so . . . there wasn't a word. Who wouldn't want to at least be friends with a woman so brightly, vibrantly alive?

His number might have been the last one she dialed, and thus the first selected in a panic. That was the most likely explanation, but it didn't matter. Tax was boots on the ground, plus he wasn't doing anything else this afternoon. It could even count as a good deed, not that it would outweigh any of the opposite he and the Squad had committed.

You didn't train a group of morally flexible motherfuckers to slip in, create maximum mayhem, and vanish just for funsies. Nor did you train them for quiet extractions and interrogations without being ready to break a few plausibly deniable eggs.

This was probably just a bit of civilian annoyance. But Tax couldn't stop thinking about that one worrying little tidbit—*they shot my car*. Maybe he'd misheard? People said funny things while in shock. He would arrive to find cops, a firetruck, maybe an ambulance, and a shaking, possibly embarrassed Meg Callahan; it would be a great story to tell Boom and Carl when they returned.

Tax didn't warm up the police scanner bolted under the dash; he had an idea they might not be quite legal in this neck of the woods and driving up with an active squawk-box was a good way to make a nosy cop even more curious. Habit as well as inclination wanted to keep him below the radar.

No flashing lights, no sirens. In fact, the entire street was so dead normal he almost drove right past the entrance to the correct parking lot, GPS not quite catching up in time. But she'd given him enough details to get a visual lock, so he cut the wheel hard and the black Honda CR-V bounced gently up a slight incline.

A huge day-bleached neon sign said *Shoresy's Eats*, but the low brick building looked for all the world like a repurposed Denny's, right up to the shape of the roof. The lot held a light sprinkling of cars in the bright buttery simmering of a desert afternoon, and Tax realized he was sweating lightly even though the car's air-conditioning was doing signal service. His nape crawled for good measure, and those fingernails were going down his back in rivulets because it was too goddamn quiet.

There was no sign of a zippy blue convertible, smashed-up or otherwise. He pulled into the spot next to the handicapped zone—*princess parking*, Klemp would call it, with a low chuckle—and popped the gearshift up to P, covering the brake and scanning what he could see of the restaurant's interior. The windows were clear except for some dancing pies painted near the swinging glass door, holding up a sign about a spring sale.

His phone lit up, so he freed it from the dash holder. The screen said *Meg Callahan* again, thank God. "Hello?"

"Arthur?" A choked little whisper. "Are you at the restaurant?"

"I am." He scanned the interior again—a briskly moving waitress in a pink polyester uniform, a glitter from the stainless-steel window where the cook would set loaded plates, three occupied tables. No fairy in sight, not a single pink-tinted hair. "I don't see you or your car. Where—"

"Are you in a black SUV?" The words wobbled, and she drew in a sharp, hitching little breath like she was in pain. "With dark windows?"

What the hell is going on? "That would be me," he said, cautiously. "Black Honda, California plates. I'm here to get you, like I said I would. Where are you?" *Calm her down, then get answers.*

"Stay there." The call cut off abruptly, and he wasn't just uneasy.

No, Tax was flat-out *alarmed* now, and the feeling only mounted when he caught a flicker of motion in the rearview mirror. His jaw threatened to drop; she must've been at the Shell station across the street, because she darted across four lanes of thankfully light traffic and hopped onto the thin excuse for a sidewalk, nearly tripped over the curb separating the walkway from the restaurant lot, and made a beeline for his vehicle.

What. The fuck?

He barely managed to get the passenger door unlocked before she was tugging at the latch. A burst of dry, hot, exhaust-laden air dumped her into the seat.

In dance class she'd worn Spandex shorts, a sports bra, sleeveless sweatshirt, and a tight, small pink-edged ponytail. She'd pulled away from Boom's in a grey twinset, skirt hitting just above the knee, tiny pearl buttons on the thin sweater, a little dark eyeliner and lip gloss, her hair in a twist with the dyed ends mostly tucked away.

Now her kitten heels were scuffed and her hair was a gorgeous windblown mess, her sweater askew and ferocious scrape-bruises marring vulnerable bare knees. Dead pale, though with two spots of high color high on her cheeks, and her eyeliner was smudged. She was breathing in great jagged gasps, and she'd lost one of her gold hoop earrings. The gold stud in her nose gleamed and thin bracelets on her left wrist jangled as she twisted in the seat, attempting to look in every direction at once. Along with the scent of sage, dust, and car-breath there was a tang of sweat, her vanilla-musk perfume, and a deeper, very familiar note.

Fear.

"We should go." Her voice was a low rough husk; she clutched her purse to her chest and regarded him with wide, terror-darkened eyes. "I'm so sorry. I don't know what to do, I need time to think."

"Slow down." The engine was still running, and sudden fierce calm folded over Tax like soft-feathered wings. He checked the mirrors, looking for anything out of place—a car circling the block, someone else hurrying across the street, any of a hundred little things the Squad's trainer Sparky Lee Jones would call a DLR—*Doesn't Look Right*. "Where's your car at? What happened?"

"They shot my car," she repeated, and if she wasn't in shock yet it was only a matter of luck, or time. Dots of sweat gilded her forehead, and a few tendrils of platinum hair, darkened with moisture, clung to her neck. "I got away, but the engine . . ." A deep gulping breath. "It was making a noise and it wouldn't . . . so I had to leave it at the strip mall." She sucked in a giant, shuddering breath, and those big baby blues glittered because they had filled with tears. "I . . . oh, God. They . . . Ella, they . . . Barton told me to run so I did but Gerry was on the floor and I thought it was a heart attack—"

"Take a breath." Tax checked the mirrors again. The bruises on her knees were glaringly fresh; if she was hurt anywhere else she wouldn't feel it until adrenaline wore off. "Put your seatbelt on, bunny. It's gonna be all right."

He wanted to bark for a sitrep, but she was already scared to death. Boom hadn't mentioned she was into anything dangerous, but even run-of-the-mill nine-to-fivers had secrets.

"Rob told me to run." Meg hugged her purse harder, and a tear rolled down her left cheek, carrying a trace of eyeliner. "He had *freckles*."

It was a wonder she'd held together long enough to call him. Tax popped his seatbelt and leaned over, reaching for hers; Meg froze, trembling like a small animal in a trap.

"Easy," he said, soft and calm. The day's heat clung to her, an invisible coat. She was probably dehydrated too, since her usually pristine-glossy lips were chapped. Her perfume mixed with the smell of a healthy woman who'd just had a hard workout, but under it all lingered the sharp chemical note of deadly panic. "It's all right." A bare murmur, and he got the shoulder belt pulled down, searching for its home. "Nothing's gonna hurt you, okay? You're with me, everything's gonna be ten-four. Breathe for me, bunny. Nice deep breath in, that's it."

The seatbelt clicked home, and he wanted to lean further into her but he had to drive. Her trembling had turned into shudders, and the fresh tear tracks on her face—tinged with that dark eyeliner, somewhere between black and grey—filled his chest with something funny. A colorless shimmer like gasoline fumes collecting, looking for a spark.

"There. See?" He got himself clipped in too, checked the mirrors once more, and reached for the gearshift. "Just keep breathing. Start from when you dropped me off, and tell me what happened."

"They're dead." Meg sniffed, heavily, and as he backed out, his arm now carefully behind her seat, he snagged the box of tissues from the passenger side of the bench behind. She flinched again when he laid the cardboard rectangle in her lap. She stared at the Kleenex like she had no idea what it was for. "Ella. And Gerry, and probably Rob too. They're all dead."

Jesus. You said your friends didn't like strangers, but this is a little above and beyond. Tax got the car moving the right way. He could backtrack to Boom's house with no problem. Still had no idea what the hell, but his thick comfortable cloud of numbness, just marking time until the wedding's finish, was pretty much gone. He felt wide awake, every inch of skin stinging-alert, and the constant seashell song of planning his exit retreated to a low murmur.

After all, this was something he knew how to handle. Any member of the Squad would be . . . well, if not comfortable, then at least unsurprised. They were trained for shit to go sideways, and besides, the soft little distressed noises she made as she buried her face in her hands, ignoring the tissues. . . .

Christ. No woman should sound like that, but especially not this one.

Fortunately—or not—he had to focus on driving. "Take your time," he said, hitting the blinker and pulling into afternoon traffic. "I'm right here."

IT HAD BEEN a hot minute since he drove while looking for tails— not long, really, since he'd stopped in Oregon to check on Klemp and found the Squad's second-in-command tangled up in a bit of business. There had been another woman in his passenger seat then, but she hadn't been crying.

Not on the outside, anyway.

You think I'm going to survive this, Rebecca Sommers had said, quietly. *That's adorable.*

Well, she had. And now Tax didn't have to worry about Klemp, because the Squad's second-in-command had Beck to keep him in line. There was a lot of that going around lately; looked like most of Tax's buddies were making up for lost time.

The rearview stayed clear but he still took a few detours, which served to fix some of the local topography inside his head as well. By the time they reached Boom's trim, locked-tight stucco house Meg was glassy-eyed, and her halting, rambling recitation of a violently truncated lunch turned him alternately icy-frozen and feverish. The waves were familiar—they happened when an operation was past the point of plug-pulling.

After that, you just had to settle in for the ride.

The garage was roomy enough for the pickup and a guest's car, plus he had Boom's extra opener. He backed in, the CR-V bumping up the driveway and nipping just under the slowly opening door. "So this guy—Barton—was Roark's fixer?"

"Lawyer," she corrected, twisting a wad of soaked tissues in her long slim fingers. "But . . . yeah, fixer too, I suppose." A bloodshot, sidelong glance, her shoulders hunching slightly. At least she was now calm enough that he could start getting some operational details. "Uh, Arthur . . ."

"Hang on." He checked the surroundings again, glancing at the street, then cut the engine and hit the button. The door began to descend with well-oiled quiet; the glare of a desert afternoon died by increments. "Who else knew you were visiting there? Think about it. Did you mention it to anyone but me and Boom, anyone at dance class? Or would your friend Ella have said something to someone?"

"N-no. I mean, not except her brother, maybe? But Rob said . . ." She frowned, wringing the Kleenex even harder. "Oh, God. Preston." She cast about, looking for her purse—a tan leather number today; she seemed to have a lot of color-coordinated bags, usually as ruthlessly organized as her office. This one filled up her lap next to the tissue box, and she lost no time digging inside its jumble. "I have to call him. He . . . oh, *God.*"

"Hey." Tax's hand shot out, and he snatched the bedazzled rectangle away. "Bad idea, bunny. Now, think. Does *anyone* else know you were going over there today?"

Finally, he had every ounce of her attention. Meg stared at him, her baby blues huge and the pulse in her throat fluttering. "That's my phone," she said, blankly.

"And it's a really bad idea for you to be calling anyone right this moment, okay?" He should be sweeping Boom's house—ideally with the 9mm from the lockbox in the Honda's trunk but he could make do with the one stashed just inside the kitchen door—instead of arguing about a reasonable security measure. But he needed her at least marginally compliant and buttoned down, not panic-dialing all her friends. "Right now the only thing I'm worried about is who knew where you were going today, because that'll tell me how long we have at this house before I've got to move you somewhere else."

"But . . . but Press . . ." She was spinning again. Civilians weren't built for this sort of thing.

Tax strangled a flare of impatience buried in a much larger jolt of copper-tasting fear, the latter so familiar he could ignore it. It didn't matter if you were scared; what mattered was doing what you were trained for so you didn't let your buddies down.

"I told Boom I'd take care of you, not . . . not anyone else." He almost said *not some dead mobster's kid*, but realized just in time that would be, as Grey might mutter, a tactical foul. "You did the right thing getting out of there and calling me."

Which, of course, made him think about how the situation *could* have gone down. Now was not the time to get all introspective about how a trip to the ladies' room had saved her, how this Barton guy had probably died to let someone else get away, *or* how she'd made it past what had been an incredibly sloppy bottleneck. All in all, it was enough good fortune to make Tax not just uneasy but downright nervous, because any member of Dez the Destroyer's Patented Wrecking Crew knew that kind of luck only gave with one hand while it sank a blade deep into your kidneys with the other.

"The cops." Now she looked horrified. Dawning realization turned her so pale her chapped lips were chalky, but at least she wasn't twisting the shredded mass of tissues anymore. "I . . . I should've called 911 instead. This could get you into trouble, and Eddie—"

If a Vegas mobster had just been erased with his fixer and daughter, inviting the cops to get their hands on the only witness was an *incredibly* bad idea at this stage. He didn't need her worrying about Boom, either. "Were there cameras?"

"What?" Meg shook her head slightly, like a cat hit with a stray drop of cold water, and it was kind of adorable. "Cameras?"

"At this Roark guy's house. What kind of security system did he have?" Tax quelled a slight, restless movement; keeping her calm was a priority, and he could be fairly sure the house was clear. A lot hinged on if the gunmen at Roark's place had identified her and how fast they could scramble a watch on her office and living quarters—now he wondered what her home looked like, a pleasant distraction there was no time for. "Motion detectors? A smart doorbell, anything like that?"

"I don't . . ." She glanced around the garage as if expecting another gunman to pop out at any moment. "There's a keypad near every door; I have my own code."

Shit. He had to assume cameras, then. Good thing her car was abandoned—at a strip mall, she'd said, and they could worry about that later. CCTV on stores and stoplights would track her movements; in a casino town, most of the pavement was likely under some glass eye. Depending on how well-funded or connected these guys were, they might get a lock on his plate number too, so he'd have to be careful.

He had too much to do and not enough time. It was just like being back in the Army, either bored out of your skull or up to your ass in blood and flying lead. He'd had all the R&R he was going to get.

"Listen." He had her phone in his left palm, tiny rhinestones digging in hard; his free hand darted out. Her nape was warm under his fingers, and he wasn't grabbing her by the scruff, really—he just needed her to stay still and calm, to stop thrashing and take in what he was saying. Her hair fell over his fingers, soft silken strands, and his arm tensed. "You called me because I'm the most recent in your phone, okay? You were in shock, and you did the right thing. Whoever took out a hit on this Roark guy is going to be looking for you, and the cops might mean well." *If they're not on the take*, he wanted to add, but that was more than she needed to be thinking about right now. "But we're not going to them until I'm sure it's safe. All right?"

She was shaking again, thin trapped tremors, or maybe she hadn't stopped. There were fine lavender lines in her irises, and silvery ones too. Her eyeliner was smeared, her lashes wet and matted, her nose-stud glittered, and her lips were slightly parted. Meg drew in a shuddering breath, blinked owlishly, and nodded, a tiny helpless movement.

"I don't want you to get into trouble." Her mouth drew down at the corners, and it was ridiculous—she'd just escaped murder and been under fire for quite possibly the first time in her life, and she was worried about *him*?

"This isn't trouble," he lied. Or maybe it was only half a lie; he was, after all, a card-carrying member of the Squad. Even a dumbass PTSD-frayed medic could handle a few jumped-up gangsters. "You're gonna sit here for a few minutes while I check the house. Then we'll do the next thing. Can you handle that?"

Another tiny nod. A little color had come back into her cheeks. The contrast with her usual seamless, cheerful practicality might've hurt, if he had time for that kind of thing.

"Good," Tax said, softly. "Just sit tight, bunny. I'll be back in a flash."

Contribution to the Cause

THIS IS A NIGHTMARE. Meg kept expecting to wake up, rolling over while her sunrise clock gradually brightened. Eventually it would give out a cascade of electronic birdsong, her bedroom walls—painted the perfect shade of white with a subtle pink undertone—flushing under its full-spectrum glow.

Every time she squeezed her eyes shut and reopened them, hoping to see a white popcorn ceiling, the antique nightstand with her phone on its charging stand, or hell, even her bathroom floor if she was hungover or really sick, she saw Eddie's garage door and the dashboard of an unfamiliar car instead. If she looked out the windows or in the side mirror, it was tools hanging neatly on pegboard and the half-open door into the kitchen. Arthur had gone straight into the house, not up the stairs to the mini-apartment overhead, and now she was kicking herself for blindly jabbing at her phone to call someone, anyone.

This was bad, and she was going to get him into really deep doo-doo. She should've dialed 911, or even Sam Morigny despite the fact that the latter's *I told you so* would reach near-insufferable levels.

That wasn't even the worst thing. If someone had broken into Gerry's house to kill him and Ella and Rob, Preston might be in danger too. He was a giant, cheating, boundary-violating douchebag, but he didn't deserve . . . that.

Nobody did. And now she couldn't even close her eyes, because if she did she saw the breakfast nook, Ella's surprised, contemplative stare, and heard Rob's harsh breathing.

Meg. Run.

Was he still alive? Oh, God, had she just left someone to die? And why had Arthur taken her phone? None of this made any *sense.*

Meg took a deep breath and tried to force her tired, shivering brain into working.

Gerry Roark was pretty much out of the business; everyone knew it. Still . . . his wasn't the sort of career you retired early from, and the underside had long memories, not to mention grudges. Press might be safe, since Gerry had been both vehement and adamant about keeping his son in daylight; it wasn't quite a point of contention, but the expectation that Press would keep his nose clean and eventually go into an aboveboard career was high, and non-negotiable.

Why would anyone hurt Ella, though? Was it a message? Whoever sent the men with guns had to know Gerry's daughter still lived in the mansion, working part-time at an ad agency near the Strip. She pretty much always did a half day on Wednesdays; Meg knew Ell's schedule nearly as well as her own.

Now Ell would never have her fairytale wedding. They wouldn't look through catalogs or rate sheets together, Meg gently suggesting options and Ella finally laughing, saying *you know best, bitch*; they would never argue good-naturedly over wedding gowns or shades of white, cream, ivory, ecru. There would be no tasting dinners, no venue tours. Ell would never mock-complain about Meg's love for horror movies again—she was a complete weenie, scared even of the most childish and clunky special effects—and Meg would never return the favor about campy musicals.

I thought you liked *music*, Ell always teased, tossing a popcorn kernel in her direction.

Gerry would never ask for a kiss on the cheek again. Nor would he gently inquire if she was doing all right, if she needed a little bit to tide her over, if anyone was hassling her. It was how he showed he cared.

Barton would never appear again, tall and imperturbable, to smooth away some minor problem or deliver a quiet message. He'd taught both Meg and Ell how to deal blackjack, how to play poker, how to read a tell and keep your bets hedged.

Meg. Fucking run.

Why had he done that? The shivers had her again. The tiny little noises were back in her throat, she realized, squashing the urge to dig in her purse. Nothing there would help; she couldn't even remember if she'd gotten everything spilled over the passenger side of her car back in its proper place.

She had to call the cops. It was the only solution. Why hadn't she done the right thing to begin with?

A shadow moving at the kitchen door made her jump, craning wildly to look out the SUV's back window, metallic fear painting the back of her throat. But it was only Arthur, who glanced at his car before he took the stairs to the apartment above two at a time, carrying a black duffel bag and moving with lithe economy of motion. Had he called Eddie?

Wait, they're glamping at Merbelows, there's no cell reception up there. It was a selling point, and one of the reasons she often suggested the hot springs for honeymoon trips if people didn't mind a bit of campfire smoke and hiking.

Meg sniffed, heavily, and fished another tissue out of the box. They were the good kind, with lotion, and she'd probably used half of Arthur's supply. She was making all sorts of problems for Eddie's friend, and that was bad.

Christ, Meg, it's all bad. Who would do *this?*

Sure, she knew the gossip about who was underside and who wasn't—this was Vegas, after all—but she stayed away from all that. She hadn't even taken Gerry up on his offer to fund her business when the bank wouldn't give her a startup loan.

God, hadn't Eddie been mad to hear she was even considering Roark money—he'd left whatever he was doing for the Army and showed up at her apartment in the middle of the night, fuming, with a check in hand. *Just take it, Meg. What else do I have to spend it on?*

"Oh." A hurt little syllable, and she was crying again, a slow hot leak from grainy, aching eyes. "Oh, Jesus," she whispered; though she regarded herself as practically an atheist, Gerry often asked if she'd gone to Mass recently. . . .

Arthur descended the stairs at the same quick, graceful clip, and he had not just the black duffel but a larger green one as well. Meg blew her nose, trying to contain the tears, but they wouldn't stop.

Don't be a weepy little bitch. Ella's voice, again. *Woman up, Callahan.*

She was trying. The black Honda's back hatch rose, and after only about sixty seconds' worth of rummaging around, closed again. He didn't head for the driver's door, though. Instead, he approached hers.

He was probably going to give her phone back and tell her to call the cops while he headed up to join Eddie and Carl. Even the most oblivious do-gooder would realize this was a hole nobody sane would jump into, and he'd gone above and beyond just picking her up.

The door opened. She balled up the hot, damp tissues, realizing belatedly that she should get out of the seatbelt. "Okay," she said, breathlessly, pawing for the release. "I'll give you a head start, and if anyone asks I'll say I hitchhiked here because I didn't want to go home. Just give me my phone, and I'll—"

"What?" He leaned down, and a faint breath of harsh, plain soap—the kind Eddie used ever since coming back from basic training, though he could certainly afford better—reached her, mixed with the indefinable tang of a male animal. Close up, it was obvious Arthur's tan was entirely natural, and he'd been blessed with great eyelashes too. Some guys were; it was maddening. "You're not calling anyone, bunny. Come on, let's get you cleaned up and take a look at those knees. You probably don't even know where you're hurt."

Bunny? Meg finally got the seatbelt unclicked. "It's okay." Her lips felt numb, and she was suddenly aware her hair was a mess. So was the rest of her. "I'll be fine. You can—"

"Meg." Very quiet, but almost steely. "Get out of the car."

Maybe he'd learned that tone from Eddie, or they taught it in the Army. In any case, Meg had a total of zero other options at the moment. So she obeyed.

THE MASTER bathroom was bright, clean, neat as a pin, and apparently Arthur knew where the Army surplus first-aid kit was—a good one, too, olive-green and stocked with all sorts of extras. She perched on the edge of the Jacuzzi tub instead of the toilet, because it gave him room to work. Her knees were still raw, and stung as he dabbed with cold, antiseptic-soaked cotton.

Meg sucked in a harsh breath. A laugh jolted in her throat; he glanced upward, his eyebrows coming together. From this angle his nose was long and his underlip stuck out slightly, and he had to shake his hair back with a quick, impatient flicker.

Eddie did that, too. He'd gotten used to a high-and-tight, not like the rat-tail and fauxhawk he'd had in high school. Of course, when he'd come home this last time, saying he was mustering out, he'd grown a full beard until Carl threatened to hold him down for a clipping—and Meg said she'd help.

The beard was tamed, but Eddie's mane was now much longer than any military regulation would allow.

"Sorry." Arthur's touch gentled still further; the skin over his knuckles was red and roughened. Even folded down on the tiled floor he was obviously much taller than her, and each time he moved she caught another whiff of that harsh unscented soap. "I've got some painkillers for after we get you bandaged."

"No, it's . . ." The sheer unreality of the situation threatened to swamp her again. Ella was dead, and Meg was sitting in a spacious skylit bathroom getting her knees fixed up by a guy she barely knew. "I just, Eddie would never have had a first-aid kit before he went into the service. He wasn't the type."

"Still isn't." One corner of his mouth curled, a lopsided grin. "This is probably Carl's contribution to the cause."

"Yeah." She tried not to wince. "You don't have to, it'll be fine."

"I'm the medic, Miss Callahan. Where else do you hurt?"

Everywhere. Her head ached, her feet were swelling—these heels were cute, but they weren't meant for hurrying block after block in spring sunshine—and her hands felt like throbbing balloons, plus her left shoulder twinged as she shifted uneasily. "I'm okay." She should be *doing* something. Getting her phone back, calling the authorities, calling Press to warn him and make sure he was. . . .

"Rule number three, bunny. Don't lie to your medic." He paused before the last word, probably because he wanted to insert a swear word.

"Number three?" What were the other two? "And . . . bunny?"

"Ah." His broad shoulders hunched, and he reached for some fresh cotton balls, the bag's top neatly sliced open and the puffs inside like little clouds. "It . . . my mom would call me *puppy* sometimes, or *little boy rabbit*. It sounds better in Korean."

"You speak . . ." *Of course he does, jeez, Meg.* At the same time, you couldn't assume someone knew a language just because they looked like they did. Her cheeks warmed; now she was embarrassed as well as scared to death.

"Korean, Mandarin, Spanish, a little Polish from my dad. Not like Jackson, he knows every da—uh, every word under the sun, though sometimes it's like pulling teeth to get him to use any. Sorry, it's just a . . . a term." He turned aside, rummaging in the green metal box.

"I thought you meant Playboy bunny. I never worked that angle." Why, in God's name, did she feel the need to make that clear?

"Huh." Arthur made a neutral noise, neither interested nor dismissive. It was, in fact, perilously close to a grunt. "We've got some Band-Aids that'll fit. Take a deep breath and tell me where else it hurts."

He had, Meg decided, a reasonably good bedside manner. "I have a headache. My feet, too."

"We'll get you different shoes soon as we can. You take those heels off now, you'll never get them back on."

She always had clothes stashed at Eddie's in case of an overnight visit, but she couldn't remember if there were any sneakers. "I guess." Meg shifted again, her shoulder deciding it hurt a *lot* now that she was asking, thanks. "Everything hurts. And my shoulder, too. I think I hit Ella's bumper." The mad scrabble in the garage was terribly warped inside her head, memory stretching like taffy. A jumble of disconnected images, from when Barton's lips shaped the words *fucking run* to the moment she scrambled into Arthur's car—and God, she'd been half sure, peering around the corner of the Shell station like some kind of sweating weirdo, that the SUV across the street wasn't his but *theirs*, the men with their huge ugly guns.

"I'll take a peek at that in a minute. We probably have some time before anyone'll think to look for you here." He produced a pair of jumbo-sized bandages from the kit's depths and tore open the first one with a practiced motion. "So, those guys. You think you can identify any of them?"

"Not the ones outside." Her voice wobbled, and she felt utterly stupid. "But the one . . . the one who . . ." The freckled redhead in the hoodie, yes.

She wouldn't forget *him*. Ever.

Arthur leaned a few inches closer, and blew gently on her scraped knee before smoothing the bandage on. When she stood the adhesive edges would wrinkle, but she felt a little better.

"My mom used to do that when I was little," he said, quietly. "It helped."

Oh, God. If this kept up she might indeed catch religion. Sitting in a pew and waiting for the Big Guy upstairs to realize he'd made a horrible mistake was a tremendously seductive idea. "You don't have to." She sounded like she had something stuck in her throat, and Meg realized how thirsty she was. "I know a cop. A detective, in fact. I can just—"

"This Roark guy was retired, but someone wanted him gone and didn't care that his daughter would be collateral. They had to know the house was full of cameras and they did it anyway. Then the two outside were sloppy, but they still had rifles. What does that tell you?"

Nothing, and it's safer that way. She hadn't been this scared since she was a kid, and back then the fear had been common and ignored as air. "That I should call the cops instead of maybe getting my best friend's Army buddy involved."

He glanced up again, and maybe this time he looked a little aggrieved. "These guys clearly aren't afraid of being caught by detectives, Meg. That means they're either semi-professional or well-connected. Maybe both. Hold still."

How do you know what 'professionals' are like? But he had a point, and her head hurt even worse trying to pick apart the implications.

Her other knee was bandaged in a jiffy; he slid each shoe partly off her heel and looked for blisters, said she was lucky, then washed his hands with quick efficient scrubbing motions while she struggled out of her cardigan. A few moments' worth of prodding her bruised, aching shoulder returned a verdict of no splint necessary, and while he was that close she was painfully aware of how much she'd sweated.

A tepid shower and a nap would've been heavenly. Instead, she pushed herself upright with creaking slowness as he dealt with used cotton balls and spent packaging. The bathroom seemed awful big when it wasn't holding her and a virtual stranger; now it was cramped and airless.

Meg swayed, grabbing at the dual-sink, granite-tiled vanity Carl was so proud of.

"Hey." Arthur unfolded in a hurry, his hand closing around her arm. "Oh, hey. Look at me . . . no, at me, Meg. Up here."

I'm trying. But her tongue wouldn't work. The world greyed out, the same way it had that one awful time when she was fifteen and Bobby Pilsden had slipped something into her red Solo cup of beer at one of the bonfire parties up at Lake Mead. If not for Eddie, that entire night could've ended really badly—there were rumors about what smiling, leather-jacketed Bobby liked to do.

Fortunately she didn't pass out entirely; her knees buckled, but she didn't fall. Instead, her eyes unfocused, her cheek met something warm, and her entire body decided it had, quite frankly, had enough of her bullshit and was going to reboot.

Whether she liked it or not.

Hideous Lesson

SURFACING FROM restless doze full of gory flashbacks from previous missions that morning, Tax hadn't thought he would end up standing in Boom's bathroom with a pink-tinted pixie pressed against him.

Meg nearly collapsed; he barely managed to get upright in time to catch her. She weighed less than a whisper—far less than a soldier in full gear, but he still had to get his arms around so she didn't slide right to the ground. Which put her face in his chest and mashed the rest of her close too, a soft living warmth completely unlike anything else in the world. It was, in fact, so novel he froze, his mind racing.

Well, what little of his brain was functioning at the moment.

Her hair smelled like floral shampoo, fresh air, desert heat, and that maddening tang of fear. He knew because his chin dropped and he inhaled, helpless not to while she sighed, leaning into him like a weary ship finally docked.

Come on, Tax. Do something.

Trouble was, there was nothing *to* do. Oh, sure, he should be moving her along, on the off chance that someone who knew about this Roark guy's schedule and could gain entry to a mobster's house might also be informed about a frequent visitor's patterns. It was a long shot, but better safe than sorry. Not only that, but his nape was itching, like Jackson's when an op was about to go bigtime sideways.

Something here wasn't adding up.

So yeah, he should be getting her packed into the car now that she was bandaged and relatively calm. But she wasn't shaking anymore, and maybe it wouldn't hurt anything to just . . . let her rest for a second.

"It's all right." He was barely aware of his lips moving, and when he inhaled again he got a full shot—shampoo, fresh air, warm vanilla musk from her perfume, and just the barest, fading tang of fear. Even the metallic edge of the last component just made the rest of the mix that much more delicious; he hunched slightly, wishing he could curl all the way around her. "You're okay, I've got you."

No reply. Probably didn't even hear him, any port in a storm and she'd been tossed around like a rowboat during a hurricane. Of course she'd be clinging to the closest thing approximating safety; it didn't mean jackshit. He should just be glad she'd called, by sheer dumb luck, the one person who could handle this with Boom out of town.

Tax hadn't been this close to a woman in a while. Shaking hands with Beck didn't count, and neither did the R&R he and the guys had hit before the last mission. That was the only reason his head was short-circuiting, all available bloodflow going in an entirely different direction.

Wasn't it?

The last thing she needed was some asshole taking advantage while she was vulnerable, but he couldn't stop a purely biological reaction. It was goddamn embarrassing; she was going to think he was some kind of randy teenager.

But *Jesus*, she smelled good. She felt like a puzzle piece finally clicking into place. The constant restless numbness was gone, as well as the stinging alertness. Instead, a completely unphysical warmth blurred from the contact between them, one of her wounded knees pressing into his leg sending its own signal to add to the symphony.

It's nothing, he thought, desperately. Even silently reciting the vilest threats he could think of in several different languages wasn't helping. *Get a hold on yourself, you idiot. You're the medic, get her moving.*

Except he was still talking, like a certified dumbass. "Everything's gonna be all right." Which was the biggest lie in the book—but sometimes it was exactly what a wounded animal, or a soldier, needed to hear.

Meg took a deep, shuddering breath. She didn't stiffen, or flinch. Instead, she leaned in a little further, and he had to figure out how to get his lower half away so she couldn't tell he was—

"God," she whispered into his chest. "This is so fucked up."

Yeah. "Uh." There was a rock caught in his throat, and all his mental circuits had fused. He was sniffing her *hair*, for Chrissake; it was unreasonable for anyone to smell so good and doubly so for a girl like this to be depending on a washed-up fuckhead like him. "Don't worry, I've seen worse."

Meg twitched. At first he thought she was trembling again—adrenaline crashes were brutal, and she probably didn't have any experience with that sort of thing. Or maybe she was crying? *That* was the wrong thought, because instead of the unfamiliar warmth of her closeness or the cool clarity he'd been trained to function with, a wave of unsteady rage threatened to swamp him.

But the sound she made into his T-shirt wasn't a sob. Thin and pale, married to a series of wracking shudders, it was another reaction he'd seen in strung-out soldiers.

Meg Callahan was laughing, forlorn little chuckles. When they faded she tensed, subtly leaning backward, so he had to let go of her.

Slowly, though. In case she crashed, he told himself. Tax loosened up, and it seemed to take forever for the most beautiful woman in the world to peel herself out of his arms. Paradoxically, it was over far too soon. Meg blinked up at him, and the slight tremor in her chapped lower lip added to the hopefulness shining in those big baby blues was enough to knock the breath clean out of him.

"I'm sorry." The wall was back up, thin and brittle but probably the only defense she had. "I shouldn't have—"

"Don't." The word was a little too loud, and he could have kicked himself as it bounced off the mirror, echoed in the tub. *Goddammit, be gentle.* "I promised Boom, okay? He'd fu—uh, he'd kill me if I let anything happen to you."

It wasn't what he really wanted to say. But Meg nodded, biting her lower lip, and crossed her arms, hugging herself. Pale but composed, she examined him like he was supposed to know what to do.

Tax found out he did, thank God. It was trained into him, and now he was glad for each hideous, painful lesson. "So let me put the kit away," he continued, "and we'll do the next thing. All right?"

She hesitated, but there was no other option for a woman in her position. A flash of hot, nasty gratitude went through him the instant the realization visibly crossed her face.

"All right," Meg said, softly, hopelessly. "What's the next thing?"

APPARENTLY SHE kept a change of clothes at Boom's house, and Tax found himself wondering just how often she stayed over. It didn't matter; not with the back of his neck and the rest of him prickling too. The feeling was undeniable as well as inescapable, so he hustled her into the passenger seat again. "Hang on a minute, okay?"

Meg nodded. This was a new side of her—a pair of butter-soft, faded jeans, a pale rose-colored tank top, and a white button-up that had to be Boom's from the size, but was so threadbare and comfortable-looking it was probably a long-held hostage. A few splashes of cold water getting rid of draggled eyeliner, her hair pulled back in a sloppy ponytail, and she looked like a girl-next-door any soldier would be proud to pass around a picture of. *A stone-cold mama,* Grey would say; *a real doll,* Footie

Lenz would intone, spreading his hands and pursing his lips with aesthetic appreciation.

Even the thought of poor Lenz didn't jab Tax right in chest like it usually did. He was too busy.

Still, her eyelashes were damp and matted, her nose a little pinkened, and she hadn't dabbed at her lips with any kind of gloss. The evidence of tears lingered, and an astute observer wouldn't miss the way she hugged that tan purse and a paper Smith's bag full of her previous outfit, blinking up at him.

She was holding together like a champ, but only just.

He closed the passenger door as gently as possible and cruised Boom's house one last time. His last stop was peering out the big bay window in the living room, careful not to let the curtains twitch or the venetian blinds move. The sun was getting low, long shadows falling across front yards full of multicolored gravel or spiny succulents—it was a nice part of town, but very few green lawns—and he was probably being overly cautious.

But the prickles just wouldn't stop. After a few missions the animal inside a man woke up permanently, and it didn't believe in things like *coincidence* or *luck*. No, it had finely tuned antennae for any variety of danger, and screamed bloody murder if even a leaf twitched the wrong way.

You realize you're eating a heaping helping of combat stress, right? And planning your exit—you would kick any one of your buddies' asses if they were doing the same thing. You are not functioning anywhere near tip-top, soldier.

"Doesn't matter," he muttered. If one of the Squad started talking to himself it would be time for concern and possible action, since Tax was the medic and supposed to look out for that sort of thing. But there was nobody around to pass the buck to; the medic was where that particular dollar bill screeched to a halt, as Sparky would say.

And besides, he was all Meg had. So Tax had to cope, and was even glad for the lack of other options.

The street looked fine. A red Toyota swam past at a reasonable speed, pulling into a driveway two houses down; it belonged, he'd clocked it at least once before. The habit of observation was hammered in, not least by Sparky Lee's rough drawl—the man didn't smoke, but he certainly sounded like he had a pack-a-day habit.

Be interested in everything, boys. That way you notice the DLR—when it Don't Look Right.

Nothing. Nada. Zip, and zilch. But the damn prickles would *not* stop. Tax returned to the garage, climbed into the driver's seat, and hit the door opener. Along with the familiar chemical mix of new-car smell, a tang of her perfume lingered. The engine woke up, right on track and purring, happy to be doing its job again.

So was he. It was a helluva surprise, but one he had no time to think over.

"Where are we going?" Meg's hands were primly clasped, and her knuckles were bloodless. "And . . ."

"Motel." *Not a fleabag, but not a nice one either.* He caught himself—she wasn't on the Squad, there was no way she'd know the procedures and considerations. "Just to be safe."

"Why a motel?" She nearly flinched when he glanced in her direction, and that jabbed him right in the ribs.

It wasn't personal. A jumpy civilian's unease might fasten on whoever was closest instead of the real danger, a purely psychological reflex. He *knew* that.

And yet. "SOP. We don't know if you were part of the deal, and we don't know how well-connected these guys are." As soon as they were clear he hit the button, aiming the opener over his shoulder, and watched the garage door descend in the mirror. "It's just safest, you know? Hedging our bets."

"Part of the . . ." She sucked in a sharp breath as they made it out of the driveway and to the corner, the Honda humming happily to itself, and god*damn* but the sense of something about to go wrong was all over him with red-hot ant feet.

The feeling didn't abate. He kept scanning, hoping it wasn't too obvious. She needed calm competence now, not a shellshocked nitwit trying to look in every direction like a paranoid junkie.

"Don't worry." Which was a stupid thing to tell a woman who had been shot at a few hours earlier. "It isn't very likely. Unless there's something you haven't told me."

She stiffened, and he could've kicked himself. Implying he didn't trust her version of events was not a good move—for Chrissake, if she was into something serious Boom would've said something or given a significant look, eyebrows slightly raised and mouth tense.

There wasn't a lot of traffic. Another black SUV—Ford Explorer, the model from a few years back when some designer had gotten funny ideas about revamping the whole line—turned onto the street upstream, windshield glaring with dusty desert light. Its privacy tinting was even darker than his own ride, which was saying something. The vehicle overcorrected, also going just a shade too quickly for a neighborhood resident.

Huh. The prickles went away, leaving only cold readiness.

"Oh God," Meg whispered. "Oh God, oh no, oh *fuck*—"

"What?" *Play it cool.* He kept it steady as the Explorer swam past, moving air between the two vehicles causing a subtle bounce. "Meg? Tell me."

She twisted violently, glaring into the backseat. No, out the back window. "No. It can't . . . I'm crazy." The words quivered, and he could almost taste the sudden jump of copper-chemical panic.

"Sit down." A touch of bite to the words, which he hated—but it brought her back to stare at him, tense and trembling. "Deep breath." Tax kept an eye on the rearview, and when the other black car turned onto Boom's street, a terrible suspicion bloomed into certainty. "Meg. Work with me here. Please."

"It's . . . they had a car like that," she whispered. Probably thinking if she didn't say it too loudly, it had a chance of being a simple coincidence. "And another SUV just like it, outside near the . . . There were two of them in the blue one."

Sonofabitch. To think he'd been arguing with himself about moving her, not to mention if he'd spent any more time with his arms around her like he'd wanted to. . . .

It didn't happen. Jackson's voice, the soft considering tone he used when there were, in Klemp's immortal parlance, bigger fuckin' fish to fry. *So don't worry about it right now.*

"Are you sure?" It didn't matter if she was or not—what were the odds, especially with the way they were driving? Still, answering a few standard questions might distract her. "Did you get the plate number, or—"

"I know what I saw," Meg snapped. The switch to frail bravado almost hurt to hear.

That's why she asked about my car, he realized. Funny how the mind made connections under stress—Christ, she was smart. "I believe you." He was also very, very glad that he'd been borderline paranoid; now he needed to get them out of the neighborhood. "Settle down, okay? We're good, Meg."

She stared at him for what seemed a long while. He kept his speed low, only half an eye on the rearview since peripheral vision would warn him of any sudden changes there.

This made the game completely different.

Burrow In

MEG COULD BARELY remember the last time she'd been in a cheap motel. This one wasn't the worst type—it didn't charge by the hour—but it was hardly one of the Strip's high-rolling palaces either. The sun was down, night falling swift as vulture who had decided to move right to the main course instead of circling to eye the buffet offerings.

With daylight gone the temperature plunged, but heat had barely started leaching from the pavements as Arthur unlocked the door. He swung it open, glanced inside like he expected to catch someone from housekeeping just finishing up, and motioned her through.

He wouldn't let her carry anything other than her purse and the bag of takeout Thai. Nor would he give her phone back, and Meg was beginning to feel squirrelly about that—just a little.

Okay, a *lot*. Even the sickening chill of realizing it was the same black Ford Explorer on Eddie's street was a little less intense than the deep, panicky feeling of missing her goddamn phone. And her feet hurt, though he'd stopped at a sporting goods store, parking in scanty shade and leaving the car running for fifteen agonizingly silent minutes while he bought white cotton socks and a pair of black Nikes in her size.

It hadn't even occurred to Meg to turn the radio on, that he'd left the key in the ignition and the engine going so she had air-conditioning, *or* that she could have slithered into the driver's seat and taken off. Not until he'd reappeared, that was.

"You take that one." Arthur pointed at the farther of the twin beds sharing the small room. A cheaply veneered dresser stood against the opposite wall, holding up a television old enough to have a cathode tube. It smelled clean, at least, and the shower water might even be a shade or two above lukewarm.

Meg moved to obey, and halted awkwardly on blue, floral-patterned nylon carpet. He swept the door closed, locked and chained it, dropped the duffels onto the other bed and went immediately to the window, getting the slatted blinds tilted to his preference. He even pulled the pale mauve drapes closed. "Check if that lamp has a lower setting," he said, not bothering to look over his shoulder. "No table, but we can at least sit down to eat. You hungry?"

How the hell should I know? "No." The smell of hot food wasn't doing anything but making her stomach roll. The big pink ceramic lamp with its faded shade did indeed have a lower setting, and she hoped that satisfied him; the nightstand didn't match the dresser, but she made herself the sucker's bet that there was a Gideon inside.

The drawer was sticky; she slid it open and stared at an ancient Yellow Pages as well as smaller book in imitation red leather. Good old King James, ready for a bottoming-out alcoholic's conversion or rolling a joint with a spare page, depending on the guest's preferences.

"Boom does that too." Arthur looked fresh as a daisy, even the ironed creases in his shirt still holding up. Meg felt even more wilted and shapeless just glancing at him. "Every hotel room, he's gotta find the Bible. It's like a compulsion—once Jackson managed to get in and hide it before he could check, and Boom about hit the roof. Said it was unlucky."

Oh, Eddie. It was an old game of theirs in high school; she'd had a housekeeping job at a place very much like this one and managed to make sure both of them slept inside most nights. Since their caseworkers were so overloaded and they both had good grades—she did the English and history assignments, he did the math and took care of everything in shop class, amen—they had not so much fallen through the cracks as deliberately taken refuge in a system of caves only Sin City could provide. At least they'd never had to shelter in an underpass or floodway.

"I should call him," she heard herself say, and had the urge to clap her hand over her mouth "No. God. What am I going to do?"

"Sit down, first of all. You look about ready to fall over." Arthur crossed to the bathroom and glanced inside, as if something might be hiding in there. "And we're not calling Boom just yet."

"That's right, they're on the honeymoon. Pre-honeymoon." The sheer enormity of the day's events towered over her in a black wave. The paper takeout bag crinkled a bit; her fingers had tightened. "My clients," she continued dully. "I have appointments. Tasting dinners. Venue visits."

"Hey." He was suddenly right beside her; Meg couldn't repress a flinch. "Sit."

She sank onto the bed, arranging her purse, settling the takeout bag on the nightstand. The mattress squeaked dully, and for a moment she thought the creaks issued from the nipping aches all over her. Now that they weren't in the car, wheels turning for some destination, she realized how exhausted she was.

And she still hadn't called Press, or the cops. Her life had veered into the underside, after all her struggle and striving to stay away.

"Here." Arthur turned back to the other bed, and rummaged in one of the duffles. "You need to eat, and something to take the edge off so you can rest. The adrenaline's gone and you're gonna stiffen up. Tomorrow—"

"I have to call someone," she repeated, hating the whine in her tone. "The cops. I'm a witness."

"Yeah, and I'm thinking about that, okay? If the guys who took care of your friend Roark knew to go to Boom's place, what does that tell you?"

Oh, God. If she hadn't called him, if Eddie and Carl weren't out at Merbelows, what could have happened? "It might not have been them," she offered, lamely.

Christ, she didn't even believe herself.

"You sounded sure before." He straightened, critically eyeing an orange prescription pill-bottle rescued from the bag's depths. It had no label, but that was no indication. "For right now we'll assume it was, and act accordingly. Scooch back a bit, and let's eat."

It wasn't the first time she'd had pad thai with tofu while sitting cross-legged on a strange bed, but the food might as well have been cardboard. Not that it was bad—far from, and she was justifiably proud of her chopstick game. Arthur went for chicken satay and an appetizers platter, all neatly packaged in white paper boxes.

He even offered her the extra peanut sauce. But Meg could barely chew and had to force herself to swallow, eating mechanically.

"Now," he said when she'd managed a few bites, and produced a small white pill from the bottle. "Take this."

"What is it?" *Like it matters,* she realized. Nobody knew where she was, even Eddie. Alone in a motel room with a man she barely knew, and he was offering her drugs.

Good God.

"Anti-anxiety. You need to rest."

She accepted the pill, tweezing it delicately between thumb and forefinger—but made no move to actually ingest it. "What about . . .?"

"We'll see if what happened at your friend's house has hit the news by tomorrow morning. Then I can figure out who we should call, and when. But for tonight we burrow in, okay? If nobody knows where we are, that's safest."

It sounded reasonable, so far as she could tell. "But if they know about Eddie—"

"If they're going to his house, they don't know he's on vacation. Once they do they'll leave him alone. If they don't I pity the poor bas— ah, I mean, you don't need to worry about him. He'll take care of himself, and Carl too. My priority is keeping *you* in one piece, all right?" A small, hard, delighted smile tilted up the corners of Arthur's mouth, vanishing a heartbeat later. "If he gets back into cell range and we've both gone radio silent, he'll know something's up and check Carl's cameras. We're professionals, Meg."

Professional what? She was getting the idea Eddie's Army career had been a little more intense than he ever let on. Which could be good news, considering—but how awful was it to think that way? Especially when she was alive, sitting on a bed and eating pad thai, while Ella was slumped in a chair with a bullet hole in her forehead and Gerry on the floor, dear God, would Tilda be the one to find them like that? And Rob. . . .

Meg's stomach seized up, a deep desperate cramp all the way from the pit of her navel to the back of her throat. She nearly retched before scrambling off the bed, almost dropped her carton of noodles and tofu onto the carpet, and barely made it to the bathroom in time to heave over the sink instead of the toilet.

For one thing, the porcelain throne was too far away. For another, she'd cleaned so many of them she never wanted to get her face near one again.

Besides, there wasn't enough left inside her to wring out more than a few undigested bits of rice noodle and some thin yellowish bile. Her embarrassment was complete when Arthur somehow made his way into the tiny tiled space and crowded close, his hand warm between her shoulderblades, rubbing gently and patting as if soothing a kid afflicted by stomach flu. He was talking, too, but she didn't care. The roaring in her ears swallowed anything he could say.

When the retching was over he produced another pill—where the first one had gone was anyone's guess—and a bottle of water; she took both without demur. He gave her a toothbrush and a half-used tube of Colgate, and she didn't even bother to protest at using someone else's personal care items.

What was the point? At least it got the taste of bile out of her mouth. It didn't even matter that she'd have to sleep on motel sheets. By the time she was brave enough to peek out the half-open bathroom door he had the bed near the wall turned down as if he'd worked hospitality before, the lamp was off, and only the thin spectral glow of the television lit the room.

Thankfully it was muted, and wasn't the news. It was the weather channel, of all things, and whatever was in the pill must have been magic because as soon as she lay down on the creaking mattress she was out.

She didn't even take her new shoes off.

Psychological Response

IT WASN'T THE first night he'd spent on the floor of a rented room, and it probably wouldn't be the last. The subliminal whine of a muted television wouldn't interfere with hearing footsteps along the concrete breezeway outside, and above him Meg's breathing was deep and slow.

The sedative was doing its job. A good thing, too—she needed it. He would've barked at a soldier to take some chow down as well, but the last thing she needed was that kind of demand on her system.

Even pale and distracted she put up a good front, which gave him a weird feeling. She'd been coping with disaster all her life, her responses shouted as much, but while Eddie talked about growing up in the system he had never really mentioned anything about *her* family or upbringing. Sure, he had a ton of stories about pranks and other friendly hijinks, and he wouldn't have asked Tax to look after her unless they were close.

What made her so determined to keep that wall up? She'd given a good impression of calm, plugging along like a soldier on punishment detail until her body rebelled. Christ, she'd mostly fooled him, even.

Once she was safely asleep he found the local news channel. Closed-captioning ran along the bottom of the screen; Tax watched for at least an hour, a pillow jammed under his head and weapons carefully stowed on his left side, where she wouldn't accidentally put a foot if she needed a bathroom visit at midnight.

She could step on him all she wanted, but a gun was another matter entirely.

Human-interest stories, a big neon-lit casino closing down, a couple drug stings, more human-interest spots. Looked like a slow day in the studio. No mention of a crime boss, millionaire, or local businessman murdered with his daughter and lawyer. Either that didn't qualify as news in this town or nobody had found the bodies yet; Meg mentioned a housekeeper who was off at some family shindig for an indeterminate time.

Or, most likely, somebody didn't *want* this getting out. Which—added to the black Explorer turning down Boom's street—had a number of interesting implications. Not least among them was the idea that Tax probably had a certain . . . latitude of action, when it came to tidying up. A few more bodies wouldn't matter, so long as the other side stayed interested in keeping this quiet.

How would Meg respond to that? Not like it mattered either, really. He could tie this off, make the wedding, and go on his merry way.

Or could he? Thinking about that was distracting, and he needed all his horses on deck, as Jackson would say.

So he had to shelve his escape plan, and think about next moves. As well as contemplating a few things about his unwilling, nervous, beautiful responsibility.

He suspected that after a little bit of rest, she'd be giving him some problems.

HIS TRUSTY TRAVEL coffeemaker had just started burbling on the counter in the bathroom, so neither of them had enjoyed a cup of caffeinated sanity yet.

"But why?" Meg folded her arms and fixed him with a glare.

Tax didn't mind. It was better than numb apathy or tears. "Because it can be tracked. I just popped the SIM card out and left both parts in Boom's safe."

"He has a safe?" Her pink-tipped hair tumbled in every direction, her baby blues were a little bit bloodshot, and the white button-up was wrinkled; all in all, she was a far cry from her usual polished, tamped-down professionalism.

He liked it both ways, Tax found. "Yeah, he's a responsible gun owner. When this is over we'll pop the card back in and it'll be good to go."

"Arthur." The glare intensified, her forehead wrinkling, and even for a grunt who had endured both Eun-Kyung Tachmann's maternal examinations *and* Dez the Destroyer's occasional displeasure, it was markedly uncomfortable. "That's my *phone*, my entire life is in there. Plus it's my property. You can't just—"

"You'd rather someone showed up at the door here with a shotgun?" He indicated the still-muted television with a short jabbing motion; thankfully, she didn't flinch. "It hasn't hit the news, bunny. That means someone doesn't want it to, and with those guys heading to Boom's house yesterday it all adds up to more here than meets the eye. My job is to keep you alive. Don't make it harder than it needs to be."

Meg straightened slightly and leaned back, weight sinking into her heels. Her chin rose, her eyes flashed, and he was right—now that she'd had some sleep, all her anxiety was going to fasten on the closest possible target. It was a regular, normal psychological response.

Tax almost wished he could remember what that felt like. Coffee-smell, rich and illusory, vied with the scent of cheap carpeting and industrial cleaners, plus a hint of exhaust and desert dust. There was barely enough weatherproofing in this place to keep the sand out, and the only reason he hadn't had to check his green Army-issue boots when he woke up was because he'd slept in them.

At least his hands weren't raw; he hadn't felt blood on them for a while now.

Meg surprised him again, sinking her teeth into her lower lip and staring not quite at, but *through* him. Watching her expression shift, tiny incremental changes flooding through, was fascinating. Once you learned to glimpse under that wall of hers, everything was telegraphed—but that only deepened the mystery.

A man could spend the rest of his life contemplating her emotional weather, and never see the same shade of meaning twice.

"Oh, God." She retreated blindly, but only two steps. The backs of her knees hit the rumpled bed and she sat down, hard; the mattress made a forlorn squeak that might've been funny in a different situation. "I have to call Sam. And Press."

Not just yet. "Let's have a cup of coffee first. Tell me who Sam and Press are, and we can make a plan. All right? You're not in this alone."

"But if what you're saying . . ." She shook her head, a small hard flicker like a surprised cat. "Sam's a detective, I told you. Vice squad. And Press is Gerry's son. You've met him."

"Have I?" He only vaguely remembered the latter's name, and that bothered him. Was he slipping? Something about it nagged at him.

"He came by the office." Her shoulders hunched. "Gerry was out of the underside, and Press never got into it. He might not even know his father . . . if something's happened to him—"

"Don't." Tax sounded harsh even to himself. True to form, she was worrying about everyone else before herself. It seemed to be this woman's default setting. "You did exactly what you were supposed to."

Another small shake of her pink-frosted head. He didn't think the situation warranted a cut and color change, which was a mercy. But a ballcap or something else to hide that distinctive dye job wouldn't be a bad idea.

"I have to call Sam at least," she insisted, soft and stubborn. "The longer I wait, the worse it looks."

Which was exactly what he didn't want her brooding on. "Not necessarily. It could just be that you're scared, and smart enough to know you shouldn't be—"

"You said coffee, right?" She blinked up at him, and the shimmer in her eyes wasn't just that she was so goddamn beautiful. No, it was tears. Less than fifteen minutes after she woke up, he'd made her cry. "Please? I'm not going to ask how you know so much about this stuff, or what you and Eddie did in the Army. But I could use some caffeine before figuring out what to do."

"Sure. There's my travel mug in there, I washed it out already. I don't have any milk or anything, sorry about that."

"You picked me up at Shoresy's without asking questions and haven't left me to deal with this on my own. Which you probably should, by the way. But I think that kind of compensates for not having creamer on tap." A tremulous smile, and she unfolded from the bed. She still looked a little shaky; his hands itched to help.

Some clear instinct warned him that she was on a particularly ragged edge right now and didn't need anyone in her personal space.

Least of all him.

"Well, I promised." *Shit.* It was awkward as all hell; how did you talk to a woman under these circumstances? Especially one so visibly determined to keep a brave, brittle calm. "We'll have some breakfast as soon as you've got some java in your bloodstream, then we'll go shopping."

"Shopping? For what?"

"Camouflage." It was hard not to sound grim. "And a couple burners. I do want to know what's going on with this Press guy. And a Vice detective might not be a bad idea either." He caught himself, because she'd halted halfway to the bathroom, staring at him, and she looked for all the world mildly thunderstruck. "What?"

"I thought I couldn't call anyone."

Not precisely. "I said your phone could be tracked, and we're not calling until we have a plan."

"And we have a plan?"

Go ahead and lie to her. "We do. But we'd better get moving."

The transparent relief on her face felt almost too good to contemplate, so he looked away. The bed was barely rumpled; housekeeping would be thankful they hadn't left much trace. A supply run and getting some intel would eat up the whole day, and he needed some coffee too.

The list of tasks inside his head wouldn't get any shorter for a while.

Good thing I'm on vacation. And he was glad he hadn't checked out somewhere between Oregon and here, too.

Which was a novel sensation as well. But a halfway pleasant one, Tax had to admit.

Neutral Ground

IT WAS A BEAUTIFUL morning, clear golden light and mountains knife-sharp in the distance, a breath of sagebrush and the promise of warmth riding the breeze. A pall to the northwest meant the spring storms were on their way; it was too early for flash floods but a good lightning storm wasn't out of the question.

Normally Meg loved the prospect of Ma Nature's light shows. Everything seemed sharper and cleaner afterward, given a good scrubbing even if no rain fell. But there was no joy in a balmy Thursday, even in a car with great air-conditioning and probably fantastic speakers, given the rest of the accessories.

No music except softly playing classical, which was fine because it was someone else's ride. But what she wouldn't give for her own car— poor thing, it was probably going to end up impounded. There went a chunk of her savings.

That was a small consideration, comparatively. In the clear light of day—one of Gerry's favorite phrases, and her chest hurt at the thought— she could admit to being sneakingly grateful Arthur seemed to know exactly what to do, even if dragging him into this was another terrible guilty weight on her mind.

The worst thing about getting into trouble was if someone else inadvertently got mixed up in it as well. All her life she'd tried not to be a burden or a bother; it was hard enough keeping herself afloat without trying to haul someone else along. Except for Eddie, of course—the two of them had been clinging to the same raft until he left for basic. Now he and Carl had their own yacht, and she was sinking fast.

She kept glancing at the clock on the dashboard and thinking, *this time yesterday, Ella was still alive*. A dry rock lodged itself in her throat despite an apple-cinnamon muffin from the closest Lucky Bean drive-thru; Arthur got himself a giant drip coffee. He only had the one stainless-steel travel mug; she felt guilty for not realizing it and offering to at least share the caffeine he'd brewed.

Eddie would call it *the reds*, a mood where everything in the damn world seemed to be her own fault. It was bleakly funny that today the feeling was unquestionably correct. At least he was up at Merbelows with Carl, and probably didn't even know a black Explorer had visited his house. But what if they'd broken in or. . . .

The pay-per-minute burner phone buzzed twice in her ear, and she was hoping Sam wasn't busy.

"Morigny." A crisp, authoritative bark.

"Hello?" Meg's voice threatened to fail her. "Sam?"

"You're gonna have to speak up." Impatient and brusque, plenty of noise behind Sam's voice—ringing phones, conversation, a general hum of busyness—meant *I'm at my desk, and I fucking hate it.* "Hello?"

"Sam." Meg stared out the window. Arthur, in the driver's seat, hit the blinker for a right turn. "It's Meg. Don't hang up."

"Hey girl hey. This a new number? I was just thinking about you."

Why? Meg realized her hands were shaking. A faded blue baseball cap covered her hair now; Arthur said the pink tips were too distinctive. Not like it mattered, everyone dyed their hair these days. "Why? Did you . . . what did you hear?"

"Hear?" A bright, only semi-forced laugh. "There's a new guy in the prosecutor's office, and I thought I could set you up. You know, a couple drinks, maybe a movie?"

Oh, God. The last thing she needed was yet *another* blind date with a lawyer. "Not right now, Sam. Listen, I need a favor. A big one."

A slight creak—shifting in a chair, finely tuned cop senses catching a perp's nervousness. "Hang on a second." More noise of movement, then a door closing and a sharp cessation of chatter. "Meg? Where are you? Are you all right?"

"I'm fine." *Stick to the script,* Arthur said. *Burners aren't untraceable, but it will give us some lead time.* She swallowed, hard. "Actually, I'm not fine, but it doesn't matter. I need you to come meet me. Gianello's, in half an hour. Can you?" *Please, God, don't say no.*

A faint touch of static scraped Meg's ear.

"You in some kind of trouble?" Soft and reasonable, but with an edge of demand. Oh yes, now she had Sam Morigny's *entire* attention.

"Yes," Meg whispered. "I am. Please, Sam. Something's happened. Come alone, okay? Not even Mike."

"I know you don't like . . ." Sam stopped, audibly realizing Meg was indeed deadly serious and wasn't asking because she didn't really get along with her detective friend's partner. "All right. Alone, half hour, Gianello's. This your new number?"

Arthur reached for the paper cup. His throat worked as he tossed back the remains of his coffee. With his sunglasses on he looked like a pilot slumming from the airbase—it was probably the watch turned to the inside of his wrist like Eddie's, or his completely unconscious air of cool, trained confidence. Or maybe the military precision of each movement.

"Yes," Meg lied. This was her number for at least the next five minutes, at least. "Thanks, Sam. I owe you. Bigtime."

"Yeah, yeah, whatever. Look, be safe, okay? Call me back if you need to, I'll put this number as priority. See you in thirty."

The line went dead.

"Good job." Arthur sounded soothing. He hit the blinkers, turning right onto a familiar street lined with small bungalows and their gravel yards. "Power it down. You're sure this place is open?"

How could she explain? "It doesn't really close." *Not if you're local.*

THE SIGN OUT front said *Little Italia's Home Kitchen*, but only a tourist would call it that. Not that any Strip-bound group of rubes would want to risk a brick building with dusty front windows, a stained green canvas awning, and a general air of dilapidation despite the neon sign blinking *Welcome - Open*. Still, the tiny parking lot saw a great deal of traffic. Gianello's sat amid a patchwork of residential and small business zones, gentrification pressing a few blocks over but not quite able to pierce a little bubble of how things used to be.

The interior was a time capsule, from the red vinyl booths to the old Pick and Win machine, the framed pictures of firefighters—dead in the line of duty—on the back wall. School wasn't even close to out for the summer, so the wait staff wasn't augmented by a few bored teen-agers; a middle-aged woman with tortoiseshell glasses and a spray-lac-quered bouffant called a cheery, "Just sit anywhere, honey," as she hefted a loaded tray. Despite the ancient cigarette machine at the front there was no smoking section anymore, but a ghost of old nicotine lingered in the slightly sticky linoleum, the carpet, even the tile under the booths.

The order-up bell dinged, and Meg had to suppress a twitch. She remembered waiting tables here part-time, the summer after high school. The back door that needed propping open on hot nights for smoke breaks, the lost-and-found under the glassed-in counter where wax models of pies and other desserts still lingered to be dusted religiously every Sunday, the heat lamps over the long stainless-steel order window, the balky old soda machine—no, they'd gotten a new one, and a few of the booths had been reupholstered too. The wait staff didn't have to wear candy-striped polyester uniforms anymore.

The happy, bubbling smell of red sauce was just the same, though. Barda Gianello would come back from her grave in what was now Bunkers Eden Vale to kick some ass if anyone dared mess with that particular recipe. It made sense, though—why change perfection? There were still only four main dishes you could order, all came with garlic bread, and a choice of two desserts except on Friday when the apple pie from Costenza's Bakery was delivered to make it three.

The two booths lingering under the memorial wall were reserved by unspoken agreement. If you sat there, it was understood you didn't order a main dish. You got a cup of coffee and maybe a slice of pie while waiting, conducted your business or other discussion with a reasonable expectation of privacy, tipped well, and left as soon as possible.

Above all, you started absolutely zero shit. Gianello's was neutral ground.

Meg had to remind herself to keep her shoulders back and not to scurry. She settled in a booth under black-and-white photos, uniformed men grinning before American flags. Tiny brass plaques on each frame gave names; the photos were starting to wrap up the long west wall, edging out a collection of Route 66 memorabilia and old-timey Chianti-bottle kitsch. The bouffant waitress brought a heavy white china mug full of boiled java. "Ya want creamer, honey?"

"Yes, please." Meg tried a tentative smile, but the woman's gaze slid away, easy and professional as a pole worker avoiding a now-penniless client.

It felt like a long time before the bell on the door gave another cheery little jingle and Arthur appeared, looking completely different with his sleeves rolled up and a pair of stainless-steel reading glasses on—the lenses held no prescription, he said, a piece of camouflage.

He wasn't quite out of place, but neither waitress called him honey or told him to 'sit anywhere.' He was shepherded to another table by the one in leopardskin leggings and a tight black top warring with her crisp red apron, her jaw working furiously at what was probably a wad of Juicy Fruit gum. For all that, he certainly acted like a local, listening to her rattling off the specials and ordering coffee with a small, polite smile Meg had to admit was kind of cute.

The glasses were a nice touch.

Another jingle-jangle, the door swung wide, and Sam Morigny

strolled in. Her hair was growing out, a wheat-colored bob that would have just brushed her shoulders if it hadn't been scraped back into a no-nonsense ponytail. Her chunky, well-shined shoes screamed *cop*, just like the lack of purse and her pantsuit with the shoulder holster peeping out when the jacket flapped; her hazel gaze scanned the interior once, passing over the other customers—including Arthur—without a hitch before lighting on Meg. A flicker of relief crossed her strong-jawed face, and she prowled to the booth with long easy strides.

Waiting for the second cup of coffee to arrive was torture. Meg folded her hands around hers and shivered despite the afternoon heat gathering outside. She could tell herself it was the air-conditioning, but that was a bald-faced lie.

"You look like shit," Sam said, when the bouffant waitress had hurried away.

Meg reached for the dish of creamer packets. Her hand shook. "I like the new hair."

"Yeah, well." Faint sweat glistened on Sam's forehead. "What's going on? Don't tell me you had some bad luck at blackjack."

Oh, God. Where did she even start? "Gerry Roark's dead." The words trembled just like Meg's fingers. Getting the shelf-stable powdered non-milk added to her cup was proving a little difficult. "So's Ella, and Rob Barton."

Sam's mouth opened slightly, her honey-colored eyebrows leaping for her hairline. She studied Meg in the dimness; the overhead fixtures in this part of Gianello's only had bulbs in every other one. No new hire would ever make the mistake of fixing that oversight. "And you know this how?"

"I . . . I saw it happen." Saying it out loud meant it was real, and a hot wad of something too bitter to be her own spit lodged in Meg's throat. Even her legs felt unsteady.

Good thing she was sitting down.

Sam reached for her own cup of coffee, but her hands settled on the tabletop midway and stayed, palm-down and forgotten. "You saw it?"

"Yesterday. I was there for lunch, Ella's getting married." *Oh, God.* "Or . . . she was."

Sam sank back, her arms stretching out, disregarding the coffee. She tilted her head slightly, glancing at the ceiling—a movement familiar from high school mischief-planning. Eddie was all-in, all the time, but it was Sam who could be depended on for a quick, reasonable plan that *didn't* involve getting caught.

Subtle was absolutely not Ed Baumgartner's style.

"I was going to plan the wedding." Suddenly Meg couldn't sit still, and couldn't shut up, either. "Gerry was making fajitas. I went to the bathroom and—"

"Hang on a second." Sam exhaled sharply, shaking her head a little. "Jesus *Christ*. You saw the guys?"

"Barton told me to run." The words wobbled; Meg's fingers ached, clutching the cup. The faint ghost of grittiness on her fingers was a bit of spilled milk powder. "I did, they had—look, Preston might be in danger. I haven't . . . fuck, Sam. It's a mess. A huge mess." *Don't look at me*, Arthur had repeated. *I'll be close by, but* don't *look*.

She was trying not to. Her shoulders were stiff, her knees ached, and her shoulder throbbed despite the ibuprofen he'd provided.

"How close?" Sam's chin came back down, and the old Morigny gleam was in her hazel eyes again. "You could identify them? How close were you? Could you tell them in a lineup, or if we got out the mug-shots?"

"It was from me to that table over there." Meg nodded in the direction of the closest two-seater. "He had freckles, greenish eyes, and was wearing a hoodie. I'd recognize him again, no problem." She shuddered; coffee slopped against industrial-grade ceramic. "The ones outside, I don't know. But they had two cars, a black Ford Explorer and a blue SUV. They shot my car, I barely got away." What else could she say? "I should've called 911 but I didn't. I didn't know *what* to do. And if something's happened to Press I'll never forgive myself."

The urge to glance in Arthur's direction mounted again, near-irresistible. He'd gone from being a complete stranger to a necessary comfort, but if Sam could get her under police protection or something, maybe Meg didn't need to drag a Good Samaritan in any further.

"Don't worry about *that* asshole, he's fine." Sam's feelings on Roark Junior were well known, and had been since ninth grade. "Fuck, Meg. Just . . . of all the shitty luck."

Not so shitty if I'm still alive. But that was a horrible thing to think. "Press." The only thing she could produce was a strained whisper. "Please tell me he's okay. You haven't heard anything, have you? Can you check? Please, Sam."

"Christ." All the blood had drained from Sam's face; she was so pale her lips looked chalky. "Okay, first things first. Who else have you told about this?"

"N-no one." Meg had to lie, and hoped she still had the old mojo for it. Adult years of pursuing a policy of tactful but near-strict truth pinched her conscience, hard. "Eddie's out of town, you know. He and Carl—"

"Good." Sam's expression shouted she didn't want to know. "Where's your phone?"

"I ditched it." Another lie. It was slippery-slope time in Meg Callahan's life, just like the bad old days. Maybe she *should* go to Mass. What would a priest do with this kind of confession?

She longed to give a quick glance over her shoulder, just to see Arthur's face. It was like a sneeze threatening during the breathless hush of *speak now or forever hold your peace.*

Some weddings left the objections bit out. Meg thought it was a terrible idea to rush over something so critical, but it was really just like life itself. No takebacks, no sudden saves at the last minute—like a slipshod venue, God never really solved a problem unless forced to, and then nearly always in the worst possible way.

"Good." Sam nodded briskly and leaned aside, digging in a back pocket for her wallet. The echo—just like Ella slumped in her chair—was deeply uncomfortable. "Coffee's on me. Let's get out of here."

Oh, thank God. But something nagged at her. Her armpits were damp, and the hollows behind her aching, bandaged knees too. Her heart had decided to start galloping as if she'd just finished running the half-mile for gym class instead of sitting perfectly still in a sticky vinyl-upholstered booth. "Please, Sam. Can you call Press right now? At least try to get hold of him?"

"I told you, he's fine." Sam laid a neatly folded ten-spot right next to her untouched cup and slid out of her seat, tucking the leather whip-stitch wallet away—that was also familiar, hadn't changed since high school.

Wait. "Sam . . ."

"Come on, Meg. We'll get the wheels turning. You did the right thing, coming to me."

I hope so. Her heart kept pounding, so hard Meg felt faint. It was hard work getting out of the booth, and even more difficult not to look at Arthur's table. "I can't figure out why it's not on the news."

"Probably because someone doesn't want it to be." Sam paused, looking down at her. Even with heels Meg was shorter than everyone, and she was only in sneakers now. "You can only identify the one guy, right?"

"I . . ." Meg's knees threatened to buckle. Why now? That strange, insistent little thought returned—the sensation that she was missing something, like a bad clause in a contract or an error in a column of prices.

She's not surprised. It was Rob Barton's voice, not gasping or strained at all. Instead it was his quiet, flat tone while teaching Ella and Meg the casino-correct way to deal—not the flashy, friendly technique for when you were having a poker party with your friends, but professionally enough to avoid both player ire and pit boss suspicion. *She said, 'guys.' How did she know it was more than one?*

And why on earth was Sam saying Press was fine, instead of *probably* fine?

Meg couldn't help it; she snuck a glance over her shoulder. Arthur's table was now empty, save for a lonely water glass.

The bell on the door jangled again.

Madness, Stop

TAX DIDN'T LIKE leaving her alone, even for the few minutes it took to recon. Still, he had to hand it to the girl, this was the perfect place for a meet—quiet, plenty of side streets to get lost in, an alley behind the building and good parking nearby. No cameras outside unless the gas station a block and a half east counted—there was a fair amount of residential zoning around, though, and nowadays that could mean doorbell or driveway eyes.

The restaurant's security was mostly passive, from the bell on the door to the ancient, probably arthritic CCTV pointed not at the Pick and Win or the entryway but at the cigarette machine. Christ, how long had it been since he'd seen one of those boxy horrors giving out coffin-nails?

Singapore. Four years ago. A shudder tried to force its way through him, suppressed with a reflexive, trained-in effort. He didn't like thinking of that particular operation, the package they'd been sent to extract nearly getting an arm blown off and Dez getting winged, every single member of the Squad losing blood before they made the extraction point.

Focus, goddammit. Tax gave the waitress a smile and did *not* stare in Meg's direction.

She was doing great, holding up under the pressure like a champ. From this angle she was simply a pretty woman in jeans and a baseball cap, clearly waiting for someone else to join her—hopefully this Vice cop was balding, and old enough to be her father.

What the hell are you thinking? He glanced at the rear of the dining area--a peeling *Restrooms for Customers Only* sign with an arrow pointing to a hallway, the swinging door to the kitchen sitting stolidly on the other side. Two middle-aged waitresses, the cook a hawk-nosed man with heavy eyelids and a highly bleached towel over his shoulder—that guy probably knew how to handle himself, but wouldn't want any trouble reported to his parole officer. The smattering of other customers, barely a dozen people all told, made a point of not looking in Meg's direction as well;

the fixtures over the booths she'd headed for were only half-lit.

For a woman Boom said was on the level, she was certainly conversant with some interesting people and places. Then again, this was Vegas; locals probably knew more than they wanted to about any number of things.

A tall blonde with no-nonsense shoes paused outside the dusty plate-glass window, as if bracing herself. The bell jangled as she entered, heading straight for the booths; Meg looked up and her shoulders turned taut.

So this was Sam. And Tax had to squash an entirely unprofessional flare of relief—which made no sense. He had one foot out the door already, why was he getting so . . . what was the word, here?

He could think of a couple. His buddies would no doubt supply a few more if he let any whisper of his current state escape. He'd razzed Klemp almost unmercifully about Beck, and couldn't wait to get a few digs in at Dez himself, too. If he did, and let anyone see even a sliver of how he now felt . . . well, payback was gonna be a bitch.

It wasn't fair; he was still considering the biggest opt-out of all once he got this situation tied off. The last thing this girl needed was a raw-nerve, combat-stressed wreck like him sticking around, fucking up her busy life even more.

Still . . . it was nice to have the fantasy. What a man kept inside his skull was his own business, even in the Army.

Wait a minute. There was a relatively good view of the parking lot from his seat, if he half-turned and gazed through dust-glazed glass like he was expecting someone to join him. A boxy, pale-blue Chevy SUV pulled in, bouncing gently as it crested the deliberately steep cut-ramp. The car wasn't that uncommon, especially since plenty of folks here liked gas-guzzlers—but right behind it swam a shiny black Explorer.

Tax snapped a glance at Meg's booth. The cop leaned back, gazing at the ceiling as if asking heaven for a little bit of help. Her expression was pained but a few fractions from what he'd expect, given the story his pink-tipped pixie was bound to be in the middle of telling. The warning bells inside Tax's head were ringing loud and clear now.

Sparky Lee would nod, his lips pursing slightly. *That's a DLR right there, son.*

The big black Explorer swerved aside. Oh, its driver could possibly be looking for a parking space—if he hadn't already passed three empty ones in a row. Or he could be heading for the corner of the building to cut off any retreat, since the wider end of the alley gave out on that side and prey looking for a quick exit would no doubt rabbit in that direction.

Fuck. Tax's priorities reshuffled; he rose, quietly, and ambled in the direction of the restroom. Neither waitress noticed; one was exchanging a volley of wisecracks with the cook, the other had a three-top in the back corner opposite the booths.

His hand itched for a weapon, not any of the knives he was carrying but something a little more robust. The rest of him wanted to skirt a few tables, put two in the cop's chest, sink another into her golden head, and drag Meg out through the kitchen. The narrower end of the alley had a halfass chain-link gate, but that was a problem easily solved, would slow down pursuit, and as a bonus got him and his package closer to their own transport.

Were the bastards out front going to come in shooting? Maybe not, but he couldn't afford to make the wrong call here. He stopped and turned, his right hand raised slightly as if he'd forgotten his phone at the table. *Nice and easy, take it slow. Play the part.*

The blue Chevy had pulled up cockeye across the lone handicapped space. Its doors promptly flung open, and two hostiles—sleeves down and hoods up—were about to effect entry, both holding their right hands low and half-hidden.

You know, I haven't even set foot inside a casino yet, just a few wedding chapels and rec centers. It was the kind of cheerful, inconsequential thought that always happened just before shit went sideways with a vengeance.

The bell on the door sounded again, a happy little jangle. And now he could see both hostiles had bandannas over mouth and nose—of course, ski masks were probably hot as hell. Not that zippered hoodies were better, but those could be removed while running.

And yes, both of them were packing heat. Looked like a 9mm on one and a .45 on the other, held with familiarity but only moderate professionalism. The first to make entry nearly stopped, his head on a swivel—attempting to get a zero, but both women were standing now, and Meg was half-hidden behind her taller companion from that angle.

Would the hostiles recognize her? She'd told him about two men outside the Roark residence shooting at her car, but their buddy inside the residence could have given a description of their current target.

It didn't matter. Tax was already moving.

THE FIRST SHOT fired went high and wide, because the second guy through the door was too twitchy to zero in. Fast reactions were nice but often useless; you had to be both quick *and* correct to play dangerous games well.

As it was, the bullet whined before burying itself in the rear wall, and the cop's shoulders hunched. She twisted as she headed for the floor, hand blurring cross-body to get her service piece out, but Tax had already hit Meg, nudging behind his package's knees to get her falling backward.

Civilians froze in high-pressure situations, it was just a fact of life. His package went down like a toppled tree, but Tax had his arm around her waist and managed to get them both mostly behind the booth, hitting heavily varnished industrial-grade linoleum with a crunch.

He was braced for the impact and hauled her the rest of the way into cover, ignoring her shocked, breathless cry and the second shot as well. Tax shoved her again—as gently as possible, but he had to get untangled. With that done, it was time to see what the hell. A yell from the kitchen said the cook was definitely the best equipped among the onlookers to handle sudden confusion, and another shot from much closer said the detective, like any nervous cop, had been startled into returning fire.

Good. Tax's lips peeled back from his teeth, a wolfish grin he would recognize on any member of the Squad. Adrenaline hit his bloodstream and the back of his palate at once, a tide of thick bright copper; he snuck a glance around an edge made of plywood and tacked-down red vinyl.

The two hostiles had separated, one screaming *get down, motherfuckers get down!* The other squeezed off another shot, and the cop returned the favor. More screams rose, civilians beginning to shake off the freeze response. One, a heavyset woman who had slithered out of her chair across the restaurant, had her phone up as she huddled under a spindle-legged table.

Holy shit, is she . . . she is. The urge to record was a fucking epidemic nowadays; maybe she was livestreaming. A laugh bubbled in Tax's chest, was savagely repressed. Meg scrabbled backward, her shoulders hitting the wall with a thump he had to imagine, since he couldn't hear it over the other noise.

He sighted, exhaled softly, and midway through his own 9mm spoke. The first hostile screamed as a hole appeared in his left leg, blood spattering the glass behind him. A shiver of breakage—a huge chunk of the window had now evaporated too, the neon sign sparking—wasn't from Tax's shot but from the detective's. She was probably soaking in both stress hormones and tunnel vision at the moment.

Fucking amateurs, Tax could just hear Jackson mutter, like he always did whenever the Squad had to deal with the enthusiastic who weren't trained to Sparky's exacting standards.

He had to hope the lady across the way was filming the attackers and not him; he had enough problems at the moment. The second hostile had spotted him and decided to start wildly spraying .45 hollowpoints in semi-auto fashion.

None had much chance of hitting actual targets, unless the bastard got lucky. Just collateral.

You dumbass. Another breath, dispelling the urge to hurry. The chemical soup of being under fire, glands open and throwing buckets of whatever they could find into the bloodstream, had to be corralled and contained if you wanted to get through this kind of shit alive.

Or get your package out safely.

The second hostile threw himself into a crouch as the cop's gun barked again. Tax bit back an obscenity; his own shot had gone wide. The Vice detective was using the booths as partial cover, but sooner or later someone was going to get lucky and there was that goddamn black Explorer to think about too.

Move it along, soldier. You've got to get her out of here.

Another deep soft breath, fighting his own tunnel vision and urge to hyperventilate. Tracking the target smoothly, a good clear sightline between tables, and the guy in the grey hoodie, black bandanna combo wouldn't get away with a leg or arm winged. No, Tax popped the second hostile twice in the trunk region, both nice solid shots—no idea if there was body armor under the jacket, a burden in desert heat but it could still be managed if you had to.

God knew he'd done it himself when the situation warranted. Not to mention cutting the Kevlar off a wounded body that had to be kept alive for whatever reason—a buddy, a package, or someone needing questioning.

More noise was screaming from the first hostile—probably hurt like hell, a chunk taken out of the thigh was bad news if the femoral artery was nicked. For a moment he was in the chopper again, Klemp's blood pumping hot over his fingers and the catechism burning his throat.

You're not dying today, motherfucker. There is no fucking dying allowed today.

Except one or both of the attackers probably would, and he didn't care. The important thing was Meg, who had hitched in enough breath to scream and was still flailing, trying frantically to push herself back through the wall. Her ballcap was askew, her eyes were wide with terror, and he had to grab her one-handed because there was still the cop to deal with.

As soon as he got his fingers around her arm, though, she froze. Meg stared at him, blue eyes wide and terrified, her mouth slightly open, and the only thing more heartbreaking than the fear in her expression was the naked hope that he knew what to do, and would make the madness stop.

Don't worry, bunny. I've got you. "Up," he barked. "We gotta go."

A Helping Hand

MEG'S HEAD RANG. Arthur's thumb ground into one of yesterday's bruises, sending a zing of pain up her arm, and her feet felt like huge clumsy hooves. He hauled her upright, and where had the gun in his other hand come from?

I don't want to know. She wasn't even sure what had happened, for Chrissake. One moment she'd been looking over her shoulder, the realization that he had vanished filling her with a mixture of panic and unsteady relief—at least he would be safe, far away from the disaster her life had suddenly morphed into.

Then everything was chaos, terrifyingly loud noises, the floor reaching up to grab her along with the sudden weird certainty that she was nineteen again, passing out during a floor show audition at the Copacabana because she hadn't yet eaten that day.

It was probably a good thing, since afterwards she'd heard the manager there was a real piece of work.

Arthur was moving, so she had to as well. There was an acrid, burning reek, and someone was screaming. Someone else was cussing up a blue streak.

He dragged her away from the booth. Her coffee cup was still sitting on the table but Sam's had shattered, a tide of brown liquid soaking the ten-spot and heading for the table's edge with syrupy slowness.

What the hell? The world sped up, as if it had realized Meg was trapped in slo-mo and had to yank her along just like Arthur was. *Sam? Where did she—*

The question was answered as soon as it arose. Sam was on the floor, her golden ponytail askew. She had to be okay, because she rolled aside, wriggling her legs out from under the table and clearly about to attempt sitting up just as Arthur paused next to her.

Sam had a gun, too, and a horrified sound blurted from Meg's mouth as it rose in their direction. The end of the barrel looked very big, and very black.

Sam's jacket was torn, she was dead pale, and she looked ready to shoot this guy who had appeared out of nowhere. Which might have been entirely reasonable, Meg couldn't quite tell because of the dust in the air and that awful, smokey, permeating reek.

"Nope," Arthur said calmly, and his right boot flicked. He actually *kicked* Sam's hand with one big ol' green Army boot; the gun skittered away. Meg flinched, sagging against his grip. "Wrong answer."

"No." Meg found her voice. Her knees were still impersonating over-cooked noodles, refusing to do their job. "No, don't, she's my friend—"

Because the gun she hadn't even known he was carrying—though she should have guessed, really—was now leveled at the blonde woman on the floor.

Sam stared up at him. Her pupils were so dilated there was only a thin ring of hazel iris, and she twitched as if she was going to scrabble-roll after her weapon.

"I said *wrong answer.*" Arthur sounded amazingly calm. He kicked again, catching the detective right in the stomach. Sam curled around the blow, making a funny wheezing sound.

Oh, Jesus. Meg lunged, nearly slipping free of his hand; her arm gave an amazing, volcanic flash of pain. "*No!*"

"Come on." He set off again, dragging her for the front. The window was broken, hot early-afternoon glare pouring past glittering shards, and bodies lay everywhere.

What the hell had *happened?*

"Back door's not the best," Arthur continued, his gun moving with clockwork precision. Now it pointed at a man collapsed amid the remains of two tables closest to the door, rolling back and forth while he clutched at his leg. The stranger wore a tan hoodie and for some inexplicable reason a red bandanna was wrapped around his face, belling out and collapsing as he panted. "Come on, bunny. Stay with me."

It wasn't like she had a choice. And now she saw a second man sprawled under the ruins of the window, also wearing a hoodie. His was grey except for the bright scarlet flower spreading on his chest, another on his belly, and his bandanna was black.

What. The fuck. She couldn't even frame the question. The cussing was coming from behind them—Meg snapped a glance over her shoulder. So far as she could tell, it was someone in the kitchen.

So the cook was probably all right. She also saw that the other bodies on the floor were moving, including both waitresses and a heavyset brunette woman who was crouched nearly under a table, her mouth slightly open and her phone gripped in one fist, raised as if she was recording all this nonsense.

Oh, good. They're alive. Except for the guy crumpled under the window, maybe? Meg's stomach cramped; she was genuinely unsure if she was going to throw up. It was a neck-and-neck race, especially when Arthur dragged her past the writhing fellow in the red bandanna.

"Fuck," the wounded man moaned, his hands clamped on his upper leg. Bright blood spurted between his fingers. "Oh, fuuuuuuck."

Meg heartily concurred. The bell on the ruined door gave a discordant jangle—it was getting a workout today—as her sneakers crunched on broken glass, and her heart stuck in her throat alongside the urge to puke when she saw an older, blue Chevy Tahoe parked cockeyed in Gianello's handicapped spot, its two front doors open, the engine still running.

It was unquestionably one of the two SUVs she'd seen at Ella's house.

"That's . . ." The word was a croak; Meg tasted acid and dust, the smell of the desert and car exhaust enveloping them both. "Oh my God."

"Just keep breathing," Arthur replied, grimly. "You're doing great."

I most certainly am not. Woozy indignation filled her at the thought of anything about this situation being even remotely close to 'great.' *I should be in a client meeting right now.*

Her poor clients wouldn't know what was happening. The office was closed, her phone going to voicemail, and meanwhile she was being hauled out of Gianello's as if they were dine-and-dashing. "Sam," she managed. "You kicked Sam."

"Who do you think brought those guys to the party?" He clearly had a plan; the gun disappeared and he drew her closer, arm over her shoulders as if they were a couple. There was no slowing down, though, they were moving along at a good clip. He also craned his neck, shooting a quick glance at the corner of the building, and let out a sharp breath as if relieved. "Get in, and put your seatbelt on."

He all but tossed her into the Tahoe's passenger seat, pushed the door closed, and hurried around the front, looking briefly through Gianello's broken front window. The car reeked of fast food and cigarette smoke even with the windows down, a drift of greasy paper bags in the backseat, and he was behind the wheel in a hot second, reaching for the gearshift. "Seatbelt," he repeated grimly, popped the parking brake, and the vehicle lurched into motion. "We aren't using this ride for long, but it's better to be safe."

HE WASN'T KIDDING. A short drive ended with him pulling up behind a very familiar car—his Honda, parked on a side street less than two blocks from the restaurant. It might as well have been another planet, gravel or AstroTurf front yards simmering under hot golden sunglow and small houses on either side with all their shades drawn to keep out the assault. Arthur cut the engine, gave the interior of the Tahoe a long critical glance and told her to sit still, he'd get the door.

How gentlemanly. The words stuck in Meg's throat. At least she didn't feel much like puking anymore, although passing out sounded like the best idea she'd had in a while.

Arthur hustled her out of one car and into another; she couldn't even feel good about the sudden lack of cigarette smell or the sedate speed at which he drove away, leaving the blue SUV behind with its doors unlocked, the driver's not quite closed all the way, and the keys in the ignition. Just begging for someone to steal it, especially in this neighborhood, but she belatedly realized that was no doubt part of the plan.

Good Lord. Eddie's teenage penchant for mischief had *nothing* on this guy.

"Here." He kept one hand on the wheel and popped the center console open with the other, fishing out a chocolate-covered protein bar and dropping it into her lap. "There's a bottle of water on your other side, wash that down. Eat the whole thing."

What? "I . . ."

"You only had simple carbs for breakfast, and you're gonna adrenaline crash soon. Trust me." He slowed for a stop sign, glancing in either direction, and rolled right through.

"Do you want to get pulled over?" Hot air touched Meg's cheeks; even parked in the shade a car quickly filled with trapped heat, and it always took a while for AC to get itself together. Her stomach rolled, the miserable urge to throw up returning like a bad boyfriend.

Like Preston, showing up with roses and excuses.

"Don't worry, my plates say Cali so it's expected. And if we do get pulled over I'll handle it." Arthur glanced at her. "You need me to open that for you?"

Open what? Her hands were numb; she fumbled with the protein bar's wrapping. "Where did you go? I looked and you were gone."

"Gone? Oh, I was just in your blind spot. Saw them coming in, blue Chevy and black Explorer." He paused, frowning slightly. "Did you think I'd leave you there?"

"Well, Sam . . ." Meg's fingers felt like sausages. "You think she . . .?"

"*I* didn't tell anyone where we were going." How could he sound so *calm?*

"Maybe they followed her. Maybe they were watching." Meg hated the quaver in the words.

She didn't even believe her own objections. *Guys*, Sam had said—how had she known? And why hadn't she seemed more surprised?

And why had she said Press was fine, instead of *probably* fine?

"It's possible, sure." He nodded a little, and reached for his jacket's breast pocket. For a terrifying, dizzying half-second she thought he was going to pull out the gun again, but it turned out to be his cell phone, with its nondescript greyish cover. "Either way I'm not betting your life on it."

"Wait, how come you get to keep your phone?"

"Nobody's trying to kill *me* yet, bunny." Half his mouth curled up in a tight smile, and it wasn't a nice one. "Give me that, I'll open it for you."

"You're busy." The unreality hit her all at once—she'd just been shot at, for God's sake.

Again.

"Never too busy to lend a helping hand." It sounded like a proverb, or an in-joke. He poked at the phone's face with a thumb, barely taking his eyes from the road. "You did great. Just get that and some water down the hatch, that's your only job right now."

"You should focus on driving." And, to top it all off, Meg realized she needed a restroom. Not desperately—not yet—but certainly a little more than usual.

"Relax, I'm a professional. Were those the guys with rifles out at your friend Roark's place?"

How the fuck should I know? "I can't tell a hundred percent." The wrapper finally parted, and now Meg was faced with trying to chew chocolate-coated protein chalk. "I think . . . I'm pretty sure that was the blue car, but . . . Oh, God."

"It's all right." He finished poking at his phone and slid it into the dash holder. Now it was showing a GPS map, their position a jaunty little moving arrow. "We know more than we did yesterday. That was the whole point."

Was it? "I thought the point was getting me out of your hair." Her throat was too dry to even contemplate eating this goddamn thing. "Wait. What do we know?"

"We know someone wants this kept quiet, and it's someone who knows you, Roark, and that crooked cop too."

"Sam's not crooked." The urge to leap to Morigny's defense was immediate, and Meg felt ridiculous just as quickly. It simply couldn't be true—they'd known each other since *high school*, for God's sake, her and Sam and Ella. They'd had sleepovers, they'd hung out, they'd pooled change and gone off-campus to get cheap gas station nachos for lunch together all senior year.

There was no way. And yet. . . .

"Sure, bunny. Start thinking about who would know you well enough to send strangers to Boom's house, and anyone the good detective back there might know in that same group."

Now she felt stupid. Meg took an experimental nibble. How was it possible for even bad chocolate to taste so wonderful? And how could she even think about eating after . . . all that?

The bright daylight world was a thin crust over a deep well of nastiness, and it was so easy to slide downward in this town. She'd worked hard all her life to stay on the surface. Now the ice had cracked, and she was sinking.

"She said *guys*." For a moment, she wasn't sure whose voice it was— the tiny, defeated almost-whisper.

Arthur glanced at her, a brief incurious check, probably to make sure she was eating. "What?"

"She asked, *did you see the guys*. I didn't tell her how many, maybe she just guessed. And . . ."

When added to the blue Tahoe, the guys with bandannas over their faces, Sam's questions—*where's your phone, did you tell anyone else*—and *I told you, he's fine* as if she'd spoken to Press lately even though the two of them didn't really get along . . . well.

There was a presumption of innocence, sure, but there was also preponderance of evidence, and Barton would be the first to mention this wasn't a goddamn courtroom, it was Vegas.

The worst thing wasn't being unable to tell who to trust. It was knowing that nobody could ever be trusted at all. Even the guy driving, occasionally glancing at the GPS on the small screen as if he knew where he was going but had to check to make sure. He'd calmly shot two people, kicked Sam, and dragged Meg away, certainly.

What would happen when he decided she was too much trouble? The foster system had taught both her and Eddie the limits of adult kindness; they were a country of two, disbanded only when he left for basic training. Sure, they'd both had other friends . . . but when it got right down to it, none of the kids who had houses or parents, no matter how dysfunctional, could understand. Even the Roarks' open invitation and Ella's friendship weren't wholly reliable.

Nothing was.

Eddie had his life with Carl now, and was safely out of the way. Meg was, in every conceivable sense, alone. Pretty soon Arthur was going to realize he was better off *not* dealing with this unholy mess.

"But she knew there were more than one, and right after that they show up. And the only guy who actually saw you close-up went for the back of the restaurant." Arthur sounded grimly unsurprised, like teenage Eddie when some dumbass authority figure decided it was a good time to throw their weight around. "It tracks. And if it makes you feel better, we probably saved her life. Unless the guy coming in the back has orders to tie her off too."

Oh, God. She nearly dropped the protein bar. "You can't . . ." *You can't be serious.*

But he was. And Meg realized she'd better get serious too.

Helluva Joke

TAX HAD ALL sorts of questions, and if this was a regular operation he—or Klemp—would be responsible for getting answers out of the package no matter how traumatized she was. They could worry about therapy later; right now there were things he needed to know if he was going to get her through all this.

But Meg was glassy-eyed and silent, the half-eaten protein bar in her lap. Staring out the windshield, pale as milk, her mouth turned slightly down at the corners—her quiet would fool an amateur into thinking she was dealing with all this reasonably well.

That thousand-yard stare under the baseball cap's bill was most common on soldiers who had seen hell. It also showed in untrained civilians; any member of the Squad was equipped to handle a sudden burst of violence, but regular people, *real* people?

Not so much.

She didn't ask where they were going, or cast longing glances at the turned-off radio. There was no attempt to set her hair to rights, straighten her clothing, or wipe at the smear of dust on her cheek; when lead started flying, any place with even an inch of drywall or acoustical tile filled up with flying particles. The baseball cap was awry, and she leaned toward the window—not much, just a few degrees off-kilter, and her shoulders were so stiff-taut they hurt to look at.

In fact, his personal fairy was probably disassociating, and that was not only bad news but spoke of past trauma.

The few details Boom dropped about his own upbringing, or the lack of it, were chilling enough. Tax was wondering if she'd endured something similar. The foster system, juvie hall, homelessness . . . a lot could happen to a child, or a pretty teenage girl. She and Boom were tight, true, but there was only so much one kid could do to protect another.

Now she was in the middle of a helluva mess. Whether or not she'd been into something quasi-illegal with this Roark guy was beside the point; everyone had to make a living. The important thing was getting her *out*, alive and whole.

Tax had a full tank and some daylight. Driving was a good way to shake a plan free of his skull, and he had to come down out of the red as well. He wasn't nearly as steady as he wanted to be at the moment. A firefight right in the middle of civilian space was nothing unfamiliar, but he was on *vacation*, for God's sake.

Besides, the Squad didn't do domestic ops. They were sent overseas to make sure there was no need for such things, or at least that was what the recruiters told you on signup. Klemp's business in Oregon had been relatively straightforward; this was looking far more serious.

Vegas rolled by outside their small bubble of air-conditioning. Dusty golden sunshine drenched cars waiting patiently at stoplights, gas stations, residential areas, mini-malls, smaller casinos, supermarkets, billboards, neon signs, twists of sand whirling in vehicle backwash, patches of overwatered green or glimpses of gleaming-blue swimming pools. He hadn't seen the Strip yet; it was probably crawling with cameras.

Maybe she'd give him a tour once this was all over?

That was a dangerous fantasy. He had enough to deal with in the present moment, it was no time for useless daydreams. At least his grasp of urban terrain was holding up. He couldn't navigate this city like a native, but a little while studying the underlying geography and urban zoning meant circling got a lot easier.

"Hey." His fingers were itching, and not with phantom blood for once. Patting her shoulder or touching her knee might calm *him* down, and he longed to feel that warmth again, no use denying it. But she probably wouldn't take kindly to any encroachment on her personal space at the moment. "Meg? Talk to me."

He had to slow for a yellow light. They stopped an appropriate distance from the rear bumper of a wallowing Dodge sedan probably old as Tax himself; its muffler looked held on by hope, spit, and baling wire.

"About what?" Two pale, flat words.

Crap. She was in bad shape.

"Anything. Whatever's in your head."

A small, restless movement, then she turned her head, staring out the passenger window. She probably wasn't really seeing the bowling alley on her side of the street, its sign proclaiming TUES KIDS NITE on the first line and THURSDAYS - $2 BEERS on the second.

What a juxtaposition.

"Preponderance of evidence," she murmured, almost lost in the sound of the engine, and twitched slightly, an arrested flinch. Then, a little louder, "Nothing."

Come on, medic. Treat her. Give her something to latch onto.

"Here." Tax freed his phone from the dash holder. A few taps on the screen had the music app he never used—satellite radio was better—open, and he made sure there were a few service bars. "Do me a favor, will you?" He offered it, keeping his other hand on the wheel and returning his gaze to the stoplight. Traffic from the cross street showed no sign of abating.

She took the phone, but automatically, with dreamlike slowness. "Who am I calling?"

Nobody, sweetheart. "Make me a playlist, will you?"

"What?"

"A playlist. You know, favorites, or things I should hear."

One of the waiting cars had their bass turned up. The ghostly thumping underlay engine hum, a sudden high note of a car horn as someone decided they wanted to turn right instead of waiting and someone else made their opinion on the maneuver known.

"But I don't . . ." She paused; Tax could *hear* the fetching little frown she was probably making, as if scanning a column of figures. His fairy viewed numbers as slightly suspect instead of comfortingly solid friends, but that was okay. He was more than equipped to handle all sorts of things she didn't care for. "You like classical, right?"

I'm neutral. Classical stations were easy to find, and contained a lot less talking than others. Plus Bach was close to math, and that was comforting. "I should branch out. Give me something to listen to driving back to California."

"Yeah." Another small movement, visible in peripheral sight. She was nodding, with sleepy slowness. "You should probably do that soon."

"When this is over." *And when I make my exit, I'll take the songs with me.* "Because it will be, bunny. This isn't the end of the world."

She made a tiny noise, neither assent nor disagreement. But when he stole a glance at the passenger seat, she was thumb-typing. "Uh, you don't have a subscription for the music app on here."

"Go ahead and sign me up, then. Or just buy the songs, it'll let you with a double tap."

"What's your budget?" How many times had she asked a client that? But a little color had crept back into her voice.

"Don't worry, it's all courtesy of Uncle Sam." He had plenty socked away, since there wasn't much to blow your pay on in the field and when he was home there was nothing to do but wait for the next op. Dad had done some investing, so along with her widow benefits Mom was set. She probably wouldn't even need her son's life insurance, which would pay out if Tax could make it look like an accident. "Pick what I should hear, give me a good education. I trust you."

She didn't reply, but when he stole another glance her head was bent. Biting gently at her lower lip, she focused on the screen as if it was the only thing in the world. There was plenty of battery on the small electronic brick, and he wasn't going to take them out into the desert just yet.

Not unless it became necessary.

The light turned green, the Dodge in front of them sputtered a cloud of white smoke as it jerked into motion, and Tax had a little time to think over his next moves and deal with the uncomfortable idea that perhaps this was the universe's way of roping him back into the endless rodeo of actually living.

Which would be, he admitted, a helluva joke.

THE HOTEL CHECKED all his current boxes—an older building; plenty of exits; half-full parking lots with good sightlines; a coffeemaker in the kitchenette though he'd use his own, thanks; cable; free wireless; and to top it all off, shopping nearby. If burrowing in was a necessity, they might as well be comfortable.

There were even two small swimming pools. He could imagine she had great bikini game, but good luck getting her into one at the current moment. Just one more pleasure he'd have to forego.

Leaving her with the car for check-in was bad for his nerves, but luck—and professionalism—meant they still had some breathing room. He'd just handed whoever was after her a helluva surprise. The cop might not even be able to give a good description of his pixie's guardian angel, between the adrenaline and sudden hit to the gut.

Should've bounced her head off the floor a couple times too. It was unpleasant to think of doing that to a woman, but anyone stupid enough to point a gun at Meg Callahan while he was around deserved whatever he had the time to dish out.

Meg made a beeline for the bathroom, and he didn't blame her. By the time she opened the door again, peering out distrustfully as if she expected more flying lead, he had the drapes drawn and the muted television on local news. A few nervous, delicate steps into the rest of the suite, holding Dad's old baseball cap from the Honda's trunk, those baby blues wide and haunted—instead of a bunny she was a doe alert for hunters, ready to leap if a leaf fell or a stray gust brushed the grass.

And, true to form, she cut right to the chase. "I think I know what's going on."

Do you, now. "Yeah?" Nice and casual, easy and quiet. "Let's get room service, and you can tell me."

"Oh, that's . . ." The hat wasn't going to survive if she kept twisting it like that. "No thank you, I'm fine. Look, I have an idea, so it's probably best if I go take care of it and you can—"

What the hell? "Come here." He didn't quite bark it as an order, but her shoulders hunched and her eyes got even rounder, if that was possible.

Still, she obeyed. Reluctantly, but he was the only security in a situation wildly outside her normal patterns.

The table by the window was a marginal risk with the drapes closed, and pushing her onto the bed could be . . . misconstrued. He had to handle the next few minutes very carefully, so Tax got her settled in the safest indifferently padded chair, lowered himself into the other seat, and pushed the pleather folio detailing amenities aside with an elbow. "I'm listening."

Meg's fingers interlaced, her knuckles bloodless. She sometimes sat like this—hands on the table and head slightly tilted—while listening to a client, but never so tense or tousled. "Gerry was moving out of the underside. For years."

Tax didn't fold his arms or lean back. Even his body language had to be nonjudgmental, accepting.

"Barton agreed it was a good thing. But it took a while." A nervous glance at the door; Meg's shoulders hunched. "And of course Ella would never ever be involved in anything like that. But Preston—that's his son, you met him at my office—a couple times he complained how his dad was leaving money on the table. Not directly, you know, and not in front of Gerry, but . . . we dated, so I knew what he thought of it."

You dated? Now he remembered the guy, from his very first day of work. "Little under six feet, dark hair, chip on his shoulder almost as big as his trust fund, right?"

"Yeah. That's him." Her mouth turned down at the corners, and Tax had the idea the relationship hadn't been a happy one.

Why that should make a bolt of hot, nearly queasy relief shoot through him wasn't quite a mystery, but it was nothing he wanted to comment on at the moment, even to himself. And now he *also* remembered Carl and Boom mentioning a stalker of an ex-boyfriend, too; was it the same guy? "Okay. So he didn't agree with his dad leaving the business."

Tax indeed hadn't liked how the tanned, dark-haired fellow had been looking at his new boss, and had ambled into the outer office for coffee he didn't really want on the off chance that she needed backup. Her polished, professional veneer hadn't cracked much, though he'd been able to sense her dislike.

Yes, he'd bet his next round of cigar-night penny-poker winnings this 'Press' was the one they'd been talking about. Now he wanted to know exactly how old the breakup was, just what the asshole had done, and a whole lot more.

But that was all beside the point. Meg's interlaced fingers were tense, knuckles bloodless-pale. "Well, Sam didn't seem surprised that . . . that Gerry was dead. She asked if I could identify the guys, plural." The words sped up, nearly tripping over each other. "And I've been going nuts all this time thinking that whoever had . . . had done that would also go after Press. But Sam said not to worry, that he's fine, which is weird because they can't stand each other. It's not legal proof, but—"

"But it's logical. She knew more than she was showing." Another slow nod, while his mind raced. Christ, this girl was smart. Even under duress she was putting together puzzle pieces. "This Press guy didn't know you would be at his dad's house?"

"He knew I was handling Ella's wedding, that's why he visited my office—or at least, that's what he said." Meg took a deep breath. "Barton said he wouldn't be there yesterday. Said he had another appointment." She shuddered, the chair giving a forlorn squeak.

Focus on the essentials. "You're right, this theory holds up really well."

"But . . ." Meg shook her head. "His *sister*, Arthur. He wouldn't hurt Ella." She blinked, and regarded him anxiously. "Right?"

Please, her eyes said. *Tell me the world is better than it looks. Tell me it's not rotten all the way through; tell me it's not filthy.*

Any member of the Squad knew the terrible things humans did to each other, and were ready to do the same if necessary. When he really thought about it, that was part of the reason he'd chosen to opt out—not the biggest component, but a significant one. Bad enough that he was a failure as a medic, unable to save so few of those he was supposed to; entirely worse was the fact that he now wasn't fit for pretty much any other career—except maybe the one he'd just lucked into.

The world was a cesspit. About all Tax could do was keep the dirt from touching her, and he was more than ready for the job. "That doesn't mean a lot to some people, especially when there's money involved. How much are we talking?"

"This is *Vegas*." A slight eyeroll, a faint tinge of weary sarcasm.

Christ knew he'd seen people kill each other over the strangest, most petty shit. "So he removes his father, maybe makes it look like a hit from a rival? There's a witness, but all she can do is ID the triggerman." Nice and slow, reeling out the logic, looking for holes. "Does this Press think you're smart enough to figure it out?"

"Probably not." A quick grimace, a tiny shake of her head. It was an extremely feminine gesture of disdain, and it cheered him up immensely.

The man's an idiot if he let you go. Still, even dumbasses could be dangerous. "You broke up with him?"

"Yeah." No further details, just the one word.

Tax was suddenly, overwhelmingly certain this Press was the stalker ex Boom and Carl had mentioned. No need to pry further, especially when she was so fragile. "Do you think that might be why he waited until you were at his dad's house?"

"I . . . I don't . . ." But the look in those baby blues before she hurriedly glanced away told a different story.

A woman might not want to believe it, but on some level, they knew. It was hard not to, especially with the statistics. He'd quoted some of those to Beck Sommers back in Oregon, not too long ago.

It felt like a lifetime.

"Okay." Tax didn't really want her thinking about it at the moment, though, and could've kicked himself for asking. "So the next step here is—"

Meg stared across the room at the television's silent glass face. The color had drained from her cheeks again, and her tightly clasped hands rose, hovering near her mouth.

He had to crane over his shoulder to see what had caught her attention.

Millionaire Found Dead, the chyron said, and the picture was a helicopter view of a stone-walled mansion with red roof tiles, the swimming pool in its backyard glittering through a light scrim of dead leaves. Cop and other emergency vehicles clustered the driveway. *Family and House-keeper Slain.*

Pictures of the victims bloomed as the closed-captioning struggled to keep up. Two older men in business suits, one with a smile and greying temples, the other sleek, dark, and humorless. One young woman, blondish and bare-shouldered in an evening dress, grinning like she knew the secret to all life's mysteries and found it hilarious. A DMV photo of an older woman with a cap of dark curls and a string of clearly cherished pearls, her dark liquid eyes solemn. Names—Gerald Roark, Robert Barton, Ella Roark, Matilda Mendoza.

"Oh, God," his fairy whispered. "Tilda? But she wasn't there."

That was troubling. There was a buzz and a soft chiming; Meg gave a violent start and he was almost as unnerved.

It was his phone, and if it was ringing through the do-not-disturb it could only be one of a few people. Tax had to drag the damn thing out of his pocket in a hurry; Meg pressed her hands against her mouth.

It wasn't who he expected. Tax thumbed the green circle. "Talk." It wasn't quite a snarl, but a signal that this was not the ideal time for a shoot-the-shit session.

"Hey, motherfucker," Grey chirped in his ear. "Boston's cold as monkey's nuts, I'm coming into Sin City early and can't get hold of Boom. You got some hookers and blow lined up?"

Plumb Busted

THE NEWS WAS horrible. Blood in the water, Barton would say; he considered journalists necessary nuisances at best.

Ella's picture was displayed more than anyone else's—it was a still from the Fireman's Relief Fund winter charity ball, someone must've had it on file. All Meg remembered of that night was the taste of sub-standard champagne and sickening tension, since Press insisted on dance after dance.

Come on, Meg. Please. He'd pretended to be ever so sorry, and it was hard to say no to a guy in such a repentant mood. Even Ell had tenta-tively remarked that maybe her brother had apologized enough, maybe Meg could just forgive and forget what had happened? Whatever it was, since Meg wouldn't give details.

"He's a buddy, decided to fly out early for the wedding," Arthur said. She couldn't even scrape up any irritation over the fact that *he* got to keep his damn phone. "He'll be in tomorrow morning."

Good for you. "Oh." Meg wished the TV wasn't muted; the closed captioning wasn't scrolling nearly fast enough. Why was Matilda's pic-ture on the screen?

Had someone waited among dead bodies for the housekeeper to return? The very idea made Meg feel sick all over again. Why hadn't she called to warn Tilda? Why hadn't she thought that Preston might have had something to do with this?

It was ridiculous, outlandish, utterly insane. She couldn't imagine Press paying someone to hurt Ella, or Tilda—who was the closest thing to a real mother he had, since Mrs. Roark was always so . . . absent.

You have to think. Getting out of town would be the best option, really. Meg could certainly start over somewhere new; people did it all the time. She and Eddie had talked about how to vanish nearly con-stantly when they were teenagers, always ending up in the same place.

It took money, and being willing to lie. Getting to her savings would require some planning—if Sam was working with Preston even something so simple as going to a bank branch suddenly became a lot more dangerous. Sam had access to the cops' systems and could easily put out an APB; between the two of them, Sam and Press knew all Meg's acquaintances, everyone she was likely to turn to for help.

She couldn't risk anyone else.

The air-conditioner under the shrouded window buzzed, cold air licking her damp face. She was sweating.

Considering the situation, Meg was surprised she wasn't screaming, too. Her vision blurred, warped, and a hot fingertip touched her cheek.

There was another option, one she'd been considering on some level all day. Risky, but what did she have to lose?

Gerry would tell you not to go there. So would Rob. Funnily enough, all she could think of was Barton's disappointment if he knew she was even *thinking* of dipping a toe in those particular shark-infested waters. *Stay in daylight, Meg. The underside's not the place for you.*

"Hey. Oh, hey, bunny. Shh, it's gonna be all right." The television vanished; a shadow loomed over her. Meg flinched, but it was only Arthur. Eddie's friend had left his seat and now bent, his palms on her wet cheeks, his nose inches from hers.

His skin was so warm. There were lighter flicks and striations in his dark irises, and this close a ghost of stubble could be seen along his jaw. His hair was slightly disarranged too, a lock over his left eye stubbornly resisting the flow of the rest.

"There's a guy," she heard herself say dully. "He's on Roscoe, not the Strip. I can go to him."

"Why?" Arthur's expression didn't shift at all. "What does this 'guy' do?"

Nothing nice, but he's really effective. Or so Barton says. Said. It hurt to correct herself, to think in the past tense. "You don't want to know. He's got a good amount of pull, and if I promise not to testify or anything he can maybe get Press—or whoever it is—to leave me alone."

Meg didn't want to think about the price for that kind of favor, either. Not right now, when she was already so tired. Not even turn-and-burns between cocktail waitressing and working a pole had exhausted her this much.

"He's going to leave you alone no matter what." Arthur's thumb moved slightly, feathering along her cheekbone. "You can tell me about this guy Roscoe while we eat, okay?"

Her stomach cramped, a swift vicious jab of pain. "I'm not hungry."

"You might not be, but your body needs fuel. Don't argue with your medic."

Oh, for God's sake. "I can get an Uber out to . . ." Except she couldn't, without her phone. Both the reflex to dig for her digital lifeline plus the utterly inconsequential thought that she was going to lose clients with no-shows kept interrupting her attempts to figure this bullshit *out*. "Or I'll take a taxi. This isn't something you should be messing with."

"Really?" Arthur wore a tight, thin, unamused smile as his thumb stroked her skin again, light and sure. "News for you, babe, I just shot two hostiles and was about to put a few rounds in that crooked cop as well. I'm in—all in, all the way down."

Nobody's ever all in. Not with something like this. But there was no use in arguing—he was, after all, male. And, as he'd so politely reminded her, he'd actually shot someone. She was going to have to figure out how to get him free of this mess, but her thinker simply couldn't cope with any additional load at the moment.

It was, as Rob would say, plumb busted.

The edge of Arthur's body heat warred with the air-conditioning's cold flow, a river of strange almost-prickles spilling down her back.

Fortunately, though, he let go of her, stepping back, his hands dropping. "So look at the menu and choose something you think you can eat. I'm gonna clean up a bit."

Yeah. Sure. "Why are you doing this? You don't even know me." The shrill voice of self-interest was shrieking at her not to look a gift horse in the mouth—who cared, right? She could let this guy get himself hurt or worse because it gave her a better chance of . . . what, exactly? Surviving?

Even if she left town, she'd always be looking over her shoulder. Running away was a nice teenage dream, but she was an adult.

Arthur hesitated.

Speak now, or forever hold your peace. "Never mind." It took two tries to push herself upright, the table wobbling a little as her palms pressed on it. "Can I lie down? Is that allowed? I really don't feel well."

"That one." He pointed at the bed furthest from the door, and she had to squeeze past him, holding her breath. Once out of the air-conditioner's blast the nausea subsided a little, but her eyes wouldn't stop leaking. "Meg . . ."

"I just want to lie down," she repeated, hating the whine in her own voice. "Please."

He let her, or at least he didn't bother giving more commands. Instead he retreated to the bathroom, so she was free to curl up on her side. Even though the tears welled slowly, one after another, Meg found she couldn't really cry.

Instead she fell into a deathly doze, still trying to figure out what the hell to do.

MEG SAT STRAIGHT up, clawing at empty air. A faint blue glow was the television, sending its mute glow into the night; her shoulder hit a semi-cushioned headboard as she scrabbled away from the tall, shadowy figures chasing her through empty alleys, copper fear thick in her throat and the realization that she'd been dreaming no comfort at all because the room was unfamiliar.

Her heart hammered hummingbird-quick, and she swallowed the scream burning her throat. It wasn't the first time she'd awakened in a strange room—far from—but she hated each and every occurrence, because it was like the bad old days.

God, she wanted to be home, in her own small, safe apartment. It wasn't much, but she could lock the door and let some of the terrible, awful weight of existing in an inimical world slide off her shoulders.

Hotel. I'm in a hotel, because someone's trying to kill me.

Just as her heart grudgingly decided it shouldn't attempt escaping through her mouth, a different silhouette loomed next to the bed, a knee sank into the mattress near her, and a pair of warm hands grabbed her arms, bare because she was in a T-shirt and jeans.

"Settle down," a half-familiar growl said. "It's me, it's all right. You're safe."

And God, how many times in foster care or juvie, in spare bedrooms or motels, had she wanted to hear that? Meg choked back another scream, and froze. Recognition arrived slowly, thunder after lightning. "Arthur?" A small, despairing whisper.

"I think you're the only person allowed to call me that." At least he sounded amused, even if his voice was full of gravel. "Bad dreams?"

"Yeah." Sarcasm lingered at the tip of her tongue—*what was your first clue?* But that was unfair, since he probably had way more reason for nightmares than she did, if what she was now suspecting about his and Eddie's time in the service was any indication. "Do you ever have them?"

"Sometimes." His fingers loosened. "Wanna talk about it?"

"Not really." She realized her new sneakers were gone. She was braless, in sock feet, and felt grit-grimy. Sleeping in clothes was awful; one of the best parts of growing up was not having to. "I'm sorry I woke you up."

"You didn't. I was thinking."

Well, thank God for that. More reflexive sarcasm—she wished Eddie was here, right before a tsunami of guilt crashed over her. "About what?"

"Tomorrow." He patted her arms before taking his hands away, as if soothing a restive pet. The television's blue glow painted the walls, skated along his cheekbones, touched the tip of his nose. Even in the half-light he was handsome. "Planning."

"Is that why the TV's still on?" It was a silly question, really.

Thankfully, he didn't seem to think so. "That's so anyone watching the room might think we're still awake. Or you leave the bathroom light on with the door closed. Someone can be in there for a long time without moving, so it throws intruders off a bit."

Huh. Good to know, actually. Her throat was dry; Meg longed for a shot of freezer-cold vodka. A hit of bourbon might do the trick as well; she wasn't a drinker, but good God it sounded attractive at the moment. "They teach you that in the Army?"

"Nah. Read it in a magazine." He reached for her pillow, plumped it with a few efficient motions, and thrust it at her. "Lie down. You need something to help you sleep?"

How many of those pills do you have? "No thanks." She should probably do a little planning of her own.

But when she settled horizontally once more, pushing the covers down with her feet, he didn't go back to the other bed. Instead, Arthur shifted, stretching out on his side with one arm tucked under his head because she now had both pillows.

He had to be perched right on the edge of the mattress. Meg froze. Caution warred with unwilling comfort.

"Don't worry," he said, quietly. "It's just to keep away the nightmares."

Will that work? She and Eddie had doubled up all the time as kids, and she'd never had a bad dream with him breathing next to her.

God, she missed that feeling. Adulthood sucked, and she didn't even have her phone and a pair of earbuds. A long shoal of music to carry her through until morning would have been heavenly, and maybe she could find some kind of direction in lyrics, the beat shaking a good idea free. "You don't have to."

"I know." Arthur was very still, carefully observing the space between them. "This guy you mentioned. Roscoe."

"His name's Franke." Her eyelids were heavy, and her pulse had calmed down. Meg let out a shaky breath, wishing she'd brushed her teeth before going to bed. "He owns the Corral out on Roscoe Avenue. I can go to him."

"Maybe." Now Eddie's buddy sounded dubious. "We'll have a plan tomorrow, bunny. Just get some rest."

I don't think I can. In fact, Meg was reasonably sure she'd never sleep again—but she was wrong. As if a switch had flipped, she was out.

And thank God, there were no more dreams.

Knows the Lay

GREY'S FLIGHT WAS only an hour late, and for a Friday morning, traffic wasn't bad at all. It was even semi-soothing to circle, watching the flow of vehicles and passengers each time he swung close to the terminal, Tax's phone handling GPS, listening for comms, and routing Meg's *For Arthur* playlist through the Honda's speakers like a champ.

Not even his mother called him that. Tax didn't mind, though.

His small, far-too-brave package was probably going crazy without her own digital assistant, and he didn't like leaving her in a hotel room by herself. But she was safe for the moment, there were a million cameras at any airport, and if this Preston guy had any ounce of brains—and resources—at all he'd have someone watching departing flights as well as buses and trains.

A bright desert morning shimmered, mercury already hovering near eighty. Despite that, heavy purple clouds lingered over distant mountains, ready to sweep down on the city itself.

It would be nice to sit somewhere and watch a natural light show with a bottle of wine and a pink-tipped pixie, another useless little fantasy Tax didn't have to tell anyone about. The secret could sit in his chest, a nice warm coal on cold nights.

He'd never heard most of the stuff on the playlist before. They were love songs, but of course most modern musical offerings are, so he couldn't read too much into it. Besides, she'd been under a lot of pressure while selecting. Tax was surprised she hadn't just thrown in a few forgettable Top Forty offerings and called it good.

Starting out slow, ramping up to a few high-energy peaks, and closing with a pop anthem which blended into the first song if you had it on repeat—Meg knew the art of the mix pretty well, and it showed.

He was almost disappointed when he spotted Grey at the edge of a clot of tourists, observing just enough space to assure himself of free play while using the civilians as cover. Tax didn't even have to fight for a spot at the curb; when the shuttle bus in front of him had to stop to let two harried flight attendants and a family of five with far too many rolling suitcases use a slightly raised speed-bump crosswalk Grey ambled out into the flow, tossed a tan canvas ditty very like Tax's own into the Honda's backseat with a burst of hot exhaust-laden air, and nipped into the passenger seat neat as you please.

"Didn't know you were a Phil Collins fan," was his buddy's greeting. Lean and just a shade taller than Klemp, Mark Grezinski was knife-nosed, dark-eyed, and scrub-stubbled, scratching at his cheek after he got his seatbelt settled, then raking stiff fingers through chestnut hair much longer than regulations would allow.

Just like Tax's own, and Klemp's and Boom's too. It was always the first signal a guy was offbase and planning to stay that way for a while.

"Is that who this is?" Tax gauged traffic, cut the wheel, and took the space opening up to his left. The family had cleared the far side, parents making sure all their ducklings were in a row, and a blare of horns sounded somewhere behind the CR-V. The current song was synthesizer-heavy; someone was telling Billy not to forget his number. "And how was the flight?"

"Dueling babies back in coach and some Karen in first-class bitching about the proportion of tomato juice in her Bloody Mary. Almost rather be on a combat drop." Grey's fingers tapped restlessly at his knee as he scanned their surroundings automatically, leaving Tax free to drive without looking for tails. "What the fuck's going on?"

"Boom and Carl are on some camping trip, pre-wedding honeymoon." The music shifted; a piano solo over a beat led into a tenor crooning soulfully about his lady love being much too sexy and murdering his heart.

"So we're house-sitting in Sin City?" Grey's eyebrows rose; he kept glancing at Tax's phone like he expected it to morph into a snake and lunge for him. "What the fuck?"

He sounded honestly baffled.

"There's, uh, been a slight snag." Tax gave the briefing in a few sentences, carefully leaving out anything that might be . . . misconstrued. "So our package is tucked in," he finished, "and she says some local piece-of-shit player has enough juice to get this motherfucker Press out of the game."

"Huh." Grey's fingers paused for a moment, then resumed tapping in a different pattern. He fidgeted almost as much as Boom, except for when they were in-country or under fire. "You believe her?"

I believe she thinks so. "I'd prefer to just kill the fuckwad."

"No, I mean, is this girl running a—"

"Lady," Tax corrected. It was out of his mouth before he could stop himself. "She's a lady, you bastard, and Boom would've told me if she was on our side of the street."

"Nobody's on our side of the freeway, bro," Grey said, somewhat sourly. "But okay. We're not calling him in?"

"No cell service, he's out of pocket." *Let him have some time off.* "It'll be just you and me. Like Mombasa."

A short, surprised laugh. "Christ, I haven't thought about that in years. *What the fuck did you do now?*" It was a dead-on impersonation of Dez's weary tone.

Tax found himself grinning too, a sardonic, wolfish expression he probably wouldn't ever let Meg see. "*It was on fire when we got here,*" he quoted back, though he wasn't nearly so gifted with mimicry. The music changed again, something that sounded like experimental jazz with a heavy club beat, and he was suddenly feeling a lot better about all this.

"Man, and here I thought a wedding would be boring. Hey, how's Klemp? You checked on him?"

"Did I ever, and you're never gonna believe what I found." If he distracted Grey with the story of Paul Klemperer's torch-carrying finally reaching its objective, his buddy might not suss out Tax's guilty little secret. "Oh, and my mom sent some pickled garlic and a big jar of kimchi for you. Be good and I'll release the hostages sooner."

"Your mama's an angel, my brother. But all's fair in love and kimchi; I might have to run a liberation operation." Grey leaned forward, peering at the phone's face. "What in fuck's name are you listening to?"

Tax nudged the Honda into the left lane, aiming for the onramp. "Music, you fucking philistine."

"Oooh, a big word. Jackson would be so proud." Grey laughed again, settling back in his seat as they hit the freeway. "So, this best friend of Boom's, the famous Meg. What's she like?"

Uh-oh. "Nice girl. Smart." He had to work for a casual tone, not dismissive but not overdoing it either. "Scared out of her mind right now."

"Huh." Grey's eyes half-closed as he resettled, twitching, but only a civilian would think him about to nap. He could probably recite the plate numbers of every car around them, and no doubt his fingers were itching for a few pockets to pick—not for business, just for fun. "How we gonna bury this guy giving her problems?"

"Figure we'll have some lunch and hash that out. She's local, knows the lay."

"Does she, now." Grey didn't grin when Tax shot him a glance, but he was no doubt aware of the motion. "Well, you know what they say. What happens in Vegas . . ."

"Apparently I'm not allowed to count cards here. But you know, Boom's out of pocket, so . . ." Tax signaled for a lane change, and hoped Grey wasn't figuring out just how much he liked their package.

It was hard to fool a buddy.

TURNED OUT HE had an entirely different problem than misleading Grey, because when he used the agreed-on pattern of knocks for the hotel door, there was no answer.

The room was utterly shipshape, beds made and towels hung neatly though housekeeping hadn't visited yet because the *Do Not Disturb* tag still dangled primly from the knob.

And his bunny had—poof—vanished right out of the hat.

Polite Fiction

EVERY BRUISE AND muscle ached, she was as stiff as a board, and it was too goddamn quiet.

Sure, there was the low sound of traffic like a large but distant breathing creature. The hum of other people going about their day was different than in her apartment building, and the air-conditioning was a constant in any desert structure that could afford it.

But the room felt like a trap, and Meg's nerves were shot. No opening the drapes and blinds, no taking the chain off the door unless a specific pattern of knocks sounded, no using the phone even for room service, no jumping on the bed and screaming.

Her choices were reading the Bible from the nightstand, trying to nap, or watching cable. What would Arthur do if she turned on the porn channel and let it play, she wondered? It was probably billed by the minute.

The second full-size bed, nearer the door, was untouched. Where had he been sleeping before he'd settled on the edge of hers? In a chair, on the floor? She didn't miss that he'd gotten a dualie instead of a queen or king room, which was awful gentlemanly.

Maybe it was the Army training; maybe Carl was wrong and Arthur batted for the home team. Or maybe he was just that unicorn, a thoroughly good guy.

Who had shot two people and kicked a cop yesterday. The recent bursts of violence seemed oddly dreamlike at the moment, probably some kind of coping mechanism. Even with that numbing, it sucked. She still felt grainy and dirty after a long hot shower—her clothes were none too fresh—and logy despite the coffee from his fancy travel machine. Pacing from the hall door to the bathroom and back again could only keep her occupied for so long, and the wild what-ifs mounted with each passing second.

What if he wasn't coming back? What if there was an accident on the freeway? What if Sam figured out who was helping her, and started using police resources to track down a Good Samaritan? What if Eddie and Carl came back early and the freckled, green-eyed man in the hoodie was waiting at their house?

The peace and quiet was nerve-wracking, awful, monstrous. Tiny distorted bits of the past two days skipped around inside her head, refusing to settle. Worst of all, there was no music to be had; the clock radio only gave out garbled static on FM bands and right-wing 'news' radio on AM.

Finally, Meg dropped onto the bed she'd slept in—there was no point in calling it *hers*, really—and used the remote. Flicking through channels was better than pacing, and God how she wished MTV or VH1 still played actual music, for God's sake.

Maybe she was getting old.

Home shopping. Morning talk shows. Reruns. Infomercials. Streaming services, but she didn't want to add anything to Arthur's bill. The scrambled mess of pay-per-view. Back to the beginning, the public channels with their usual midmorning news and traffic breaks.

What the hell? She had to flick back two numbers, the remote could only transmit so fast.

"—lahan, a person of interest in the slayings that have rocked the local business community." Channel Four's newest anchor was blonde and personable in a blue twinset, the exact shade to match her eyes. She looked cool, confident, and imperturbable, and in the top right corner of the screen was a picture of Meg herself.

It was a strange, slipping-sideways sensation to see her own face on the news. Meg remembered the heat, the photographer—Swanson, a little pricey for most weddings but the clients were always satisfied—raising his camera with an inquiring look, how her armpits had been soaked and her skull ringing with the venue kitchen's din. She'd had to soothe the head of the catering crew because the AC had gone out and everything was melting. Even the heavily overwatered frangipani and jasmine had been looking a little wilted.

One for the books? Swanson had asked, and Meg put on her best smile. The result was good enough to be cropped and added to her business's website—soft tendrils of pale undyed hair flattering her face, her nose ring glinting to match her earrings, and the layer of sweat looking dewy instead of heatstruck. Still, all she could remember was the crowdsourced humidity, her heels pinching unmercifully, the headache, and wishing the damn wedding was over so she could go home and take a cold shower.

"Police are asking anyone with information—or anyone who sees

Ms. Callahan—to call the tipline," the anchor continued, her smile banished for the moment. She was all appropriate gravity, probably grateful for something to break up the recitation of traffic and weather statistics. "Again, that number is . . ."

Meg was sweating again, she realized—the heavy, cold, greasy moisture of fear instead of the body's natural climate control. She'd even had to use Arthur's antiperspirant, and the faint tinge of its unfamiliar smell made her stomach roll despite its undoubted comfort.

Try to rest, he'd said on his way out the door. *I'll be back with Grey and we'll make a plan. It's going to be all right.*

Fat chance. Her face had hit the *news*, for God's sake. It was a good thing she didn't have her phone, because it was probably blowing up with clients canceling well into next year, tabloids hoping for a scoop, caterers and venues calling off tours or upcoming events, and people she'd thought were friendly either hungry for a bit of gossip or—much rarer—offering some kind of help.

Ella was dead and Eddie was better off as far away as possible from this rapidly escalating disaster. Of all the people she knew, they were the only two she'd call actual *friends*; it was best not to use that word lightly. Meg had a zillion acquaintances and quite a few clients or business contacts, but nothing approaching family.

No family alive, that was. Except Eddie, and how long until Press figured out threatening him was a good way to get Meg to play along?

She was going to end up buried out in the desert, if she was lucky. If she wasn't, Eddie and Carl—or Arthur—would be buried alongside, and she'd probably go to hell for dragging good people down with her.

Worst case, though, was that they wouldn't kill her. Not quickly, anyway.

"Fuuuuck." Meg's own voice startled her; she hunched guiltily and pressed the power button on the remote. The television died, a faint patina of dust on its screen fluorescing for the barest moment. A wave of heat slid from her scalp all the way down her body, followed by an icy tingle. A frozen glass could shatter if set on hot pavement or patio during a summer afternoon out in the desert, shivering into pieces with a terrific crack Eddie always laughed crazily at.

Don't do it, Meg. Do not even think about it. Funny how she wasn't hearing Ella, or Gerry, or even Tilda—how on earth had they killed the housekeeper? Meg didn't want to know.

No, she was hearing Rob Barton, maybe because she'd been the last thing he looked at before that freckled guy shot him. Or maybe because he'd saved her life, though she wasn't a Roark. Loyalty—or kindness—like that was rare. She should listen to him.

But that would mean letting Press get away with what he'd done. The more she thought about it, the more certain she was of her theory—at least, the parts concerning the younger Roark.

It just explained everything too neatly. Why had he visited her office? A last-ditch attempt to get back together?

Did it matter? She had to at least *try* to make him pay. The cops most likely couldn't do it; she didn't want to think Sam was crooked like Arthur assumed, but . . . this was Vegas.

Her purse was lying on the bed. She bounced to her feet, scooped it up, and halted, her heart pounding. What the fuck was she thinking?

In poker, you're not playing the game, Rob had said over and over, teaching her and Ella about chance, betting, and etiquette. *You're playing the other person.*

Well, the last thing anyone would expect was good little girl Meg Callahan visiting the man who had taken over most of Gerry's underside business.

A few minutes later, Meg stood in the hallway, the room's door swinging shut. The point of no return.

There was a click as it latched, but she was already walking away, head down, her purse hitched high on one shoulder, and the burner phone clutched grimly in her right hand.

ROSCOE WASN'T the Strip. Still, there was plenty of neon, as well as no shortage of tourists looking for cheaper vacation packages—she wondered, almost idly, if Arthur could calculate the rate sheets for Vegas tours as quickly as the ones for wedding venues—and the Five Palms anchored the top of the street, one of the better casino-hotel destinations. Prime real estate, and a hundred percent squeaky clean.

At the other end loomed the old Corral, its wagon wheel sign spinning day and night. Its hotel rooms were deliberately not available to more than a smattering of out-of-towners, usually those with connections but sometimes a few day-trippers just to keep everything looking right.

Sure, it looked and even smelled like a bona fide historical institution, right down to the faint tinge of nicotine from the times when you could smoke in the pit and ashtrays were attached to the arm of every slot chair. The girls working drink-and-dab duty had vest-fringes longer than their shorts, the tips brushing tanned thighs, and the buffet featured such delicacies as Chuck Wagon Stew and Rootin' Tootin' Root Beer. Croupiers were issued old-timey armbands and the lounge's entertainment offerings leaned in the *Bonanza* and Patsy Cline direction, with a heavy helping of Lawrence Welk. For all that, the popping of fake gunshots was muted, the lights were low, and just like every other casino, the lack of windows on the first couple floors forced time to lose all meaning.

It wasn't a bad place to work if you kept your nose clean and the pit boss happy. Better than the Xanadu, where a full drink tray plus roller skates meant sometimes a crash was taken out of a waitress's pay. Meg had filled out an application at the Corral once, while eighteen and freshly graduated, and was deeply glad she'd never had a callback.

The real action wasn't at the bright flashing machines or the tables—roulette, blackjack, Texas Hold 'Em, and even some baccarat. Most of it happened on the floors above, and if you were very unlucky, the basement.

Most places in Vegas didn't have below-ground levels, since building downward meant attempting to drill and blast into hard caliche. But the Corral had a floor or two no tourist would ever see, probably because the core of the building had been put in when dynamite was cheap and Prohibition made concealed entrances a very good idea. Brought up to code during the last construction boom, little remained of its original appearance, at least on the outside.

Meg kept her chin level and her tan leather purse carefully against her side. Withdrawing the daily maximum cash limit at an ATM was a calculated risk, and she timed it just right for the arrival of a cab—not a rideshare, but one of the union cars a gig economy was slowly strangling out of business. The driver, a heavyset and somewhat morose middle-aged guy with well-oiled hair and an unlit stogie clamped in his teeth, didn't even seem happy for the sizable tip she forked over, but he did mumble *be careful in there honey*, and there might've been the suggestion of a paternal wink in the rearview mirror.

It was hard to tell through the cataract-clouded plastic shield supposed to deter carjackings.

She knew where to go—a particular VIP elevator on the other side of the pits, its doors burnished steel behind a red velvet rope, a single beefy, uniformed security guard eyeing her narrowly as she approached. But she'd dug in her purse before getting through the front door, and held up the gilded, glittering poker chip.

Emergencies only, Gerry muttered solemnly in her memory. *Don't abuse it, Meg. I know you won't, but some things have to be said.*

She was gestured in, the guy nodding slightly—probably because of the earpiece visible on the left side of his crewcut head.

The elevator dropped, her stomach flipflopping, and Meg kept the chip clearly visible, trying not to look up at the corner she suspected a camera was hiding in. She didn't need to press a single button; it was probably a bad sign that it was going down instead of up, but she was committed now.

At least Eddie was safely out of the way. Arthur would get back from picking up their other Army buddy and probably heave a sigh of relief that she'd taken care of the whole business without involving him further. Unless the gun he'd used at Gianello's could be traced, but that was out of her control and at the moment, Meg Callahan had all the trouble she could handle without borrowing more.

She wasn't sure what to expect when the door opened, but it certainly wasn't rotund, smiling Bert Franke himself, his sober dark suit very like an undertaker's except for the rich red of his tie. Behind him, a carpeted hallway receded, bright and tidy as any mid-tier office building downtown, lit by fluorescents, and he could've been a call-center manager greeting a new hire.

His dark eyes peered out of perpetually bruised-looking circles as if he hadn't slept in a week, and his smile was expensively capped. Plus, there was the pinkie ring, though he wore the flashing gem as if it were an in-joke. Maybe it was; he certainly grinned like he knew the world's biggest knee-slapper and was just waiting to invite everyone in on it.

"My oh my," he said, in his rich resonant tenor. "Meg, isn't it? Gerry Roark's little foster kid? You grew up, look at that."

Happens to the best of us. "Mr. Franke." Meg's headache had mutated to a strange, airy feeling, probably the result of no breakfast and constant tension. She held up the poker chip, hoping her fingers weren't trembling too badly. "Thank you for seeing me, I'm so sorry to bother you. How's Nancy doing?" It paid to remember details—like the name of a businessman's daughter, even if she was a nasty little backbiting socialite neither Meg nor Ella could stand.

"Enjoying New York, shopping up a storm. Come with me—I hope you won't mind talking while we walk? Busy day." He indicated the hall and set off, leaving her to scramble in his wake. "Terrible business, about Gerry. Just terrible."

"Yes. Gerry always said you were a good man, sir." Which was a complete damn lie—*no more conscience than a shark, but understands appearances*, were the exact words—but a little polite fiction certainly couldn't hurt. The throbbing in her head matched her feet, her shoulder, and her knees. Maybe she should have stopped for ibuprofen, or asked for some of Arthur's pain meds. "I'm sorry to cause problems, but—"

"Oh, no problem at all. In fact, you're doing me a favor." Doors passed by on either side, and Franke slowed down just enough to let her draw level with him. "Have to say I'm surprised, though." He turned to the left, reaching for a brushed-nickel doorknob. There was concrete under the thin carpet, a reminder that this was stage dressing, and the lack of windows wasn't because of casino science but the fact that no daylight could be allowed on whatever happened down here.

"Me too." That, at least, was God's honest truth. She had come to some decisions last night, and the first one came tumbling out of her mouth. "Mr. Franke, all I want is a way out of town. Gerry said this chip was good for one favor, and I know it's a big one but I won't cause any problems. I just want to leave."

And once I'm over the state line I can maybe talk to someone who isn't bought and paid for. It was certainly a more achievable goal than somehow trading enough to this man to warrant being left alone inside Vegas city limits.

"Leave?" He swung the door open and motioned her through. Meg's body was moving smoothly, though a cold trickle of dread slipped down the channel of her spine. "I suppose that's a possibility. Roark did always have a romantic streak."

Relief turned her knees wobbly. "Thank you—" Meg began, but a slight air-conditioned breeze ruffled her hair. Hard hands grabbed her upper arms, and before she knew it she was trapped between a pair of goons, blond on the left and curly-brunet on the right, both in matching off-the-rack suits that did nothing to hide their gym-bought muscles or the sidearms they were packing.

"You're welcome," Franke said, urbanely. "Young Preston's been very worried about you, Meg, but don't fret. We'll keep you nice and fresh for him." Then, clearly addressing the goons, "Put her in storage, boys. *Gently*, no funny business—and that means you, Rex."

The blond actually pushed his lip out like a sulky teenager. Meg pitched aside, violently, but it didn't matter. Their fingers bit her bruises, adding fresh ones, her feet dangled, and she was whisked into the darker reaches of the Corral's basement.

Lady Luck

THIS MADE TWICE in a month he'd lost a package, and Tax thought sourly it was a good thing he was planning a permanent exit. This shit was *embarrassing*; he should've tied Meg to a chair.

Or the bed. That thought called up all sorts of images, none of which were even close to helpful.

"Maybe she went out for a beer." Grey had a sleek black laptop open on the table, his fingers dancing over the keyboard while he frowned. "Girls get bored, you know."

"Can you track it?" Tax considered throwing something at his buddy—a pillow, maybe, or a knife, could go either way.

What the fuck had he done wrong? He scooped up the remote and pressed the 'on' button; the television woke with a slight electronic whine.

"All things should be so easy, bro. Unless the bug's fucked up." Grey shot him a sideways glance and stretched, cracking his knuckles. He looked remarkably fresh for a six-hour-plus flight; he must not have hit the in-flight booze very hard. And he was swinging straight into an operation without a single bit of bitching.

It was good to have buddies.

"Please. Have *some* faith in me." Tax stared at a commercial for laundry detergent, a smiling woman folding her presumed child's oh-so-fresh shirts. The front desk said there hadn't been any calls or messages; there was no sign of forced entry. Meg had been wide-eyed and nervous when he left, but not overly jumpy.

A professional team could bust right in and take a single civilian; a good one could do it and leave no trace, but that kind of contractor didn't come cheap. He'd warned her not to open the door unless he gave the right knock—still, all it took was a cloned keycard and she could be bundled out and away with nobody the wiser.

That feat was far beyond someone who could only afford a three-man collection of hoodie-wearing jackasses, though. It was far, far more likely that she'd flown the coop. But *why?*

Maybe because he'd pushed it too far last night? Lying frozen on the edge of a hotel mattress listening to a beautiful woman breathe, knowing she was safely within arm's reach . . . well, it was far from the worst way he'd passed the dark hours, but maybe she hadn't agreed. The bed no doubt still smelled like her.

That thought wasn't guaranteed to help him concentrate, either. And how could he take any sort of exit now, even if he got her through this safely? The woman needed some serious looking after, and anyone he could trust with the mission had other concerns.

Huh. Tax frowned slightly at the screen. He'd checked the weather channel right before leaving for the airport, but now it was tuned to a local affiliate. Noticing that kind of detail was grasping at straws. The reasonable thing to do was to let Grey work.

"Yeah, yeah." His buddy magnanimously didn't point out that Tax had been so unprofessional as to lose a fucking civilian. At least he didn't know about the previous one—what was it with women leaping into the deep end? "Anything good on?"

"Probably just a talk show." Tax glanced at his watch, snug against the inside of his wrist, and had to look again because he wasn't tracking very well. Two minutes to noon. "Or soaps."

"*Like sands through an hourglass,*" Grey quoted, and laughed. The sound went right through Tax's head. "My grandma loved that shit."

Will you just do your fucking job? But that was unfair. His buddy was fresh off the plane and no doubt wishing for a leisurely lunch and a cold cerveza, not this bullshit. "My mom too. Calls 'em doramas."

"Huh. Don't mean to be rude, but maybe you could open up some of that pickled garlic? They didn't feed us much on the plane."

There was no way he was feeding any of his buddies something fermented and willingly sleeping anywhere near them afterward. "Not even in business class?"

"Fuck, man, you know they're . . ." Grey trailed off and the clicking resumed, a song of concentration. It was his job to keep them connected with each other and the mothership; he was also what they called a born organizer. He could saunter out into a strange city and return with half a dozen necessary articles as well as a whole carful of pleasant additions. Pulling rabbits out of hats, literally or figuratively, was damn near a vocation for him.

Tax was hoping he'd be able to work some actual magic with this particular bunny.

Where had he gone wrong? Maybe her silence last night hadn't been slumber but fear of a strange man sharing the bed. How could he have been so fucking *stupid?*

Tax stood, hands dangling, and stared at the colorful blur without seeing it. The volume was on low instead of muted; the impatient synthesizer tune heralding another round of *if it bleeds, it leads* scraped his nerves. He should turn the damn thing off; they'd probably already moved on from a few murders, no matter how juicy.

But Grey liked a little noise while he worked. Meg's phone and its SIM card were safely stowed, but the burner—even powered down—had a telltale attached. Just a little insurance, added right after purchasing because that was SOP whenever you handed a piece of gear to a package.

Everything hinged on whether or not she'd ditched it.

Wait, what the hell? Tax returned to his physical body and the room with an internal thump he was surprised didn't register on the Richter scale. Grey was still tapping at the keyboard, his eyebrows drawn together and a bright thin blade of desert sunshine slipping between the drapes to neatly bisect the table behind his laptop.

"—a person of interest in the slaying of a Sunset Park businessman." The noon anchor, his expensively styled hair a set of plugs if Tax had ever seen one, gazed into the camera with what he probably fancied was studied gravity. "Again, if you've seen Ms. Meg Callahan, police ask you to call the tip line at 1-800—"

"Fuck," Tax breathed. The screen inset glowed, and it was—of course—a picture of his personal fairy, wearing the particular set little smile that meant she wasn't quite having a good time but gamely determined to carry on. Either there was something magic on the lens or the light had been just perfectly right, because she glowed, her blue eyes wide and dark with hidden pain and her sweet mouth curved tightly, a secretive half-smile.

Of course, she was just that pretty. Any picture of her would be a work of art.

"What?" Grey's clicking halted, and he peered across the room. "Tax? What the hell?"

"Fuck me." Tax sounded like he'd been punched right in the gut, he realized. *Christ, she's beautiful. Now everyone in the goddamn city is going to recognize her. Meg, baby, is this what happened?*

A chair squeaked. His buddy approached, cautiously, as if he suspected a fellow soldier was about to have an episode—and that was wrong. The medic was the one keeping everyone else bolted together;

Tax was the one supposed to be calm even when a friend's guts were hanging out.

Thinking of poor old Lenz was a distraction. He was much more concerned with the present, for once, and didn't have to wrench his attention out of the past. He hadn't even scrubbed his hands more than once that morning, and had no desire to get out the sanitizer.

"Don't tell me that's her." Grey made a soft clicking noise with his tongue, a familiar *oh boy this is gonna be good* sound. "On the news? And wow, she's—"

"Don't." *Be very fucking careful what you say right now.* The warning in his tone was red rags fluttering from a maddened bull's horns.

"Ah." His buddy took a sideways step, keeping enough distance. He hadn't even tried to pick Tax's pocket for fun or done any conjuring tricks with spare quarters yet. "Well, you want the good news, or the good news?"

What about this is even remotely good news? "Tell me you have a lock on her." Tax sounded hoarse even to himself.

"Well, I have a lock on the burner you say she's carrying. That do ya?"

It's a start. "Let's go." He considered winging the remote right through the goddamn idiot box, managed to restrain himself with an effort that made sweat pop out along his lower back, behind his knees, and probably visibly on his forehead as well.

"Yo, wait a second." Grey had his hands up, palm-out, the classic *hey man calm down* stance, but he was braced and ready. It was the exact posture he used when Jackson got *that look*, the one that meant their wildcard was about to go well and truly postal. "I haven't even gotten to the best part."

Tax was aware of his own pulse, running far too high and hard. "Tell me while we move."

AT LEAST HE was calm enough to drive. Tax glanced at their objective, blinked, and decided to circle the parking lot at least once. "Christ," he muttered. "You're seeing this, right? I'm not having some sort of desert hallucination?"

"Yeah, it looks like *Bonanza* got blackout drunk and fucked *Gunsmoke*, then died of embarrassment halfway through sobering up." Grey peered out the windshield, and his personal aesthetics were obviously offended by the view. "She said the guy here's a local player, right?"

"Yeah, his name's supposed to be Franke." Tax added up the exits again, scanned the front of the casino, and decided it was built around the core of an older building. "Apparently he's got some weight. Or so she thinks."

"That probably ain't all he's got. Man, Boom never said his hometown was *this* interesting." Grey laced his fingers together, cracking them with small popcorn sounds. He wasn't bitching about balancing his precious laptop on his knees while someone else drove, nor had he made a single joke about a civilian jetting off to play roulette in a Roy Rogers fever dream—all of which meant he grasped the gravity of the situation. "Yeah, the telltale's definitely inside. Can't get more of a lock, though. Either it's switched off or there's too much building for the signal to get through. Or both."

Five stories, plenty of concrete and glass, even more neon festooning the façade and a billboard squatting on top proclaiming it the *Home of the Six-Shootin' Slots*. It was a Friday just after lunch and the lot was half-full already, cars like hungry piglets clustering as close to the entrance as possible. The sunshine was a migraine attack, a steady wind carrying veils of golden dust across every street, eddying between vehicles and rasping corners. It was a day for static electricity, or maybe the unsteady zap lurking at Tax's fingertips was purely internal. Certainly the purple smudge over distant mountains was bigger than it had been yesterday.

The idea of walking into this Corral place and tearing apart the entire fucking building was deeply, unsettlingly attractive.

"Okay." Tax eyeballed the pattern of security cameras atop the lot's streetlamps. *What's the objective, soldier?* It was the sort of question Dez might ask just to make sure a grunt was paying attention. "How we doing?"

"Three and a half minutes, tops." Grey produced a small black USB stick and popped it into the side of the laptop. "Go in and count a few cards, or something. Win us enough to buy drinks."

You don't pay for drinks while you're in Vegas and working for me, Mr. Tachmann. Was she sitting across from some piece-of-shit mobster, pleading politely for a way out of this tangle? Had they patted her down and taken the phone before spiriting her away? A hundred things could've gone wrong.

Thinking like that was a good way to get a bad case of sideways. Tax cut the wheel and parked a few empty spaces from a red Corolla that had seen at least one fender-bender. "I'm under orders not to. Maybe I'll just see if there's an Elvis impersonator in the lounge."

"You're under orders not to have any fun? Man, she must be some girl." Grey tapped at the keyboard. "You got your phone and the other burner?"

"Safe and sound." Tax patted at his jacket's breast pocket. He probably wasn't dressed like a local; security would peg him as tourist the moment he walked in. The urge to ask *are you sure this will work* was useless, so he discarded it. "What are the odds the guards in there are packing?"

"This is *Nevada*. Although it's a little past high noon." Grey sounded for all the world like he was enjoying himself. "You pop in, get the package, waltz out, and we vanish. And you owe me dinner."

"I know a nice place." Once this was all over he could even take his bunny back to the restaurant Boom and Carl had treated them to, since she seemed to like it. They could talk about the weather, and maybe he could . . . what? Tax exhaled, nice and slow, watching the front of the building. The first step was getting inside. "Boom's got a full liquor cabinet too, and some steaks in the freezer."

"Now you're speaking my language, bro." Grey made an irritable little shooing motion, pushing his sunglasses down his nose and frowning at the screen. "Timer's ticking, I'll be in like Flynn in under two. Get your ass moving."

"See you on the other side." Tax popped the door, stepping into a bath of dry desert heat. Grey would slither over to the driver's seat, and the second Tax's smartphone and the burner were inside and active he'd have a connection to the casino's network. The decryption software and other goodies he had access to were in some cases experimental, in others flat-out illegal, and uniformly useful; of all the Squad, he was probably the best backup for this. Another little piece of luck, and Tax was uneasy at how much was swirling around.

Well, it *was* Vegas, after all.

Just be alive, Meg. They were going to have to talk about this save-everyone-else complex she had; that sort of shit only ended in grief.

After all, he should know. But now he wasn't thinking about his exit or even about the lives he couldn't save. His focus was entirely on snatching just a single, solitary person from the fire, and as solutions to his own problems went it was one he could live with.

The walk seemed to take forever. He took his time, ambling as if he had a pocket full of cash and was looking forward to burning it.

At least, until a black Explorer, a model from a couple years ago with dust-screened windows bearing heavy privacy tinting, rolled past the front door. Though bigger, the silhouette did look a lot like his own car at first glance.

A cold finger brushed Tax's nape. *You have got to be kidding me.*

The vehicle slowed, sharklike, and when it reached the corner of the building it hooked a left and vanished.

What do you want to bet he's heading for the back to pick up a certain package?

Tax kept his pace even, and continued covering ground. It couldn't be the third player from the diner. The coincidence was just too outlandish.

Either way Lady Luck was spinning, and the prize was Meg Callahan's life.

It was time to play a little dirty.

Invisible in Life

STUPID. YOU STUPID little bitch. Her wrists hurt like fire, and her ankles followed suit. The concrete floor was cold; this space had once been a walk-in freezer. The only light was from a single bulb trapped in a heavy cage of frosted glass and wire, and its anemic glow barely penetrated the gloom in the back corners. Whatever was hanging on the overhead rack along that wall was large, bulky, wrapped in black plastic, and there were two of them.

Meg didn't want to know. She'd managed to get herself mostly upright, bracing her bruised, aching shoulder against a heavy metal rack holding plastic Rubbermaid bins; their sides weren't frosted because it wasn't refrigerator-cold in here, just a few degrees under really good air-conditioning.

The dark stains on the floor were disconcerting, and so was the drain in the middle. You could hose a rectangle like this down with bleach solution, and any evidence would swirl into an oblivion of dripping pipes.

Quit thinking like that. Get your hands free, and then you can think about your ankles.

The goons had zip-tied her, and she supposed she should feel grateful that the blond had only squeezed her tits once before dropping her on the floor and swinging the heavy door closed. At least the light hadn't gone out; she was just lucky all over.

Her breathing was ragged, the sound echoing against hard surfaces. So long as she was counting her blessings, she could chalk up the fact that she hadn't dragged anyone else into this particular dead end as a big one. Had Arthur picked up his friend yet?

I hope they're having a beer together. Hope Eddie and Carl are soaking in a hot spring right now. I hope Sam is okay.

She couldn't guess what time it was; for all she knew she'd been sitting for hours, her forehead on denim-clad knees and her wrists straining against tight plastic. She could barely remember what *day* it was, for God's sake; would Eddie and Carl come home to evidence of a break-in?

Should've guessed Franke was in it too. He probably wasn't happy about Gerry leaving the underside, even if it meant a lot of profit running the business—either that, or Press made a good case for even better percentages to be had once he was in control of his father's other holdings as well.

The only fly in Preston and Franke's ointment was a certain witness, who had waltzed right in the Corral's front door. She was lucky Franke hadn't ordered the goons to drive her out into the desert yet, but maybe Press was looking forward to doing that himself? Maybe getting rid of a witness was some kind of gruesome buy-in, to make sure he couldn't back out of whatever deal Franke was offering.

Oh yes, *now* all the puzzle pieces were fitting together, though she couldn't figure out why or how on earth Sam was involved. The cuff of Meg's white button-up brushed a sharp metal edge and she exhaled sharply, twisting. Her shoulder flared with hot, dull pain.

It was stupid, it had no chance of working—but she got the plastic of the zip tie on her wrists against that edge and made a few experimental passes. This type of industrial shelving could bite when you were least expecting it, a fact she and Eddie had both learned while doing warehouse work one long-ago summer. Paid in cash at the end of every day, sweating buckets in what amounted to giant ovens, sleeping wherever they could find a safe place, avoiding trouble except for when he could get his hands on some firecrackers or construction blasting supplies. . . .

Oh, Eddie. I'm sorry. Carl and Arthur would no doubt keep him from doing anything inadvisable, though. And any halfway competent planner could step in where Meg had left things for the wedding. They'd hardly notice she was gone.

The sense that she was invisible in her own life was an old, frequent visitor, a constant companion since the bad old orphanage days. Eddie never did well in adoption or foster interviews, too fidgety and loud; Meg had been returned twice when things didn't work out, the first time when the parents decided they were divorcing after all and the second time when it became clear the 'dad' of the family liked little girls too much.

Getting put in juvie when she aged out of the orphanage had been a relief. *I missed you,* Eddie's fierce hot whisper. *Nobody else gets me.*

Well, now Carl had the job, which was great. Everything nice and neat once Meg was out of the way.

Her arms cramped and she realized she was holding her breath as the light dimmed; when she whooped in a deep, faintly sour lungful everything got a little brighter.

She worked steadily, not really expecting much. Everything below her elbows was numb, so when the plastic finally parted her right wrist banged against a vertical strut, making a hollow noise.

The door was so heavy she could scream her lungs out and get exactly nowhere; it was ridiculous to think they'd hear her moving around. Still, Meg flinched and her heart hammered. The sweat was all over her again, and she tried to think of what music to set her efforts to. Maybe Metallica? She could do with some *Master of Puppets* now that her hands were free.

Great. Now deal with your feet.

Meg sat, flexing her fingers despite the pain, trying to think. Her ass was numb, and so were her feet. Maybe if she took her new black Nikes off?

Let's see what we've got. Two heavy zip ties, one around each ankle, snugged to her socks. Another between and connecting them, a crude but effective hobble. If she could cut the middle one. . . .

Betcha wish you had a pocketknife now, Eddie crowed inside her head, and Christ she was glad it wasn't Rob's voice. Both agreed a man should carry such an article as a matter of course, not to mention a handkerchief. Meg always answered Ed's teasing with the reminder that she didn't need a pocketknife when she had him around.

She hoped from the bottom of her heart that he and Carl were eating canapés in a hot tub right now.

There was another rough spot in the shelving, a glint of bright metal on a vertical section. Her fingers were still numb, but when she clumsily ran a bit of the broken wrist zip tie over the jagged bit, plastic parted grudgingly. It meant getting her sneakers off and lying on her back, her hands wedged under her ass to provide the right angle, but she could just about get her ankles up and make the small, straining movements, hoping she wouldn't put a hole in her sock or the skin underneath with an ill-judged twitch.

The world narrowed to those small moves, her heart thundering in her ears and her eyes stinging, her hair rubbing cold concrete and her throat dry as the desert where they would dump her body.

Please, she chanted inwardly, not in time to Metallica but to a Jackson Wang song, heavy on the synth beat. *Please, please, pretty please. . . .*

Two things happened at once. An almost-inaudible *snap* was the central tie parting as she shifted to get a better angle, her thighs burning as if she'd just finished a spinning invert in pole class, and her legs were suddenly free.

The other event was much louder by comparison. The door's heavy latch clicked, plus there was a hollow boom as if someone had misjudged the distance and collided with the heavy, insulated metal exterior.

Oh, for fuck's sake. She was flat on her back in her sock feet, and her toes were numb too. A bright copper tang filled her mouth, adrenaline singing in her veins.

Meg scrambled upright—or at least, attempted to. Her ankle rolled painfully and she landed hard on her side as the door shuddered again and began to swing open.

Well, at least I tried.

In Play

IT WAS LESS noisy than he expected, or maybe only in comparison to mortars and live fire. The roulette wheels spun, the card tables weren't very full just yet, but the slots were doing a land-office business. It hurt to look at their neon glares, but he did because it was part of his cover— a hayseed gawker, come to Sin City for fun and fleecing.

"Welcome to the Corral," someone chirped, and Tax found himself confronted with a pert blonde-streaked cowgirl, her nametag announcing *Sondra* and her ponytails swinging since she'd put on the brakes from a brisk trot. A big round tray loaded with drinks, braced on her shoulder and one flattened hand, showed she wasn't just decorative, and the bright smile as well as her chipper tone was oddly familiar.

Was this how Meg had learned to put up that wall of hers?

"Help you find anything? The lounge is right over there, and the buffet's got prime rib today." Her gaze was hazel and entirely professional; she gave him a once-over any hardened duty officer would be proud to deploy.

Shit. He had to think of something reasonable. "Quarters," Tax heard himself say. "For the slot machines, right?"

"Oh sure." She shifted a little, one hip stuck out to balance the load. The costume here included a pair of tight white shorts, a fringed polyester vest that was probably dry-clean only, and he wasn't sure whether or not the tank top underneath, showing generous cleavage, was approved by management but it probably brought in no end of tip money. "See those cages back there, honey? Just go on over, they'll take care of you. Want someone to walk with?"

Good God. "No thanks. I think I can make it that far." He tried a smile, got a megawatt tooth-baring in response, and the thought of a pink-tipped pixie wearing those shorts instead was distracting in the extreme. Sondra ditty-bopped away, the drinks on her tray barely rippling but her hips moving with a slow roll that probably emptied more than one pocket; Tax ambled for the row of barred, bulletproof-glassed windows under an old-timey wooden BANK sign.

Exits were in the usual places, two rows of elevators, the lounge had a pair of real swinging wooden saloon doors, and he pegged at least five plainclothes security, none who had zeroed him yet. Still, there were bound to be people watching the cameras. He stopped as if fascinated by a row of brightly lit machines; an elderly woman with a tight silvery cap of permed curls pulled a lever with metronome regularity, feeding in coins with dreamy slowness and watching the rollers spin. Her thin fingers reminded him of his own mother's; Mom would probably scoff at people wasting good money on a silly light show.

She was cutthroat at backgammon, though, and might clean a few clocks if they had betting in that particular direction around here. It was likely; there was no game invented someone wouldn't lay at least a nickel on.

A haptic buzz in his pocket interrupted his slow progress toward the cages. He fished his phone out, glanced at the screen, frowned as if getting a message from an irate spouse, and tapped into the encrypted chat app.

2 fl dwn, basmnt, Grey said, *Go getter tiger.*

Christ, the man couldn't type worth a damn. It was a wonder he was in charge of comms. So the phone—and presumably Meg—were both below his current location, which was thought-provoking. How many casinos out here had basements? Probably just a few of the older buildings, and the fact that she was visiting one. . . .

He glanced up, and met a cool, professional gaze. It was uniformed security right next to the 'cages,' and the guy looked like a retired cop. The high-and-tight haircut added to that kind of tactical belt and thick Vibram soles could've belonged to a weekend warrior, but the assessment in those eyes and the ready stance shouted that this grizzled ol' pard had chased down one or two fleeing perps in his time.

Crap. Tax's hackles prickled, and he decided there was no reason to be quiet anymore. His thumbs danced on the screen keyboard.

Pin loc & gimme cvr.

He pressed send, shoved the phone in his pocket, and turned slightly to the left, plunging into the slots arcade. That took him out of the cop's sightline, closer to the bigger set of elevators.

Less than ten seconds later the fire alarms began to scream, and his phone buzzed again.

They were in play.

FINDING A STAIRWELL was easy, both from common sense and

since Grey had access to the building's layout by now. The bastard was probably enjoying himself, watching security footage on a split screen while tracking Tax's progress. The only thing he'd like better was popcorn with extra butter, or being on the ground himself while pulling this kind of bullshit.

Of course, Grey was also listening to emergency services chatter, keeping track of Tax's location through the nag in the second burner phone, watching for response patterns on the security cameras, and hoping his buddy wouldn't get shot. And all this after a long flight and a hurried protein bar.

It was goddamn good to have backup. And, Tax realized as he careened down metal stairs in an echoing concrete well, he hadn't thought seriously about his grand exit for a while now.

Don't get distracted.

Four flights down, a heavy fire door—unlocked because the alarms were blaring, thank God and gravy for building codes and inspectors— banged against the wall as he piled through, and he was suddenly in a fluorescent-lit hallway, lighter doors on either side. He had to fish his phone out again, but Grey was one ahead of the game, as usual—he'd already sent a layout, Tax's location and Meg's burner phone both marked with pulsing red dots.

His goal wasn't far away. He burst into a wide-open space, the cheap industrial carpeting gone. The fire alarm's howl bounced and echoed, only slightly dampened by a walled-off portion probably full of offices; as for the concrete cave there were structural pillars standing in rows, good for cover if you were skinny enough. But the location he wanted was along the far wall; Tax forced himself to slow down and take in what he was seeing.

Bingo. A row of four industrial-looking doors with heavy standard pin-latches marched along the wall, and a freight elevator some distance away to the right.

Freezers in the basement? Great. He didn't think they were for holding restaurant supplies.

Just as that happy little idea tiptoed through his head, his phone buzzed in his pocket. Two quick jolts, then a longer third. Grey, again, calling from a specific masked number.

The code meant *incoming*, and Tax ducked behind a support pillar just as he realized he was grinning. The noise of the wall-mounted klaxons—as well as their flashing—was an irritant, so he tuned both out.

The heavies skidding to a halt at the door of the second freezer from the left had their backs turned, so they never heard him over the din, or even saw him. Two gorillas, both gym-bulky in untailored off-the-rack suits, the brunet with a rat-tail going down his thick neck and the blond hanging back while his buddy lifted the door latch.

Not professionals. Maybe they'd learned the hard way to have a guy in the pocket while opening the door, but neither gave a shit about watching their buddy's six. They were no doubt coming down to deal with a certain troublesome loose end, and Tax could barely believe his luck.

Don't get cocky. Could be someone else having a bad day down here. But there was a blur that looked suspiciously like his bunny's tan leather purse, hanging on a short row of pegs right next to the freezer doors.

The blond went down like a sack of bricks; if God loved him, he'd wake up with a mere headache. The brunet twitched, maybe glimpsing motion in his peripheral vision, but Tax had momentum and simply bounced him off the door once, used the recoil to get him down, and stamped a couple times to make sure he'd stay.

Funny, how the anatomy and physiology taught to save lives also made the application of violence that much more efficient. Of course, wounding or killing was the easy part.

Recovery was exponentially slower.

The alarms blared, echoes layering over each other, bouncing in every direction. Yes, there could be something or someone else stashed in this particular walk-in freezer, but Tax didn't think it likely. How long had she been in there? She wasn't dressed for subzero temperatures.

He damn near ripped the door off its hinges, and Lady Luck had decided to be kind for once.

Swaying unsteadily on sock feet, Meg stared at him with huge, fear-darkened baby blues. Her fingers curled over the edge of a big plastic tub on the shelving next to her; Tax realized it was only moderately cool instead of frigid inside the insulated box. A faint reek of pain and old blood lingered on sour, trapped air, and he glanced at the drain in the center of the floor.

Huh. Okay. You could do a lot worse for interrogation or storage. Tax's mouth fell open, and he had no idea what was going to come out.

It didn't matter, because his nape prickled and he dropped into a crouch as something whizzed overhead. Meg lunged for her new sneakers, and maybe they'd sedated her because she reeled like a drunk, scrabbling without her usual grace. But she was breathing and moving, which was two better than he'd feared.

Now he just had to deal with whoever was shooting at them, and get her out of here.

Has It In For Doors

OF ALL THE THINGS Meg expected, the very last was Arthur in the same jeans, T-shirt, and jacket he'd been wearing that morning, his dark eyes blazing and black hair ruffled. A flush lingered on his cheekbones, and he stared at her for a brief moment before dropping into a crouch so swiftly she thought he'd been tackled.

"Get down!" he yelled. The muffled sound turned out to be fire alarms echoing through the basement, and now she could see two lumps past the open door.

It was Franke's goons, both of them sprawled unconscious like overenthusiastic drinkers at a wild casino party. Something whizzed overhead; she flinched as her left hand finally found her shoes. A whine and a strange barking noise—for a moment she thought it was a dog, but why would they would have a puppy down here?

Arthur pitched aside, his shoulder wedged against the door's bottom edge, and somehow he had a gun in his hand, pointed at something on the far side of the open space. A brief bright muzzle flash, the din ratcheting up a notch, and there was another whining sound. The lightbulb overhead shattered, and the thought that she might be trapped in the dark if the door swung closed forced Meg into moving as nothing else could.

Slipping, scrambling, her left hand full of sneakers, she lunged for escape and almost fell on him. The freezer door shivered, a dent magically appearing as if banged by a sledgehammer on the outside; Meg realized someone was shooting at them as Arthur cursed, his foot slipping. It was his turn to nearly fall, and blind instinct pushed her right hand out to grab his shoulder, bracing both of them.

Or at least, trying to.

He surged upright, a complicated flurry of motion ending with Meg staggering past another freezer. She barely recognized her own purse, hanging on a peg nearby.

What. The hell.

Arthur grabbed the bag on his way past, bumping into her back like an enthusiastic sheepdog with a particularly confused member of its flock. "Keep moving," he yelled, and she intended to. Her socks slapped concrete, each step sending a jolt through various bruises and other aches, but terror filled her mouth with the taste of pennies and she didn't care *what* hurt so long as she could get away from all this insanity.

Another popping *zing* and Arthur changed direction, aiming them toward a freight elevator she hadn't noticed before. Its metal cage-mesh flexed slightly, rattling in its tracks, but right next to it was a bright, reassuring EXIT sign.

Oh, thank God.

"Keep going," Arthur yelled. "Keep going keep going *keep going!*"

Chrissake, it's not like I'm slowing down. Meg's arms pumped and she hoped the exit was up to code; if it was merely cosmetic because of cost-cutting, this would be a very short jog indeed.

She hit the panic bar on the fire door at warp speed, tumbling breathlessly into a confined space full of strobing light. Someone was screaming and her throat was afire; she belatedly realized the cries were her own. Arthur's hand closed around her arm and he dragged her aside—no small trick since she was still trying to run. Instead, she collided with him, driving them both into a much-repainted concrete wall right next to stairs.

Beautiful, solid, wonderful steps. A whole flight of them, going *up*. The door banged against the opposite wall, its overhead closer pinging as something broke. On its way back home it shuddered, metal confetti spraying from a sudden tiny hole on one side—the wound was bigger on the inner surface, because someone was shooting from outside.

Jesus Christ, whoever that is really has it in for doors. The sheer boggling unreality of the situation hit her, and the big soft black flowers were blooming in her peripheral vision again. The strobe was a fire alarm stutter-flashing, and her eyelids fluttered as well.

"Meg. *Meg.*" Someone was saying her name. "Come on, bunny. We gotta go."

I would love to. Honestly. "Uh-huh," she said, but it was lost in all the noise. There was a quick yank on her elbow; Meg jolted back into her own body, her face buried in Arthur's shoulder and his arm around her in a brief, crushing hug. His mouth pressed against her sweating temple so hard she felt his teeth for a moment, and there was a sharp, acrid smell around them both.

She knew it now. Gunfire.

"Up." He let go only to grab her arm, hooking her purse over her wrist and pushing the straps up to shoulder-height, then crowding her toward the stairs. "Move, bunny."

A FLIGHT, a landing, another flight, turning endlessly as her feet slapped harder and her head rang. Her legs were on fire, her lungs heaved, and she nearly threw herself through another fire door at the top. But Arthur grabbed her arm again and she nearly overbalanced, teetering on a sharp concrete edge. There was rough safety tape on every step, and it ground under her sock heel.

"Hang on," he called over the fire alarm's wail, and snapped a glance down the stairs. His expression changed a crucial fraction, a stranger peering through his dark eyes, before he calmly pointed his gun down the stairwell and squeezed the trigger again. Echoes boomed, but he was already moving, popping the door open and yanking her into a bright haze of afternoon.

Fresh air broke over her in a wave, oven-hot and full of exhaust, sand, a distant tang of sagebrush, and a breath of ozone.

Storm's coming. Meg gulped a huge mouthful—did it taste so good because she wasn't in a decommissioned freezer anymore, or because she hadn't been shot? It was an open question. "Shit," she heard herself say, and bent over as her midriff cramped hard.

A pair of dumpsters crouched inside a chain-link rectangle, nestled against the Corral's flank. There was a loading bay on the other side, probably leading to the freight elevator, and the parking lot spreading before them had to be for employees. The rooms on this side of the hotel were no doubt cheaper with that kind of view.

Arthur glanced at their surroundings. The gun vanished under his arm and he dug in his jacket pocket, fishing out his phone; he glanced at its face and nodded as if a text he'd been expecting had just shown up. His other hand closed around her shoulder; Meg straightened, wiping at her dry mouth.

There probably wasn't time to throw up right now.

"You hit?" He tugged—rather gently, all things considered—and Meg reeled obediently along, sock toes slipping in sandy pebbles over hot pavement. "Hurt anywhere? Talk to me, sweetheart."

The practically new Nikes bumped her thigh; she was still miraculously carrying both sneakers. Purse-straps slipped against her aching shoulder. "How . . . ?" What on earth could she say? She hurt everywhere, but that was beside the point. Nothing in her entire stock of English or high-school plus caterer-specific Spanish covered this. "Who . . .

what the *fuck* . . .?"

"You're doing great." He pulled her past the dumpsters; a padlock on the enclosure's gate glittered angrily. Even the simmering smell of garbage was oddly sweet, since she wasn't tied up and lying on the floor anymore. "Just stick with me, bunny, and everything'll be ten-four. Hey, you wanna see a magic trick?"

What. In the fuck. The ground was rocking underfoot—maybe an earthquake, or maybe her body simply couldn't cope with all this nonsense. "What?" she managed, blankly.

"Bet you do," he continued, as if she hadn't spoken, and snapped a glance over his shoulder. "It's a good one. Any time now."

Meg realized he was looking to see if whoever was chasing them had made it up the stairs, and she sucked in a harsh breath, trying to stagger along more quickly. A flicker of sunshine reflected off a windshield—a car in front of them was moving.

It was a black SUV with tinted windows, coming right for them. Her heart lodged in her throat; she was still trying to scream when the vehicle braked hard. Arthur reached for the rear driver's side door, yanked it open almost before the wheels stopped turning, and nearly threw her inside. Not only that, but he scrambled after, landing pretty much on top of her, and as the door slammed she found herself flattened under Eddie's buddy on a leather seat, a faint touch of welcome air-conditioning caressing her sweating forehead.

The Honda reversed, tires chirping as the driver hit the gas, and swung sideways. The brakes grabbed, the tires squealed again, and they jolted forward. Acceleration pressed her deeper into the seat, and Meg's breath sobbed in her throat.

"Abracadabra," Arthur muttered.

"That's my line," the driver said. "First-aid kit's right on the floor there. How's she doing?"

Oh, God. She really was going to throw up.

And in a nice car, too.

Doesn't Sound Healthy

ONCE THEY WERE out of the parking lot Grey kept it to civilian speed, even pulling over a few blocks away to make way for a shiny red fire engine, its lights jabbing the desert afternoon.

Response times were good in this part of town. Or this Franke guy could arrange to have priority, which was equally likely.

Tax didn't care. The only thing that mattered was sprawled underneath him—pale, trembling violently, her pupils huge and a stripe of blood on her bruised cheek. If she was hit she probably didn't feel it yet, so as soon as he got them both untangled and upright he began checking off the list of possible combat wounds.

She flinched when he touched her left shoulder. Her eyelids were red and lashes matted, her socks were filthy with sand, and she clutched her sneakers like a teddy bear, only loosening her grasp when he took each arm in turn to examine—nothing dislocated, nothing sprained or strained except possibly that already bruised shoulder. She wasn't hit anywhere, and when he took her face in his hands to gauge if she had a concussion Meg stared at him, a tear streaking down her dust-powdered cheek as well, leaving a glistening trail.

Oh, sweetheart. The jab of pain in his own chest could have been a bullet, but he didn't care. Fingertips slipping under her tangled hair, no contusions he could feel. Velvety skin, slightly damp—she was probably heading into shock. "It's all right," he said, softly. "I got you, bunny. You're okay now."

"Any change?" Grey wanted to know if they had a different destination than previously planned. It was a reasonable question, even if Tax wanted to shoot the man for interrupting.

"Negative," he said. "You cover our tracks?"

"Fu—" Grey audibly realized there was a lady in the vicinity. "Ah, I mean, you wound me, good sir. I had plenty of time to wipe their entire morning's footage, and put a little somethin'-somethin' in their offsite backup."

Good enough. "Really earning that steak dinner, my friend."

"Yeah, well, I'm gonna stretch out beforehand and tune my liver up too, so you'd better make sure your wallet's in shape." Grey tapped the brakes as traffic thickened, and signaled for a right turn. "How's our package?"

Tax realized he still had Meg's cheeks cradled in his palms, one thumb moving gently over the un-bruised side. "Little shook up, that's all." There was a sticky sliding sensation under his left jacket sleeve; he ignored it. "Meg? Meg, honey, this is Grey. He's a buddy, you probably heard Eddie talk about him. You're safe, okay? We've got you."

"Oh." Her chapped lips shaped the word, and Christ it was distracting. She blinked, another tear welling free and cutting a path through dust, dirt, and that smear of bright red. But *she* wasn't bleeding; he was satisfied of that, at least. "Um. Yes, nice to . . . it's nice to . . ." Her mouth crumpled, and she inhaled hard. "How did you find me?"

"Magic." Tax tried a smile, hunching slightly to seem less threatening. He wanted to shake her, demand to know what the fuck she'd been thinking, then get the full report on anything and everything the motherfuckers had done to her before locking her in the freezer, and finishing up with a lecture on never, *ever* fucking doing that again. But the last thing she needed was a drill sarge shouting in her face. "How'd they get you out of the hotel, bunny? I need to know, then we'll get you treated for shock. Okay? Just tell me, how did that happen?"

"Oh, I . . ." She blinked, and her lips trembled. "I . . . I was on the television, so . . . I left."

For fuck's sake. The urge to make it *very goddamn clear* she was never going to wander off again was overwhelming, and maybe it showed through the poker face he used for getting intel out of a wounded package. Her expression shifted, and she twitched.

Not a flinch, but close enough. His fingers loosened, his hands dropped, and Tax cleared his throat.

She beat him to the punch, though. "I thought you'd be relieved," Meg whispered. "Because this . . . it's a lot of trouble. You shouldn't be doing this. You . . . you could get hurt."

There was a soft, mostly strangled noise from the front. Grey had his phone in the dash holder, GPS showing on its face; he did his best to muffle the laughter.

Tax's arm twinged, hard. He'd have to deal with that next. "Get your seatbelt on. There's a bottle of water right there, I've got some electrolytes and a protein bar for you too. And you want a painkiller—you're not feeling it now, but you will be soon."

"Oh, I'm feeling it," she said grimly. "Where are we . . . I'm sorry, but where are we going?"

"No need to worry, ma'am." Grey hit the blinker, Tax's car slowing obediently. "You're on the rollercoaster with Dez the Destroyer's wrecking crew. You just sit back and enjoy the ride."

It took Tax only a few seconds to shimmy out of his coat, and he found his arm was indeed bleeding, a simple graze. Meg's gaze fastened on the wound, and she turned even more transparent-pale, if that were possible.

Fuck.

IT WAS NO BIG trick to vanish in any city, even one crawling with cameras. Grey had already done the honors of finding them a post-op berth, and a little under an hour after all the fun and games, Tax put the chain on another hotel room door. He turned to find Meg standing near the beds, arms wrapped tight around herself, her eyes still huge and dark with anxious pain.

"Don't worry, if he doesn't want pasta he'll get himself a bacon cheeseburger on the way back." Tax tested his left arm again—the bandage didn't interfere with range of motion, and in any case he'd seen far worse. Hell, he'd *had* worse.

It had been difficult to extract some kind of food preference from her, but getting a civilian to focus on anticipation of a meal rather than replaying recent traumatic events was better for all concerned.

"Oh. Yes." Meg's hair was damp from a quick shower; getting the dust and fear-sweat off was another good move, even if she was now stuck with a T-shirt from his luggage and a pair of cut-down sweats from Grey's. Her gaze fastened on his left arm again, and she sucked in a deep breath as if just noticing the glaring-white bandage, though she'd watched him apply it. "Does . . . does it hurt?"

"Nah, just brushed me." He tucked his chin, examining his upper arm; it was always weird to see your own injuries. The disconnection necessary to calmly regard violated flesh ran right up against the *hey, that's mine*, and discomfort lingered between the two sensations. "Just a splinter, I think. Lot of ricochets with all the concrete down there."

He didn't even need ibuprofen, though he should probably have some after chow. The freezer door had banged him a good one, stopping a bullet. The bastard in the hoodie had been a much better shot than a civilian, the two dipwads from the restaurant, or even most semi-professionals; Tax had gotten a glimpse of a freckled face and pale eyes near a support pillar a goodish distance across the basement. It could have been the third party from said diner, but that was a problem which could wait for debrief.

At the moment, there were other fish to fricassee. "We need to talk," he continued. "Sit down, right over there."

She looked at the bed furthest from the door. "A two-top," she said, softly. "Like the other one."

Yeah, and don't worry. "Whoever's not on watch will have the other bed. But we've gotta get a few things straight, Meg. Please."

She sank down, slowly, still hugging herself. Tax thought it over, and decided sitting on the other bed across from her was probably best, though it would put his back to the door. It felt good to get off his feet, bracing his elbows on his knees, and he could look at her all he wanted across a few feet of empty air.

Meg uncurled one arm, but only to reach for the nightstand drawer. A quick peek in and she nodded, then slid it closed. "Good old Gideon." A ghost of a smile, but her lower lip trembled.

She was scared out of her wits, and trying to keep that brave, brittle wall up. The strange, piercing pain in his chest was back; if he was having a cardiac event it would have to wait. "I'll make it quick, then you can rest. You cannot do anything like that ever again, Meg."

Her lashes swept down, veiling those baby blues. His shirt was too big for her, the neck slipping aside to show the vulnerable arch of her collarbone, and her long pretty legs bore a fresh crop of rapidly darkening bruises. Her right ankle was slightly swollen, her knees were scraped again and re-bandaged, and her bare feet were probably swelling too.

Every single injury was a sign that he hadn't done his goddamn job.

"I'm sorry." Barely audible over the hum of the air-conditioning. She took a deep breath, and lifted her chin. "My face is on the news. I thought I could get out of the state and maybe get in contact with some federal authorities, or something. I can't let him get away with it, and I can't let you get hurt. They were shooting at us, Arthur. Both times." The words hurried up, tripping over each other as if she thought he was going to interrupt. "You could have been *killed*."

Jesus on a stick. "And you couldn't? I get shot at for a living, Meg." Except he was off-duty at the moment and had been contemplating an even bigger retirement, right? Switching to civilian life had given him a helluva kick, PTSD had thrown him for a loop, but he was back on the rails now. In a big way. "It's fine."

"It's not fine." Her eyes weren't dark and wounded anymore; the annoyance in her tone was far better than that terrified numbness. "Eddie would feel awful if something happened to one of his buddies. I can't drag you into—"

"I dealt myself in, Miss Callahan." Frustration gave each word an edge, and Tax knew he was probably not doing himself any favors with this girl. But God *damn* it, she was too stubborn and self-sacrificing for *anyone's* comfort, let alone his. "And what the hell you think Boom'd do to me if I let those numbnuts mobsters ice his best friend, huh? Until this is tied off, you're going to stay where I put you. Understood?"

He could've told himself it was to give her something to focus on— if she was mad at him, she wouldn't be thinking about what *could* have happened in that fucking freezer.

But it would be a lie. His motivations were entirely different, and he was glad Grey wasn't witnessing this little chat. The ragging would be goddamn near endless, especially once his buddy told the rest of the Squad.

"You don't understand." The serene, confident front she was so used to putting up had vanished; Meg glared at him, her mouth turning down at both corners, and Tax realized he wasn't just in over his head but sitting on the ocean floor, because he found the expression completely goddamn adorable.

Just like everything else about her. "I think I do," he said, and had to clear another dry obstruction from his throat with a halfass facsimile of a bitter chuckle. "But either way, you're *staying where I put you*. Is that clear?"

Her shoulders came up, an evasive little shrug. She'd probably used that movement a lot as a teenager, and it was just as heartbreakingly cute as her glare. "People are dead, Arthur. I can't just—"

"I'm not going to die." At least he sounded certain instead of like he was just finding it out at that very moment, and his mouth fell open again. "I don't have time. Got my eye on a girl."

Oh, fuck. There went his exit plan. And wasn't that a bitch—bowing out wasn't the hard part, no sir. The worst was having something to lose.

And she was looking right at him, her lips slightly parted, confusion passing over like clouds across the sun on a windy day.

"Oh," Meg said, blankly. "That's . . . I didn't know. Will she be at the wedding?"

"Yeah." *I'll personally make sure of it.* No matter what he had to do to this Preston guy, that Franke bastard, or anyone else in the way. "You bet."

"Okay." Meg's shoulders firmed, her arms loosening, and wonder of wonders, she actually looked interested. "Does she have a favorite color?"

Huh? The change was welcome, but Tax had the sense of gears slipping. He would never get used to this woman's quicksilver turns; fortunately, keeping up promised to be an entirely pleasant occupation. The kind that could keep a man occupied for decades, really. "What?"

"For a corsage." She laced her fingers together, and it was her intent, client-facing expression now, head slightly cocked, all her attention focused on a single goal. "I can have a special one done, you know."

Oh, hell. "I don't know." Because he didn't. Pink might count as her favorite, but he couldn't assume. Still, there was the dye in her hair—

"Oh." A slight, forgiving nod, as if they were in the office. All she needed was a legal pad to make notes on while listening to a bride-to-be pour out preferences. "How about your song? You guys have a song, or she has a favorite? I can have the DJ play it at the reception."

What had he gotten himself into now? "I don't know what her favorite is." So far she hadn't played the same one twice.

"All right, fine. No, I can work with this." Meg didn't pinch the bridge of her nose, but she did inhale deeply and set her chin. "Okay. What does she like to eat? I can have the caterers—"

He hadn't had time to figure that out yet either. "I *don't know.*"

His rumpled, breathtakingly gorgeous fairy stared at him, her eyebrows drawing together. "Jesus, Arthur." The irritation was a wonderful change from fear or apathy. "Do you know anything about this woman at all?"

Some things. "I know she's beautiful, and she drives me fucking insane." Watching her try to manage this particular situation was a painful pleasure, like lancing and irrigating an infection; Tax couldn't stop himself if he tried. "I don't know her favorite anything because she's so busy arranging things for other people she doesn't take care of herself, or do anything *she* enjoys. We're gonna have to work on that."

"Yeah, that doesn't sound healthy," Meg blithely agreed. The pale pinched look was gone, some color was back in her cheeks, and she wasn't hugging herself anymore.

"You think?" A wild urge to laugh crawled up Tax's throat. "But that's what my CO would call a long-term goal, and right now we've got other problems. So are you gonna listen to me?"

Silence filled the room, spreading like the haze of desert sunset outside. Meg bit at her lower lip, worrying gently, and if he wasn't going to make his exit Tax had to start planning an entirely different operation—a difficult one, sure, but interesting, deeply enjoyable, and if it failed, well, he'd make other decisions.

But it would be . . . nice, to find out what Meg Callahan liked instead of what she could stand. It would be even better to provide what she preferred. She'd be a fierce and uncompromising commanding officer, to be sure.

Convincing her that a washed-up Squad medic was a good prospect would be hard work, and he wanted the position. In fact, he outright craved it.

"Okay." Meg didn't quite slump, but the fragile tension of a woman bearing the entire world's weight eased for a few moments. Her walls would go back up, sure.

He had an outpost behind them now. "Good." Tax nodded, holding eye contact. "You'll stay where I put you?"

"I promise." A good little soldier, even if she didn't salute. "Arthur?"

The guys were never going to let him live this down, but Tax found he didn't mind so much. "Yeah?"

"Thank you. For, you know." Another tiny shrug, neither dismissive nor hopeless. She even tried a timid, hopeful smile. "Saving my life. And everything."

"Anytime." He pushed himself upright; there was kit to organize and planning to do. "Lie down, I'll wake you up when the food gets here."

Coping Mechanisms

FALLING ASLEEP with a virtual stranger in the room was usually a no-go, but Arthur was there too, and that was a powerful comfort. Besides, Meg was so exhausted she probably didn't need the small blue pill he produced after a dinner of yet more takeout, this time Italian instead of Thai. Five minutes after she finished eating, she couldn't have said what she'd chewed, and the discomfort of using someone else's toothbrush was also muted.

Being zip-tied in a decommissioned freezer really put some social niceties in proportion, she decided, and was out almost as soon as she burrowed under the covers, despite the still-burning electric lights. A few vague mutters back and forth, Arthur and the new guy—Mark Grezinski, *but call me Grey, ma'am, Boom's told us a lot about you, all good*—deciding who would be 'on watch,' and she fell into a deep black hole.

She half-woke once, the room bathed in blue light from the television set to the weather channel, a shape on the other bed coming into hazy focus as a dead-asleep Arthur on his back, breathing softly. His profile was clearly distinguishable even in the dimness, and deep relief curled through her entire body.

He came down into the basement for me. Even if he'd done it simply and solely because he was Eddie's friend, it was a damn sight more than Meg had ever expected or dreamed of. People like Arthur Tachmann were rare indeed.

Especially in Vegas.

Mr. Grezinski had a laptop open on the small table near the dresser. He frowned slightly as he tapped at the keyboard, a shadow of stubble on his cheeks and his hair looking like a bird's nest, and she vaguely remembered Eddie telling her about this guy's yen for sleight-of-hand tricks.

Well, they'd pulled a good one that afternoon. Meg passed out again, and didn't surface until the scent of coffee tiptoed up to inform her she had to get up and face this mess afresh.

It was like some mad version of the Witness Protection Program.

She barely had time to sit up and stretch, rubbing at her face and hoping she hadn't snored, before Arthur's stainless-steel travel mug was thrust into her hands bearing a cargo of blessed caffeine and hazelnut creamer that had magically appeared from somewhere. The guys had somehow managed to get her clothes from yesterday washed at a nearby laundromat as well as acquire a substantial breakfast from room service, were both showered and shaved, and took down the morning meal double-quick but with relatively good manners while organizing what seemed a prodigious amount of 'gear' that had somehow ended up piled on the other bed—all while Meg was still blinking at her plate of piping-hot pancakes, eggs, and very crispy bacon with bemused wonder.

And Eddie made fun of *her* for having a bullet planner.

"We could run it like Johannesburg." The new arrival snagged a piece of bacon from the loaded tray settled on the dresser's top, just below the television. "Still can't believe Dez made us turn the rocks over."

"What, like you were gonna go up to Amsterdam and unload 'em on your next leave?" Arthur finished tying his green boots and straightened. The bandage around his left arm was half hidden by his T-shirt sleeve, and his shoulders were absurdly broad. "Leave me some godda— I mean, leave me some bacon, you hog."

They refused to cuss around her, like Eddie had after basic training until she broke him of the habit. It was kind of cute.

"If you want to eat, show up." Mr. Grezinski crossed the room with swinging strides and peered at his open laptop, one finger on the trackpad. "Huh. We have chatter."

"Yeah? What kind?" Suddenly Arthur was all business, rising and clipping a sheathed knife to his belt. The two of them weren't taking any chances; both had handguns, and she'd glimpsed Mr. Grezinski making other small sheathed blades disappear into his clothing.

Was that what the Army did to you? She hadn't noticed Eddie packing a lot of heat, but then again, she hadn't been looking. Meg kept glancing nervously at the TV; the morning news had put up her face again, but there was nothing about a fire or shootout at the Corral.

Which was . . . unsettling.

"Someone's knocking over a convenience store about two klicks south." Grezinski let out a soft tuneless whistle. "No news is good news, but we should move and get secondary transport."

"Yeah. Figure we'll run it like Budapest." Arthur leaned over his friend's shoulder, peering at the screen.

"Which time in Budapest?" A soft laugh; this new dark-haired, lanky guy seemed easygoing, and from all appearances typed even faster than her old assistant Frannie. "Oh, *that* time in Budapest."

"We can have this wrapped up by supper, if we can just find the bas—ah, I mean, the jerk." Arthur glanced at her, but Meg had her head down and was pretending deep absorption in her coffee.

They were talking about Preston. Both of them apparently believed her theory of his involvement, which was . . . pleasant? Was that the word?

The only thing she couldn't figure out was *why*. Press was rich, and connected. Even if Gerry hadn't been one of the underside's movers and shakers, his son would've had advantages others couldn't dream of. And Meg had been very careful not to tell Gerry or even Ella the precise details of the breakup—or about Press's behavior afterward.

Rob had probably guessed, though. Once or twice he'd looked at her with a line between his eyebrows, and he'd been the one making the arrangements for Gerry's son to be sent out of town for a few months on a so-called business trip.

"Well, we could ask the lady." But Grezinski didn't sound like he thought Meg was lying or holding out. The difference—a tone, a look— was subtle, but she was used to listening for what people actually thought instead of what they were saying. "When she's ready, that is."

Whatever reply Arthur would have made was lost in a melodious chime and buzzing. He strode to the nightstand, giving her a brief, casual glance—probably to make sure she wouldn't disappear again—and scooped up his phone, flicking the power cord free with a swift efficient movement. "Huh." He tapped at the screen, lifted it to his ear. "What the hell, dude? You're supposed to be on leave."

A blistering torrent of staticky words poured out, muffled by distance. Arthur winced and Grezinski turned from the laptop, tilting his head curiously.

It was Eddie. And he sounded madder than a wet hen.

CARL'S GRANDFATHER had bought the property up on the back side of Mount Charleston. Stunted pines and junipers grew in waves wherever the storms dropped moisture as they lifted their skirts to step over the heights. The dirt road—they called it 'improved' because there were berms on either side most of the way, and also because most of the arroyos managed to run parallel to it instead of perpendicular—was winding, bumpy, and choked with dust. Yellow-green light lingered over the trees, and it looked like a storm was caught on the peaks. There would probably be a lightning show later.

Meg's hands hurt, because she was clutching them so hard; the Honda bumped over washboard ruts easily, rocking like a small boat.

"Jesus," Grezinski said under his breath. "We could already be there by now."

"I'm not ruining my suspension just because your bladder's full." Arthur leaned forward slightly, checking the sky. "How much farther, Meg?"

"I don't . . ." But she saw the familiar trident-shaped lightning-struck pine on the right-hand side. Some of the scrub had grown since the last time she was out this way, Carl in the driver's seat and Meg in charge of the snacks cooler. *Let's get out of town*, he'd said. *Just for the weekend, Meggers. You need a break.*

That was right after the Preston Incident had concluded, Eddie on active duty and both Meg and Carl feeling the reds. Clearing her schedule to get away had been difficult, but well worth it in the end. Just being able to sleep without jerking into wakefulness every time someone walked down the hallway outside her apartment door had been nearly miraculous.

Carl was fond of taking off for a couple days to fix up things around his grandfather's place anyway; Eddie went along when he was on leave and dolled the tiny wooden structure up with gadgets and other appliances homemade, scavenged, or built. What had once been a simple dynamite shack on a busted claim had its own septic tank and woodstove nowadays, as well as cheerfully mismatched dishes, cookware, an old fridge, a weathervane made of salvaged scrap, a comfortable back bedroom, and an old ratty couch that folded out into a surprisingly pillowy sleeping surface.

"Not much longer," she continued, realizing both men were waiting for confirmation. "Sorry, it's been a bit since I've been up here."

A few minutes later the dusty ruts widened into an imperfectly graded driveway-slash-parking lot, and the shack's windows glittered with reflected sunset. The porch even had a slightly crooked swing, one chain a single link longer than the other.

"Jesus Christ," Grezinski said, and she couldn't tell if his horror was real or feigned. His beaky nose wrinkled. "I can hear banjos."

"Or horror movie music." Amusement shaded Arthur's tone. This was a new side of him, watchful and tightly contained instead of diffident and almost-shy. "We've bunked in worse, though. And if I know Boom he's got the entire hillside ranged."

Boom. It was a great name for Eddie; he'd always been fascinated with firecrackers of all types. Getting hold of leftover dynamite was his idea of a fabulous time and there'd been no shortage back in middle or high school, due to all the new construction.

It was, she reflected, a goddamn miracle they had both survived those years.

The front door opened. Her best friend appeared, shoulders stiff and curly hair bouncing; Meg's heart leapt into her throat. Carl crowded behind him, and even at this distance the worried pucker to the big blond man's brow was visible. Ed was halfway down the porch steps before the engine cut off.

It felt good to stretch her aching legs. Whatever painkillers Arthur was carrying around would be worth a few bucks backstage at any club; she felt halfway decent despite the variegated bruises all over her body and the throbbing in her shoulder. She took care to close the car door gently, and picked her way across weed-starred gravel, bracing for the explosion. "Hey," she began, tentatively, but her best friend made a beeline for the other side of the car.

"Mother*fucker*," Eddie snarled, and threw a punch.

Meg let out a blurt of dismay, Carl hurried down the steps, but Grezinski's hand curled around Meg's elbow.

"Don't worry," he said, as Eddie added another strike and a kick for good measure. Arthur evaded both, stepping back gracefully. Sandy pebble-laden dirt crunched underfoot, and Ed spat yet more highly uncomplimentary terms at his buddy. "Tax won't hurt him."

Oh, shit. "I can calm him down," Meg said, numbly. It had been her job in high school and it was probably what she should do now, too, even though—

"Are you okay?" Carl descended on her, and Meg was swept into a familiar hug redolent of fabric softener, coconut-scented sunscreen, and grilled onions. Clearly he'd been cooking, either a sign of stress or the two of them had driven straight from Merbelows without a stop. "Tell me you're okay. Oh, sweetie." He took in her bruised face, and Meg hoped she didn't look half as bad as she felt. "Ouch. Damn."

Well, guess I won't win any prizes at the county fair. She twisted, straining to look on the other side of the car. "Shouldn't we try to—"

"There is no calming him down at this point," Carl said, sagely. "Just let him run. Hi, you must be Grey. Pleasure."

"Likewise." Grezinski acted like it was no big deal that one of his 'buddies' was attempting to pummel the other into the driveway. "Is that steak I smell?"

"Sonofa*bitch*," Eddie yelled. "I told you to *take care of her!*"

Arthur said nothing, and he wasn't smiling. He fended off Eddie's strikes, giving ground, and his hair flopped over his forehead as he moved. It wasn't quite the tight, focused look he'd worn at Gianello's or the Corral, but it was close.

Meg squirmed against Carl's hold. "Eddie's got a temper." How could both of them act like this was normal?

"Yeah, but I'll tell you what." Grezinski stretched, catlike. His gaze moved in smooth arcs, taking in the shack, the high slope past it part of the ridge that rose into Charleston Peak proper, and the canyon-riven hills on either side. Then he turned, studying their backtrail with the same interest. "We're the crazy bast—ah, the guys who run into live fire. Tax does that too, but he's *extra* insane because he's the one stitching us up while all hell's breaking loose. Medics, man. Different breed." He shook his head, and ambled for the house. "Hey, is there plumbing? Or do I just go into the bush?"

"It's inside, left side of the hallway. Look for the stuffed singing sturgeon over the door." Carl's arms tightened. "Come on, let's get you something to eat. Why didn't you call us?"

"Carl, for God's sake." Meg couldn't believe they were all taking this so *calmly*. "Eddie's really upset and—"

"Yeah, he got out a box of matches on the way up here but I told him I wasn't having the entire hillside go up in smoke just because he has shitty coping mechanisms." Carl pushed her gently for the house. "Let them figure it out and bring in the luggage. You look like you need a drink."

Jesus, do I ever. She wondered blankly if she should mix booze with whatever Arthur had given her, and craned to see what was going on.

"I *told* you!" Eddie shouted. "Why didn't you *call me*?"

"You were out of pocket." Arthur slapped a punch aside, dodged another kick, and kept retreating. He was leading Eddie in a circle, a matador facing an exceedingly foul-mouthed bull. "Chill, Boom. She's right there. Safe and sound."

"Safe and sound my *ass!*" her best friend fumed. "You sonofa*bitch*, Imma beat that grin right off your face!"

"Come on then." Arthur backed up a little further. "Quit yapping and do it, soldier."

Ed's reply was an inarticulate roar.

Oh, hell. But there was nothing Meg could do, so she let Carl fuss her up the steps. Over the mountains, thunder rumbled.

Four on the Floor

BOOM'S ANGER was like one of his signature door-clearings—loud, quick, and effective. He'd probably fretted all the way back from camping, and the sitrep Tax had been able to give over the phone hadn't been detailed for very good reasons.

Cue explosion, about ten minutes of steam-venting, then sunny calm. The only bad part was Meg's nervousness when both of them trooped in carrying gear, but Boom dropped his cargo, strode past the visibly lumpy couch decorated with colorful crocheted acrylic afghans across its humped back, and swept her into a hug. "Fuck," he said into her hair. "Fuck a rubber *duck.*"

"Yo' mama," she replied, muffled against his shoulder, and there was a quaver to the words Tax didn't like. He wanted to tell Boom to back off a bit, not to squeeze her so tightly, but her arms crept around him in return. "I'm so sorry, Eddie. I know you were excited to go to Merbelows and—"

"*Fuck* Merbelows," Eddie snarled. "Right in the ear. A ranger came out to our campsite because there was a break-in at the house and that nosy-ass Parkington next door called the cops, and when I get back into town your phone's in my gun safe and the fuckin' news is full of bullshit about Gerry-fuckin'-Roark. And *this* asshole's radio silent." Boom lifted his chin enough to glare in Tax's general direction. "I leave for five fuckin' minutes and what the *hell.*" He softened. "How are you? Hurt anywhere? Tell me everything."

Carl was busy in the kitchenette, and it smelled magical—steak, grilled onions, the works. Looked like this place had electricity *and* indoor plumbing, which just went to show appearances weren't everything. Tax met Grey's questioning gaze and shrugged slightly—Boom was fine now, and their chances went up astronomically with three of the Squad on deck. Of course there were two civilians to look after, but that was fine.

It was all copacetic, especially since Meg was looking far less pale and jumpy. She gave the particulars in a low tone, glossing over some bits like the diner shootout, but Boom's eyebrows were in his hairline after about sixty seconds and by the time Carl said *dinner, everyone, everyone wash your hands and that means you, Ed*, the bare skeleton of events was laid out.

They'd go over the real rundown later. For now, it was enough to see her wan, wounded look drain away, and she perked up even more after a round of steak, caramelized onions, salad, ready-made dinner rolls—*didn't have time for dough*, Boom said somewhat sheepishly—and lemonade. Grey tucked in like a starving wolf, cheerfully letting Tax know he wasn't off the hook for dinner but saving any ragging about yesterday's op for later.

It wasn't the sort of thing to air out with civilians in the room.

Tax contented himself with keeping an eye out the front window while he ate, barely tasting the fuel. Of course Boom had the entire hillside ranged and a cache of weapons handy—Tax could probably even guess the latter's location.

But the operation wasn't over yet. There was too much invested for this Preston guy to stop, and the jackass who owned that pile of cowboy-themed shit on Roscoe probably wasn't going to take this lying down. Meg was not just a witness but a distinct liability, and men like that believed in cleaning up loose ends with a vengeance.

Even if Tax got her out of the state, she'd have to live looking over her shoulder. Out of the country was a possibility, but not one he thought she'd go for and wasn't he getting a little ahead of himself? Much better to just deal with the problem at its source, and Tax found out he had little to no trouble contemplating just how to arrange the solution.

The only question was logistics, and how much of Sin City he wanted to burn down. Tax felt someone staring at him and glanced at the table.

Oddly enough, it was Carl. The surfer's forehead was puckered again, and he looked quickly away; his shoulder touched Boom's, their chairs squeezed companionably close. Maybe he was holding Tax responsible for Meg's bruises, or simply unsettled by current events.

Carl also pressed a shot of vodka from a condensation-covered bottle on Meg, who glanced in Tax's direction before accepting. It wouldn't do any harm and might even bolster her nerves, but Boom and Grey both declined any liquid courage and that told him they agreed with his private estimation of the situation.

No R&R until the mission was done.

"You didn't," Meg said, and a disbelieving smile lit those big baby blues.

"Well, the shortcake's store-bought," Boom said. "But Carl wouldn't hear of whipped cream from a can. And the strawberries were big enough to bother with, so dig in."

"Almost worth getting shot at." As soon as she said it, anxiety clouded her expression, and she very carefully didn't look at Tax.

It was entirely natural; he probably reminded her of things she didn't want to think about ever again. A thin needle pierced his chest, but he ignored it. At least she was alive, and safe as possible.

"Amen, ma'am." Grey laughed, taking over cheer-up-the-package duty. "Pass me another roll, please?"

THE PORCH SWING wasn't a bad idea at all. It was the first time since arriving Tax had a chance to really look at scenery, and the view turned out to be . . . well, kind of restful, even if his nerves were raw and the rest of him not far behind. Mountains purple with dusk and storm clouds, slopes full of scrub brush, sage, chaparral, plenty of pines and juniper, the city's feverish glitter just a dull orange glow on the other side of the mountain—no wonder Carl's grandfather had kept this place. A spectacular vista, and if the concrete tentacles ever reached this far someone would probably pay a pretty penny to plonk a McMansion on this site, ruining everything.

Footsteps and voices inside. The screen door squeak-thumped; Boom stepped out, his boots deliberately heavy in case Tax was looking the other way.

You didn't sneak up on a buddy who'd given *himself* watch duty. It wasn't healthy.

Boom had two big speckled-blue enamel camping mugs, and judging from smell the coffee in it was strong enough to chew a silver spoon to pieces. He offered one silently, handle turned out—an apology, if necessary.

Tax took it. The swing wasn't bad either; he could see why people had them. He could hit the postage-stamp porch in less than a heartbeat if it became necessary, and he was tucked in the shadow beside the front window, not backlit by the glow from inside. That was probably why Boom kept it hanging here.

His buddy studied the driveway, the slopes, the rising dusk. Boom's chin jutted, and he wore the same resentfully patient scowl he always did when a mission was underway and there was nothing to blow up yet.

Sunset was kind, made him look younger. Would Meg recognize this expression?

"She's in the bedroom," Boom finally said. "Carl's got the air mattress, he'll stay in there too." In other words, the civilians were finally bedded down. Which was a relief.

Tax blew across the coffee's trembling surface. The caffeine wouldn't make much of a difference since he was already amped, but it gave him something to do. "Good," he said, finally. "She needs rest."

"I hear you went into the Corral's basement." Boom's nose wrinkled slightly. "Bert Franke's a bastard. First thing he'll do once Meg's out of the way is get rid of Press, but I'd be surprised if the little shit's thinking that far ahead. You know she dated him, right?"

"She mentioned it." Tax could even admit a certain gratitude that she was so clearly over the guy even before all this.

Not like it upped his own chances, really, but . . . a man could dream. Couldn't he?

"Well, old Roark wanted her to marry the heir. Probably thought she'd make something out of him, but he was always a gilded turd." His buddy grimaced, and his voice turned soft. "She saw it?"

"Some of it, from what I can tell." Tax didn't like thinking about the initial incident, not least because it could have ended so very differently if she wasn't brave enough and bright enough to give him several heart attacks all at once. "She got the fuck out of there, called me because my number was in her recents. Smart girl."

"One in several million." He half-turned, pinning Tax with another patented glare through the gloaming. "So, uh, Grey seems to think you . . ."

Oh, fuck. "She's a lady, Boom." In other words, he had his manners on.

"Good. Because you're my buddy, but if you hurt her I will fucking hunt you down and kill you slow."

"Thought that went without saying." Tax exhaled softly; his left arm ached. Just a graze, and he was glad it hadn't hit anything vital. This was a good hiding spot, but it wouldn't be effective forever. They were going to have to hash out an active method for dealing with this Preston, and with Franke as well. "This wouldn't be something we could solve with a good rifle and a spotter, would it?"

Boom was silent for a moment. "Now you're sounding like Jackson."

Which could even be a compliment, given the circumstances. Their resident wildcard was crazy, sure, but he was also goddamn effective. "Thanks. Hey, how solid is the roof on this place?" In other words, Tax wasn't in the mood for deep conversation, and who was taking the eyrie tonight?

"Like a fuckin' dance floor. I'm going up soon as it's real dark." Another hesitation. "Hey, you know . . . are you okay?"

"Me?" *Well, I wasn't, but now I'm too busy to off myself and anyway, she really needs someone looking after her.* Even if she didn't want a washed-up fuckhead like him, he could . . . well, there was time enough for that later. "Four on the floor, good buddy."

"Glad to hear it." Still, Boom didn't move. "Tax?"

"Hm?" *Jesus, just go get up on the roof. I want to think.*

"Thank you." He took a slurp of coffee, probably out of embarrassment. "You know we were in the same orphanage? And juvie, and school. She's all the family I've got."

"Pretty sure she feels the same way about you." Tax shifted on the swing; no cushion, but the wood was worn satin-smooth. "She was really worried this Preston guy would come after you out in the woods."

"Wish he had." Boom's teeth gleamed; full dark was nigh. "Shoulda shot that motherfucker years ago."

"Cheer up, you might get a chance." He shouldn't sound so grimly gleeful, Tax realized, but there was no civilian around to hear. "Thanks for the coffee; get your ass upstairs."

"Ten-four." Boom hesitated again, just for a moment. Then he went back in through the screen door.

And he left the rifle leaning against the wall, within easy reach.

Extra Credit

FOR A TERRIFYING moment Meg wasn't sure where, when, or even *who* she was. The room was small and fusty, indistinct shadows of shelves clinging to one wall; the thought that she hadn't escaped the freezer after all and had been left in the dark brought her into full terrified wake-fulness, a scream trapped deep in her throat.

But there was a line of dim golden glow around a door left slightly ajar, and hushed voices. She could see the air mattress Carl had settled on, insisting she take the double bed in its antique iron stead. Carl's pillow was rumpled and the blankets thrown hastily aside.

Oh, no. She scrambled to get upright, bare soles cold on varnished wooden planks. Arthur's T-shirt was comically oversized and the bor-rowed boxers weren't much better, but at least she was decently covered. Meg peered out the door, blinking.

The light was from a mostly shuttered Coleman lantern set on the floor near the kitchen table. All the drapes were pulled, windows tightly covered, and she realized belatedly why they did that.

Light travels a long way in the desert.

Her face ached, and her shoulder hurt. Her legs were beaten all to hell, and she was sure her hair was a mess. But all in all, Meg felt . . . pretty good? At least, far better than she had any right to.

Carl was right outside the door, mid-yawn, rubbing at his face with both palms. "Hey," he said, softly. "You okay?"

No. Who could be, at a time like this? "Peachy," she whispered. "What's going on?"

"Headlights." He looked down at her, blinking furiously. "Might want to get dressed."

Says the man in tighty-whities and a tank top. "Yeah." It felt like ages since she'd had a decent shower, a good latte, a night's sleep, or even a chance to do her hair properly. And forget about makeup; even her nose stud felt disarranged.

But headlights meant a car, and that could mean . . . well, who else knew about this place?

Anyone who knows Eddie and Carl. Property records were easily searchable, too. She was dragging all of them right into a tornado of trouble, and Meg couldn't feel good about that.

"Hey." Carl touched her shoulder, a light brush of fingertips. "Get some clothes on. I call bathroom dibs."

She hurried, and there was time for a quick trip to the restroom herself before the back door opened silently. Grezinski appeared, his chestnut hair slicked down, ghosting over the floorboards like he'd lived there for years and knew when each one would squeak. He took in both of them with a glance and nodded, then pointed at the bedroom. "Back there," he said, quietly. There was none of the amusement, the teasing, or the small magic tricks he'd displayed cleaning the table after dinner—making a fork disappear, the salt shaker jump, a fascinating bit of sleight-of-hand with a trio of quarters that would make any casino nervous. "Stay down."

"I was going to make coffee—" Carl began.

"Not right now." Grezinski carefully kept his hand away from the gun at his belt, and Meg realized he was in dark clothing to blend with the night. "Better safe than sorry, okay? Go on back, get down on the floor, and stay calm. We've got this."

It wasn't until she was sitting on the air mattress next to Carl that the sheer unreality of the situation hit Meg all at once. The room was dim but at least someone was with her, and he put a comforting arm over her trembling shoulders. "It's going to be okay," he said, and she wondered how in the hell he knew.

"I'm sorry." She was saying it a lot lately, two useless little words. "I wish . . ." *I wish this never happened. I wish I hadn't called anyone and just left town. I wish I hadn't gone to the Corral.*

"It's not your fault," Carl whispered back. "Chrissakes, Meg, *you* didn't kill anyone."

But oh, God, it felt as if she had. The guilt was terrible, and only got worse the longer she sat still.

What if the headlights were Press? What if it was the black privacy-tinted SUV, almost like Arthur's but larger? Her imagination worked all too vividly.

It turned out to be none of those things. The front door banged open, footsteps sounded, and the next thing they heard was Eddie's voice, clear and hard.

"Sit the fuck down, and don't get cute. Or I might shoot you myself."

The reply was a familiar voice, though Meg couldn't quite place it at first.

"You shouldn't threaten me, Baumgartner. Especially since I'm here to save your ass, and Callahan's too."

It was, of all people, Sam Morigny.

THE VICE DETECTIVE looked as battered as Meg felt—split lip, one eye puffed almost shut, bruises crawling up the side of her neck, and she winced as she shifted on a straight-backed yellow vinyl chair pulled well away from the table. Plus, her sleek wheat-gold ponytail was mussed, and her waffle-weave thermal as well as flannel overshirt both bore significant loads of pale desert dirt. Her jeans were caked with sand at the knees, too.

There was no sign of Grezinski now. Eddie folded his arms and stared at Sam, his head cocked and a small smile lifting one corner of his mouth. It was the same mask he used on teachers who thought a contest of wills was the only way to handle a roomful of restless kids, or on one of teenage Meg's dates who didn't quite measure up.

But it was Arthur, quiet and focused, who looked the most different. A type of static seemed to spread from him, a cold bath of readiness, and he didn't look at Meg at all. He studied Sam like a bug on a windshield, in fact.

Of course Sam wouldn't back down. She eyed him right back. "Let me guess. Army buddy?"

"None of your business," Arthur said, pleasantly, but the ice in the words was new as well. If Rob Barton had ever decided Meg needed the living hell scared out of her, he might've used the same tone. "You'd better start convincing me you aren't working for Preston Roark, Detective. There's a lot of mineshafts in these hills."

Sam's gaze flickered to Meg. "You okay?"

I've had better weeks. "Not really," she said. "Did you tell Press we were meeting at Gianello's?"

"No, but I don't expect you to believe me." Sam's shrug arrested itself halfway as Arthur visibly stiffened; after a moment, she continued. "Your friend there put down one of Tammy the Greek's altar boys, and Chad Beaumont finished off the other one. I should thank this guy for kicking the shit out of me, though. Beau probably thought I was a goner too."

"Wait a sec." Eddie had tensed, too. "Beaumont's back in town?"

"Flew in from New York last week." Sam's smile looked painful, and she winced again. "And I'm surprised you know about him, though I suppose I shouldn't be."

"Who?" Meg realized she was hugging herself again. It seemed the only possible response. "I've heard of Tamzoukis, but who's this Chad guy?"

"Little freckled shit, couple years ahead of us. He went to Chaparral High, not our scene." Sam was back to watching Eddie, but tiny sipping glances at Arthur showed she wasn't quite as comfortable as she wanted to appear. "Used to run protection rackets with Tammy's boys until he did a drive-by that ended up with a five-year-old girl getting shot, and they sent him out of town. The Greek's got an eye for good soldiers, set Beau up for contract work in the Big Apple. Either Press has more juice than we thought or Franke called in a favor getting him here, because Beau hooked up with two local dumbasses for the hit on Roark." Sam paused. "Sorry. I know you and Ella were . . ."

"A redhead? Freckles and green eyes? Wearing a hoodie?" Meg's knees felt suspiciously gooshy. Elias Tamzoukis was serious underside business, a man even Gerry avoided mentioning if possible; she would have never *dared* to go near his businesses with a poker chip requesting a favor, even in this extremity.

"That's him. He was right after you at Gianello's, came through the kitchen and only stopped to pop a couple rounds in the guy your friend there left breathing. Cleanup, I guess, since he didn't want to take them to the hospital and they let you get away twice." Sam exhaled softly, shaking her head. "I've been trying to call the last number you gave me."

"That phone's off," Meg said, numbly; she'd only used it to set up the meeting at Gianello's and call a cab to take her to the Corral. Yet Arthur and Grezinski had found her with it anyway, they said.

Just like magic.

"Yeah, well." Sam returned her one-eyed stare to Eddie. Just looking at her swollen face hurt—Arthur hadn't done that, had he? "You know I can't stand Press. I went by your place and found a couple black-and-whites on a burglary check; the neighbor who called it in remembered you'd said something about camping. Took me a day of calling every KOA and mom-and-pop RV hookup before I got lucky with Merbelows and got them to send a ranger out to you, then I remembered your boyfriend had some property up in the sticks. I thought what the hell, why not check it out."

"That's nice." Arthur made a brief sketching motion, pointing at his cheek. "But I didn't hit you that hard, Detective."

A flash of the old high-school Sam peered through, a tiny defiant grimace. "Hard enough."

"What's the rest of it from?" he persisted.

"Roark had a couple cops on the payroll. Looks like his son inherited them." Sam shrugged, more easily this time, but her good eye was dark with pain. No translator was needed for that look, and Meg's heart hurt even more.

It sucked to have nobody to trust. She'd always had Eddie; Sam's father was an unapproachable beat cop who spent most of his off-duty time in a bottle, accomplishing the feat of drinking himself to death pretty much right after his daughter's high school graduation.

Still, Sam had followed in his career footsteps, maybe hoping that she'd find some kind of backup there.

"Including Mike," Meg said, softly. The two times she and Press went to dinner with Sam and her partner Mike Vitebski, the two guys had acted like long-lost frat brothers. "Oh, Sam. I'm sorry." Two little words, unable to carry the weight of all that loneliness.

"He's got a mortgage." One shoulder hitched up, dropped. Sand fell from her knee, a tiny whisper-patter hitting the shack's ancient linoleum. "And kids. Turns out I'm just, you know. Expendable."

"Fucking hell." Eddie half-turned, shaking his head and staring at the front door like it had spoken out of turn. "So, finding this place makes you the smart one."

"That's all cop work is. Remembering a couple things and guessing others." She addressed Arthur next. "Like where exactly you came from. I didn't even clock you at Gianello's."

"So your partner called Preston?" Arthur studied her, his head cocked. "How'd he get the drop on you?"

"I went to meet him because I had to be sure." Sam's chin set, stubbornly. "He had a few of Bert Franke's boys along for the ride."

Arthur nodded, not particularly surprised. "They make you dig your own grave?"

Meg's mouth was parched as the highway on a summer afternoon.

"That's what they thought." Sam's bruised, split lips skinned back from her teeth. "I say never give a woman a shovel if you don't want her to use it."

What? Meg blinked, and the way Sam was dressed as well as the sand all over her made sense now. Horrible, chilling sense. *Oh, God.*

She swayed. Carl's arm landed across her shoulders, and she wished it hadn't because she didn't feel capable of holding him *and* herself up at the same time. Still, having no choice meant her knees locked, and she swallowed dryly.

"Sit her down." Arthur's voice was very far away through the sudden rushing in her ears. When the noise receded she found herself on the lumpy couch, Carl bustling in the kitchenette—running water, the well here was a deep one—and the smear in front of her dazed eyes was Arthur himself, nearly nose-to-nose with her. "Look at me, bunny. Right here."

"Sorry," she mumbled, numbly.

"For what?" He was cupping her face, she realized, and his thumb stroked her cheek again. The touch felt familiar, and absurdly soothing; her heart gave a strange, unsettled but not fearful leap. This close she could see the laugh lines at his eyes and mouth, the hint of epicanthic folds, a shaving nick from earlier in the day. A funny little earpiece, clunkier than the ones casino security used these days, was hooked into his left ear. "Are you dizzy? I have glucose tabs, and Carl's getting you some water."

"I'm fine," she lied. "Sam's hurt. You should help her." That part was true, at least.

"You're my only concern right now." He didn't look away. Good Lord, the man was *dangerous*. Whoever the girl he mentioned was, she'd lucked out in a big way.

Don't think about that, Meg. Worry about what's happening now.

"I have a contact in Carson City," Sam said, and there was a faint hint of pleading to the words. "Federal, not local. He's waiting for me to call back with something usable—the Feds have been looking to take Tammy out for a while. Press is extra credit, but they like that sort of thing. If we can get Meg to him for a deposition . . . come on, Ed. You know me."

"Thought I did," Eddie said, grimly. "But I gotta say this doesn't look good, Morigny."

"What? You *know* how much I hate Preston, for God's sake—"

"Yeah, but Tammy's big New York boy riding right on your heels to a meet with a witness? And you don't see him *or* Tax? Either you were on the take until your partner double-crossed you, or you're not very good at your job."

"I'm Vice, you jackass, not SWAT." The words shook. "And I—"

I'd better calm everyone down. It was just like being in school again, caught between Eddie's intransigence, Ella's blithe cheerfulness, and Sam's deep and abiding yen for doing things by the rules.

"Eddie," she said, quietly, but with the flat finality of the person elected to keep the peace. "It's *Sam*, for God's sake. At least get her a Band-Aid and some aspirin."

"Hey." For some reason, that made Arthur smile—a tight, grim little curve of his mouth, but she found out she liked it. "I'm the medic here, bunny. I think . . ."

Whatever he thought trailed away. He straightened, his earpiece giving a formless mutter and his hands dropping to his sides. Meg found she missed the contact as well as his nearness; that was an entirely new troublesome fact she had no time for.

Arthur half-turned, glancing at Eddie, whose hand flicked for his belt and came up with a very businesslike-looking gun. The movement seemed habitual, and the realization that perhaps she didn't know her best friend as well as she thought was another torment.

"What do we do with the baggage?" Arthur asked.

"Well . . ." Eddie paused. A flicker across his face as he glanced at Carl, who had turned from the sink, eyes wide and bits of his streaked-blond mop sticking up every direction. "Insurance, I guess."

"Then you're babysitting." Arthur turned on his heel, and was half-way across the cabin before Meg realized he was heading for the back door. "And douse that fuckin' shine."

"Tax—"

A few more strides, an angry creak from the door, and Arthur was gone. Meg stared at Eddie, who now grimly focused on Sam.

"So," he said, quietly. "You brought 'em here, too."

Ambush

YOU BROUGHT ME *out here to play grabass with cokeheads in the woods*, he'd told Klemp, but it looked like the real grabass was in the desert.

"You got eyes?" he muttered, knowing the throat mic would pick it up.

"Bright as day, baby," Grey answered, a familiar whisper through a hint of static. There was a click—night vision goggles resettled, ready for action. Eddie indeed had no shortage of boosted gear lying around. All Tax had to do was stay out of Grey's way.

And vice versa.

As soon as he cleared the cabin's corner, Tax saw them too. Four sets of headlights bobbing on the access road, and if he could get to the bend half a klick away he might be able to take out the lead car. Then it would be night games, and while he wasn't as fond of them as Jackson, he wasn't the worst player in the Squad either.

Far from.

It was just like any other desert op, hydrophobic air freighted with dust and sage hitting the back of his throat, the rifle a reassuring weight as he moved parallel to the dirt road, the berm alongside a helpful friend though he didn't have to be particularly quiet.

Not yet.

At the same time, it was different than the usual *Okay boys, time to dance*. Behind him, huddled in a cabin, was the only thing in the world that mattered. He didn't like leaving her with an unknown, but Boom was a professional first and a friend second.

At least he'd better be. Fierce one-pointed concentration filled Tax to the brim. All thought of his nice quiet exit were gone; did he have to be under fire before he found life worth living?

No, he decided as he avoided a patch of loose scree just right for turning an ankle on. He wasn't doing the adrenaline-junkie bullshit suicidal soldiers pulled if nobody got them off the line at the right time, nor was he trapped in a tangle of repeating, ricocheting memories, complex trauma revving his nervous system endlessly into the red until it snapped.

Instead, he was thinking about maybe, if he was lucky, being invited into Meg's apartment and guessing her favorite color. Taking Grey out for a hideously expensive dinner—with her, of course, and listening to her run verbal rings around his buddy. He wanted to drive her to work in the morning, making sure she had hazelnut in her latte, and witness her solving whatever little problems arose at Boom's nuptials. Who knew cutting traffic and running interference for a wedding planner would be so interesting?

If she didn't want to stay in this town he could take her home, let her pick the music the entire way. *This is the one*, he'd tell his mother, *and I think you'll like her.* Mom would be overjoyed and immediately start asking about grandkids, but that was a hurdle for another day.

In order to reach that extremely satisfying state of affairs, he had to deal with a few little annoyances. Like the convoy coming up the hillside, all bunched up instead of observing a safe distance.

Fucking amateurs.

Boom should've lifted a grenade launcher. He tried to imagine what Dez would say about all this, and decided their CO would just shrug and maybe let out a sigh before squaring his shoulders and snapping orders to *get your shit together, soldiers, we got incoming.*

The first car had rounded the hairpin curve before he was ready, but Tax was on one knee and steady as the second one slowed to wallow-bump through the rutted corner-curve. The time-honored principle of *don't kill the driver, kill the car* was a good one, but his first round might have done both because there was an immediate screech of tearing metal and overstretched belts before the vehicle veered wildly aside, almost but not quite tipping over the berm to plunge into an arroyo. As it was, the third SUV—they were all tall, high-centered vehicles, he couldn't tell if any were armored—was either driven by a lunatic or a jackass, because it proceeded to plow right into the rear of the second with a crunch Tax felt even as he was up and moving again.

Dark-adapted pupils so wide the headlights were a stinging blur but he was used to that, and no member of the Squad had to see in order to fight.

Squeeze off another shot to keep the bastards in the third car guessing, find cover because the fourth car had slammed their brakes and someone clearly had a little professionalism since there was a tinkle of glass shivered into pieces—dumbasses didn't even have bulletproof windows—

as the bark of something semiautomatic and probably borderline illegal shattered what peace remained in the desert night.

These fellows are frisky. Moving again, though they would be blinded by focusing past headlight glare. By now adrenaline was dumping into his opponents; he knew it because he could taste the metallic chemical soup at the very back of his own throat.

The heavy *thuk* of a car door's latch giving, and someone spilled from the third car's side. Tax let him, even though his rifle could have spoken; it was a good shot, but *easy* don't necessarily mean *best for the situation*, as first Sparky Lee and later Dez had drilled into their soldiers over and over.

No, the best shot was at whoever was spewing lead from the fourth and final vehicle, so Tax took it and faded aside into spine-thorny scrub huddling next to a stand of fragrant juniper. Bullets whined and pop-pinged, sand puffing into the air adding a haze to the headlights. A brief shutterflash from the cabin was Grey, most likely taking a shot at the car Tax hadn't been able to stop; he had to trust his buddies would keep her safe.

Don't get any ideas, Meg. He fired again at the chattering muzzle flares on that fucking fourth car. Thankfully they were making enough noise the local wildlife was alerted, and keeping well away.

It would be embarrassing to step on a rattler during all this.

More dust, more popping, hoarse shouts. Ears ringing, the ground crumbling under his boots—the lip of a small sandy depression, and he dropped gratefully into its shelter as bullets hummed overhead. They were shooting high and probably wide too, the dipsticks. Tax hunkered down, and began choosing his shots again.

One, two. The fourth car listed heavily now, since a ricochet had popped a tire. Whoever had the big piece in the backseat was now hanging half out the window, a ragdoll shape with a twitching hand. The third car, fastened to the back of the second, had its doors flung open. Three hefty bastards in tac gear had piled out and were shooting wildly into the bush. The second SUV—now with reflected shine he could see it was a green Chevy, newer than the blue Tahoe he'd left for stripping—rocked as bullets plowed into its hide and whoever was inside realized the lead car in an ambush was nowhere to be.

It was almost like training, except for the horrified scream of a gut-shot sonofabitch from the third car, dropping his weapon and staggering away in zigzags. The poor bastard's head jerked violently aside and he folded like a dropped rag—not a shot from the cabin, nor from Tax, but from his own supposed side.

Friendly fire isn't, Tax heard the chant again, and if Jackson was here he'd have to worry that the Squad's wildcard was going to do something insane. As it was, all he had to care about was being outflanked, which wasn't very likely.

The dumb bastards hadn't even figured out which direction to shoot in, let alone where to move.

It was over relatively quickly. The fire petered out, and Tax dimly heard Grey swear through the earpiece. He stayed on his own task, sweeping the three cars—crumbled safety glass winking like stars, sharp stink of gasoline and live fire coating a cool night breeze. A bright flash sent him crouching even lower but it was only lightning, the concomitant rumble of thunder married to a drench of greenish scent saying a spring storm was ionizing everything in its path.

Maybe it would rain. Though it felt too damn dry for any real drops to hit the ground, falling water just topped any operation off. Tax suppressed a weary laugh, glared at the wreckage in front of him.

It was so easy to make a mess, and they'd done most of it to themselves. Served 'em right for coming after a package held by professionals.

"*Sonofabitch!*" Grey barked in his ear, married to a piercing feedback squeal and a grinding, rending, splintering crash.

Past Stapled

"DON'T WORRY." Eddie was remarkably calm, all things considered. "Just stay in there, and stay *down*, all right?" He pressed a kiss onto Carl's cheek and duck-walked out into the main part of the cabin, staying low because they could all hear the gunfire. It sounded like a particularly enthusiastic Fourth of July party, the kind usually leading to an emergency room visit.

Ricochets happen, Eddie had remarked grimly, as he hustled her and Carl back into the bedroom.

Sam was in the living room, hunkered down behind the couch, and Eddie'd outright laughed when she—somewhat tentatively, it had to be said—asked if maybe she should have her service weapon back. Meg hugged her knees, her back braced against the iron bedstead, wishing Sam was in here too.

Huddling together seemed a lot safer. Carl's shoulder pressed against hers again as the racket outside mounted. There were popping and shattering noises too, dimly familiar from her first nightmarish escape; she squeezed her eyes shut and leaned into him.

"It's okay," Carl was repeating, his breath hot against her temple. "It's okay, it's okay. We're gonna be okay."

Christ, I hope so. I'm so sorry. At least they'd both had a chance to go to the bathroom before all this got started; having to pee under these conditions would be the final insult.

Another fusillade. Distant yells. Eddie, shouting something. Two shots crackled nearby—where was Grezinski? Somewhere outside, helping Arthur? That was probably best.

How were they all so *calm,* still? The pointless urge to scream filled Meg's throat, cresting just as the gunfire settled into desultory spatters, then halted. A staticky, dangerous calm descended, broken only by a low rumble she thought was thunder or maybe just the ringing in her ears from all the firework ruckus.

Carl uncurled a bit. "You okay?" he whispered.

"I . . ." What could she say? "I think so?"

Sam said something, out in the living room. The words rose interrogatively near the end.

"I think he's gonna . . . Get back!" Eddie yelled. "*Get back get back go go go!*"

A horrific crash rocked the entire cabin. Meg let out a scream, Carl swore, and for a moment she thought there had been an earthquake, or lightning had struck.

She scrabbled for the doorway in Carl's wake. Dust puffed, a sword of white light poured through the shack, and a heavy rush of chill, storm-scented night air accompanied the glare.

What the hell?

Someone had driven right into the porch and through one of the front windows. Meg blinked, peering past Carl's bulk in the half-open bedroom door. The engine revved; whoever was in the driver's seat was still pressing on the gas. The vehicle snuggled further into the living room—god*damn*, the porch had to be gone.

And Meg saw, with a sinking sensation, that it was a dust-caked black Explorer. There was precious little heavy privacy tinting left, because the two front windows were shattered and the windshield full of spider-webbed cracks. One headlight was cracked too, but the other still sent a venomous white halogen sword into the kitchenette, highlighting the bathroom door, the hall, the back door as well. A shadow moved—Eddie, crouched next to the couch, dust frosting his hair and his hand rising as he aimed at the car.

Sam crawl-scrabbled past the table where they'd had dinner, knocking over a chair as the engine revved again.

Does homeowner's insurance cover this? Meg could barely process what her eyes were seeing.

Sam made it to her knees as the car heaved forward again. Wood splintered, the house groaned, and now crap was falling from the ceiling too. The detective scrambled behind the table, and her good eye settled on Carl.

"*Come on!*" she yelled, beckoning frantically. "*Out the back!*"

Carl didn't wait to be told twice. His hand closed around Meg's upper arm, grinding on a bruise, and he banged into the door on his way out of the bedroom, barely noticing enough to cuss with uncharacteristic ferocity.

Pow. One shot, glass shattered. Darkness fell, sword-sharp. Blinded by the sudden change, Meg teetered sideways, Carl losing his grip on her as he collided with Sam. The two of them went down in a tangle; Meg fell the opposite direction, nearly ending up on one of the mismatched dining chairs.

HER VISION CLEARED swiftly—after all, she and Carl had been in the dark bedroom for a long while. Shadows danced crazily, there was a banging, and another shot close by. Wood splintered, groaning in protest; Sam swore and there was a burst of half-seen motion as she and Carl tried to heave each other upright.

"Eddie?" Meg was trying to yell, but her throat was a pinhole and only a strangled whisper escaped. "Eddie, for God's sake—"

"Run." At least he sounded calm, and nearby. "All of you, fucking *run.*"

And oh, God, but she was in Gerry's kitchen again, Rob grappling with the man in the hoodie while he said the same thing.

More wood-breaking sounds. Then, from the darkness outside, came a new voice—male, baritone, pleasant, with a slight whistle as if congested by a spring cold.

"Meeeeg," the stranger said, drawing out her name. There was a ratcheting—car doors, pushed open against a heavy weight. "Where you at, Meg?"

What the hell?

Bam. A white flash painted the cabin's inside. Her ears rang.

"RUN!" Eddie roared, the past folded over and stapled onto the present. Meg's feet slipped on dust, she tripped on fallen debris and nearly fell atop a warm living shape, either Carl or Sam. Someone's hand found hers, squeezed tightly.

"Let's go!" Sam barked, and yanked her along. They blundered through the hall, following Carl's taller shape, and burst into the desert night.

Bad Feeling

THE MOANING MAN was one of the tac-suited assholes, mostly unconscious and full of agonal twitches. The machine in Tax's head responsible for calculating triage returned the same answer no matter how many times he ran it, and in any case the opposition wasn't his responsibility.

Whatever was happening uphill had turned into the bigger problem now, to judge by the feedback and the quiet, fierce, "*Oh, fuck this noise,*" from Grey through the earpiece before comms cut out.

Because of course they would, it was how these things always went. Tax longed to yell for details, but his buddies had their hands full and in any case couldn't hear him. His current job was to flank or mop up whoever had been in the first car, since they were now causing problems. He cast another glance over the ambush site, decided the situation here qualified as 'pacified,' and loped back for the cabin, keeping to cover.

One shot, crackling through the night. Hard work to move carefully, since it was dark as sin and he had to let his eyes adapt all over again after the confusion of ambush, headlights, and muzzle flash. A bright white pop of lightning showed him the hill, dirt road, low scrub, twisted trees clinging to desiccated life waiting for a few inches of rain, veils of hanging dust, pebbles and spiny bushes standing out in stark relief before swallowed again by the night. The world held its breath, waiting for thunder.

And Tax had a bad feeling about this, the same sure instinct that warned him when shit was about to go sideways and someone was about to take a hit he might not be able to fix with supplies on hand.

He hopped up the berm, the rutted dirt road silver-lit for a brief moment before the waxing moon hid behind scudding cloud, and began to run.

Worked Out

SAM SEEMED TO knew where she was going. Or perhaps she was just following Carl, who hooked around the corner of the cabin and ran for the front, his head bobbing and the tiny puffs of dust squirting from his huaraches visible as a flash of lightning filled the mountainside to bursting. Meg staggered along, hoping none of them were about to step on a scorpion, and wondered just where in the hell they were going anyway.

The road. If they could reach it . . . but what about all the other gunfire? The sudden quiet was eerie.

Thunder arrived, and with it the heavy ozone scent of rain trying to reach the ground hurried down the mountainside in a soft brushing whoosh. Carl ran past the shattered porch, probably heading for Arthur's SUV, backed in alongside Eddie's pickup at the edge of sandy dirt serving as both driveway and turnaround.

Maybe they'd put the cars there to escape being dinged by someone crazy-driving into the front of the cabin. Sam's sedan was parked past them, also backed in but a distance, as if it feared its reception by the others.

The shack was in a deeply sorry state now. The black Explorer's back doors hung open like bedraggled wings, and Carl nearly plowed right into a shadowy shape stumbling from the broken porch steps.

"The *fuck*," this new addition barked before falling flat, and Sam didn't hesitate, letting go of Meg's hand to throw herself on the guy with an *oof* sound that might have been funny in another situation.

"Fucking *go!*" she yelled, as Carl reeled away, saving himself from falling with an astonishing pitter-patter of dance steps.

He was indeed heading for the cars. Meg decided that was as good a destination as any, but Eddie was still in the house and who the hell—

"Meg." A half-familiar voice, and a bright flash that wasn't lightning because it was a gunshot. The bullet hit something on the ground, whined away into darkness, and Meg skidded to a halt. "Meg, *stop*."

Oh, crap. Her breath came in great shuddering heaves. She turned, slowly, and now the lightning decided to take another celestial picture. There was the SUV, nuzzled into the cabin like a nursing kitten, the roof crumbling almost as she watched. Sam was rolling on the ground with a bulky shadow, and from the muttered swearing it wasn't a friendly wrestling match.

And halfway between Meg and the Explorer was a tall shadow, his face lit by that helpful, freezing flash.

It was Preston Roark, and he had a pistol trained on her.

WHAT. THE FUCK. She was vaguely surprised he'd show up himself; getting other people to do the work for him was always Press's preferred strategy.

The end of the gun looked very big, and very black. She'd gone most of her life without having weapons pointed at her, and she couldn't wait to get back to that state of affairs—if the world would just *let* her, for God's sake.

"Press," she heard herself say, blankly. "What are you doing?"

"You weren't supposed to be there." For an absolute fucking lunatic, he sounded almost placid. "Why didn't you call me?"

Why would I? "Gerry." The name stung her lips. "Barton. Ella—your own sister, Press. Why?"

"He always liked her better." Press took a step toward her. There was a grunt and a cracking sound from the rolling tussle to Meg's left, close to the shattered cabin. More thunder muttered uneasily, a greased cannonball rolling through the sky. "You should've called me. I could have worked something out."

"How?" She was genuinely curious, Meg realized, but also if she kept him talking maybe she could figure out something to do about that gun. "How could any of this be *worked out*, Press?"

Was that footsteps? Someone was running. She hoped it was Carl getting the hell away from this. If she kept Press busy, maybe he could escape.

"All you had to do was come back to me," he said, almost sadly.

Crack.

The gun jerked in his hand.

Civilian Dying

THE LIGHTNING was pitiless, and so was Tax's dark-adapted vision. The motherfuckers in the first car had driven right into the cabin, which was either a crazy desperate move worthy of the Squad itself or a consequence of unfriendly fire taking out something critical in the SUV's steering. Someone was down on the ground, tussling and throwing up a bunch of dust, and there was Carl, booking across the gravel for the pickup and Tax's own car.

Good move, heading to cover; Boom had picked a smart one.

The only thing Tax had eyes for was the hostile at his eleven o'clock, the motherfucker's hand out as if he had a pistol trained on Meg, who was standing frozen. Tax had a sidearm too, plus the rifle, but getting a shot in before this sonofabitch pulled the trigger might not—

No. Just get there.

Conversation. Meg's hair was silvered by fitful moonlight, and even in that indistinct glow she looked tired, shoulders hunching.

Pow.

They said you never heard the one that got you. A padded hammer smashed into Tax's left side, walloping his legs right out from under him. He was still trying to run when he hit, skull smacking pebbles and desert dirt. A vast feathery calm filled his ears, and he blinked, expecting pain.

Nothing. Just the world turned on its side, the cabin skewed as if a movie camera had tilted.

Because you're on the ground, soldier. Get up. She needs you, get the fuck up.

He couldn't. Still no pain, just an odd disconnected stillness. Thunder grumbled again, dissatisfied, and darkness swallowed him for a brief instant.

WHEN HE SURFACED there *was* agony, and a goodish amount of it.

"Keep pressure on," Grey sounded grim. "Fuck, Boom, are you trying to hit every goddamn pothole in the state?"

"—soon as we're in cell range." The lady cop—Sue? Sandra? Tax couldn't quite remember her name. "Just keep your eyes on the road!"

He was across someone's lap. The pain was everywhere, a giant beast with clawed iron teeth, and worst of all was the knowledge that he'd failed. Someone was making a low hoarse sound, human being reduced to suffering animal, and he thought maybe it was him.

Well, I wanted to die. Fucking figures it would happen like this.

"Don't you dare," she said, and the vice clamped to his midsection tightened another half-twist. "Don't you *dare* die."

"There's the highway." Carl, grimly calm. "Sweetie, the turn, the turn, *turn now!*"

"Will you just shut up so I can drive?" Boom barked, the vehicle slewing wildly. Each bump and shift sent a fresh flood of razor-edged smoking hurt through Tax's bones. "And of course it'd start tryinta fuckin' rain."

"Two bars!" the cop crowed. "Dialing now. Gonna get backup, don't worry."

"Don't you dare," his personal fairy continued, and hers was the only voice he wanted to hear. Tax blinked, but there was something warm and sticky in his eyes, and in any case soft dark flowers were blooming all across his field of vision. Which made sense, it was night.

Night op. Someone was badly injured. Boom and Grey were on deck, so that was good, but it was Tax's job to patch up whoever was making that sound. He couldn't make his arms work, or his legs.

Am I paralyzed? To be trapped in his own body, like a starving mammoth sunk in a tar pit. . . .

"Fucking ricochets," Grey said, grimly. "Can't tell if it's lodged in there. Just keep pressing, Meg, you're doing great."

"At least you got Roark." Boom exhaled sharply, the road smoothing out under the tires. Which was a relief, except for him promptly flooring the gas and the car lunging forward, acceleration pressing an entirely new burst of red-hot metal through Tax's entire frame. "Piece of shit."

"This is Detective Sam Morigny, LVMPD." The lady cop, nearly shouting, enunciating crisp and clear. "I'm on Kesby Canyon Road at mile marker 158, that's one-five-eight, and I need medical to meet us. We have injured civilians, I need EMT and police escort *now*. I also need Agent Gideon Fitzhugh up at the Carson City FBI office alerted, he's expecting a call." The detective was good at issuing orders—enough urgency to prod whoever was on the other side into action but not enough to hike their adrenaline into the stratosphere. "Yes, I know, goddammit. Kesby Canyon Road, mile marker 158 now and moving eastbound, we're in a black Honda CR-V with California plates. Get us some fucking EMTs, I have a civilian dying in here, and get Agent Fitzhugh on the line now. Not tomorrow, not in five minutes, *fucking now.*"

Civilian dying? Tax struggled to think. *That doesn't sound. . . .*

"Don't you dare," the only voice he wanted to hear repeated. Damp, cool fingers on his forehead, and the vice in his guts tightened another full twist, pain so massive it was cold through the gush of sweat drenching him. "Don't you dare die on me, Arthur. There is *no dying allowed* today, you hear me?"

Funny, he wanted to say. *That's my line.*

But he couldn't make his mouth work either, and all he felt was dozy gratefulness that Meg was still alive.

Done Good

A DAMP, STEAMING dawn swallowed Sin City, water evaporating under the sun's lash even as the hills turned green with brief growth and the arroyos were foam-brim full. Normally Meg liked rare spring gullyfillers, even if the humidity gave her hair the fits and washouts turned so many roads into stuttering hyphens.

She'd never seen the sun come up from inside the federal building downtown, though. And she didn't like it, even if the 'deposition' room— it was an interrogation chamber, not a conference space, and she knew it—had a great view, the coffee was fresh instead of boiled, and they fed her all the takeout a girl could want. By midmorning even adrenaline had given out, and if they were going to put her in a cell she wished they'd get on with it so she could at least sleep.

"You're damn lucky, ma'am." Gideon Fitzhugh was a lean raw-boned man with broken-in Tony Lamas to match his equally well-worn grey cowboy hat, though his suit was standard-issue federal and his tie bore a few shiny patches. "Beaumont is known for not leaving any witnesses."

They'd warned her they were recording her statement, and Meg figured the tape was still rolling. She clutched a blue mug with a gold FBI seal on its side, wishing the scorching liquid inside could touch the ice filling her stomach. "Rob told me to run," she repeated, dully, knowing she probably sounded stupid but unable to help herself. "I . . . Sam said this Beaumont guy killed someone at Gianello's, too?"

"Yeah, well." Fitzhugh didn't shift uncomfortably. A rotating cast of others came in and out of the room, some taking notes, others asking quiet questions and listening to her halting, rambling answers. At least they'd had the EMTs take a look at her after an ambulance carrying Arthur screamed away into the ozone-thick precursor to the rains. Grezinski had finagled his way onto that particular bus—*we're Army buddies,* he'd kept repeating, *he needs someone with him, I'm going.*

Eddie and Carl had been whisked away; so had Sam. Meg was on her own, in a federal-issue sweatshirt and blue cotton scrub bottoms—

her own clothes had been bagged for evidence, her hands swabbed for residue, the whole nine. She'd been allowed to take a shower in a locker room, at least. A yawning, redheaded woman in a hastily buttoned suit—Agent Milner, who reappeared at intervals with more coffee or paperwork—had lingered right outside the stall, in case of emergency.

It was beginning to feel less like Meg was a witness and more like she was a suspect. Or a loose end.

"And . . . Preston." Her knuckles were white. "He had a gun, he was going to shoot me. Mr. Grezinski was defending me, and himself."

"We've pretty much established that, yeah. Man goes messin' with Army boys like this, he oughta expect getting his ass beat." Despite the down-home drawl, sharp intelligence lingered in Fitzhugh's eyes—strangely similar to Chad Beaumont's, greenish with yellow tones as he examined her. "You do know you're not in trouble, right? You didn't do nothin' wrong."

I know enough not to trust a cop when he says that. "It doesn't matter." She hitched her bruised shoulder up, a half-shrug like Sam's pained motion in the shack's living room. "This is Vegas."

In other words, they could *make* trouble for her, whether she was clean or not. She hadn't even asked for a lawyer; whatever they were going to do, she just wanted it over with.

Especially since she could still feel Arthur's hot slippery blood on her hands, hear the faint noise he made through gritted teeth each time the car swayed or bounced, clearly trying to keep quiet while in a lot of pain. The EMTs who treated her and Sam wouldn't say whether or not he had a chance.

"Ayuh." Fitzhugh nodded as if she'd said something profound. "Well, we raided the Corral this morning. Bert Franke's already rolling on Tamzoukis, looking to save himself a few federal counts. We might not need you on the stand . . . but I do still recommend you think about our offer. Witness protection's come a long way, past few decades."

Great. Franke and Tammy both had long reaches. On the other hand, it looked like they had far bigger problems than one small wedding planner. "Yeah." She dropped her gaze, staring into the coffee cup. The building's deathly silence near dawn had changed; now there was a breathing hum of papers filed, phone calls made, keyboards clicking and computers talking in electronic streams, all reaching into this quiet room with its long wood-veneer table, too many chairs, a coffeemaker on a hutch at the far wall, and the windows full of rain-washed sunlight.

A tap on the door made her jump, but when it opened, a hot burst of relief rose to the back of her throat like hangover vomit.

Sam had been able to grab a shower as well, plus some fresh jeans, T-shirt, and blazer, but she still looked beat all to hell. "Hey girl hey." Her smile was lopsided because of the swelling; butterfly bandages marched across the gash on her forehead and she winced as she pulled the door closed. "How's it going?"

Oh, God. "Sam." Seeing a familiar face was better than coffee. "Thank God. Is Eddie okay? And Carl, and—"

"Ed's hopping mad, threatening to get the best lawyer in town on our asses if we so much as sneeze at you wrong. Some DoD legal aid showed up for him and his friends." Sam's stride wasn't quite as brisk as usual, and as she lowered herself into the chair to Meg's left she sighed, clenching her teeth like the exhale was a personal affront. "And Tachmann is out of surgery. He's stable, they say."

The bright, clean room vanished for a moment. Roaring filling Meg's ears, Fitzhugh and Sam's words filtering through only dimly.

"What about that Vitebski fellow?" the FBI agent wanted to know. "Last I heard they were wiring his jaw, he'll need to drink his meals for a while."

"He'll live," Sam said, grimly. Her partner was lucky to get away with just a few broken bones, that tone said. "They've put him on admin leave. He's got a wife and kids so they're keeping him on payroll for medical insurance. Janine will probably stand by her man."

"Damn shame." Fitzhugh sounded like he meant it. "Also a damn shame to lose a fine cop like you to this bullshit. You know how they treat IA folk, especially once the investigation's done. We'd love to have you on our side of the fence."

"Is that an offer?" Sam's grim amusement edged every word; it wasn't really a surprise to find out she was Internal Affairs. "Or just you expressing some personal feelings?"

Huh. She must like this guy. Color and full sound returned to the world; Meg was glad she was sitting down. Arthur was stable, not critical. The hospital wouldn't say that if he was going to die, right?

It sounded like Sam's partner was going to pull through as well. Meg wondered about the other guys—Tamzoukis's goons—who had made Sam dig her own grave out in the desert.

She freed a hand from her mug. Her fingertips landed on Sam's forearm, and Meg hoped she wasn't pressing on a bruise. "Sam."

"Huh?" For a moment Morigny looked like she had in high school, distracted by the sudden bad news of a pop quiz she hadn't thoroughly studied for.

"I'm sorry. About all this." Meg hesitated. "And about Mike."

"Well, you and Eddie were right, he's a shithead. Should've listened." But the tension in Sam's shoulders eased a fraction. "And for Chrissake, Meg. You've been shot and beat all to hell, and *you're* sorry? Can it. Ed would tell you the same thing."

"I guess." Meg's lips cracked as she tried a wan, tentative smile. "I . . . can I go home? I'm really tired."

"Well . . ." Sam paused. "Beaumont and his local support went to your apartment looking for you, broke in through a window. Didn't toss it too badly, I think, but are you sure you want to stay there?"

Oh, God. Meg's stomach cramped. "There's nowhere else," she said, dully.

"Bullshit. You can crash at Ed's, or at my place." Sam was in full-on management mode; did other people feel this guiltily grateful when Meg descended upon a wedding situation to set all to rights? "Or hell, have Fitzhugh here put us up somewhere nice. We've earned it."

"Wouldn't recommend a casino hotel at the moment," the FBI agent said. "But there's no shortage of options, and I'd be happy to. Y'all deserve it."

I'm so fucking tired of hotels. "I want to go home." Meg tried to sound firm, definite, and no-nonsense. "Please."

"Then I'll help you clean the place up." Sam's glower, even through the contusions and scrapes, warned against trying to argue. "And crash on your couch, too, so long as we can stop by my place to pack a bag."

"I think we've got everything we need right now." Fitzhugh paused. "And I mean it, ladies. You done good, both of you, and oughta be proud."

It doesn't feel like it. But Meg was too relieved to do more than nod. She would have liked to ask about visiting the hospital.

But she was pretty sure Arthur wouldn't want to see the woman who had gotten him shot. It was probably better if she just . . . refrained. Eddie could notify that mysterious girlfriend of his, and that would be that.

Except for whatever she owed him for saving her life so many times. She was too tired to think about the going rate for a guardian angel right now, or about the funny piercing pain in her chest thinking how happy he was going to be when whoever he was dating showed up.

It took two tries to stand, but she managed with the help of her palms flat on the table and a half-swallowed groan like Gerry's as he bemoaned getting older.

It hurt to think about that, too. She pushed the pain aside; if she just focused on the next problem, and the next, she'd get through this. Somehow.

She'd been doing it since the orphanage, she could damn well continue.

"Okay," she said, grimly. "I'm ready. Let's go."

Getting the Message

DRIFTING ON painkillers was nice, except for the persistent fuzzy sense of forgetting something important. He surfaced a few times, hearing regular beeps, and a mix of disinfectant plus industrially laundered cotton told him he was in a hospital. It was missing the tang of floor wax and the faint auditory notes of hurried footsteps, not to mention barked orders and salutes, that meant Army or VA.

Huh. Processing any sensory input required effort. After a while, foggy memories began filtering into the twilight. A vulture circling high in a desert sky. Music. A pair of wide blue eyes brimming with tears.

There is no dying allowed today, you hear me?

Tax lunged into full consciousness, or tried to. He managed a twitch, and the smear in front of him resolved into acoustic ceiling tiles and a fluorescent fixture. A metallic gleam was the arm of an IV stand; looked like they had him on saline. Which explained the chill; that shit was cold when it went in.

A faint cough nearby, and a shifting. "Hospital," a familiar voice said. "They had to patch up your spleen and replace most of your red stuff."

Tax turned his head, his hair rasping against the pillow. Slowly, Boom came into focus, his forehead wrinkled as if he was working out exactly how much charge was needed to bring down a door without taking his buddies—or the entire building—with it. He was on a chair next to the bed, his hair a mess in every direction, and behind him a window was full of bright desert light held back by a wholly inadequate beige cloth shade.

Tax's throat was parched. He attempted to clear it, and the effort almost sent him back into the warm fog. "Meg?" he husked. "Carl? Grey?"

"Carl's dealing with last-minute wedding stuff and getting your car detailed. Grey'll be here in about an hour to take over watching your sleeping beauty ass." Boom leaned forward, resting his forearms on the bed's railing, inspecting his buddy's face. His dark eyes were shuttered, and his curls far too long for regs as if they'd just been in-country for a particularly dirty operation. A shadow of stubble lingered on his cheeks. "You owe him a beer, by the way. He fell through the ceiling, crawled through fucking Beaumont's fucking car, and took out that mother-fucker Preston. Who squeezed off a shot as he went down, and near as we can figure you just happened to be in its way after it hit something on the floor."

"Good to know." It didn't matter. There was only one thing Tax wanted to hear about, but it looked like Boom was going to work through the list in his own way.

"Sam took Beaumont out of commission, so that's not on us. Some spook and his legal handler dropped by a while ago, making sure this wasn't connected to anything at work. Gave Grey and me the ol' hairy eyeball, but Sam and her Feeb friend convinced them it was purely local trouble." Boom shrugged, consigning the CIA, FBI, JAG, Vegas Metropolitan PD, and every other soup made of initials to the realm of annoying but ultimately unimportant. "You'll be happy to know our pensions are safe."

Tax didn't give a damn. "Okay."

"And . . . about Meg." Now Boom looked like a man about to give bad news.

Tax swallowed hard. *Well, it won't be difficult. There are ways to go in a hospital, I just need to find the right one.* "What about Meg?"

"The funeral's today. For Gerry Roark and his daughter. Rob Barton's was yesterday, but she missed the one for Señora Mendoza. She's holding up."

So she was alive. The world threatened to fuzz out again before roaring back into sharp color and detail. Painful, exquisite relief filled every inch of him, and Tax let out a soft breath. The beeping from machines crouching on the other side of the bed didn't alter much, thank God— or his mother's ancestors, who were probably watching all this with sardonic amusement.

Boom's left eyebrow was up while the right one stayed put, a sure sign of impending trouble. "She asked me about your girlfriend," he continued. "Wanted to notify her that you're hospitalized. You been holding out on me, Tax?"

What? "My what?"

"Girlfriend. Meg said you told her a certain lady would be at the wedding, but Grey and I can't figure out who the fuck she's talking about. So, you've been holding out, and I'm under orders to get the name and details from you so we can get this mystery woman notified you're in for repairs." When he finished, Eddie's mouth settled into a thin line, and by God and garters, as ol' Footy Lenz would have said, he looked *disappointed.*

The sense of having slid into an alternate universe mixed with lingering painkillers, and Tax wondered for a brief second if he was in hell. Or some other kind of afterlife.

Then it hit him, right between the eyes. Of course. The woman was oblivious, and he couldn't blame her. "No need." The dry nasty grit in his throat wouldn't go away. "She already knows."

"Tachmann." Boom was dead serious, and it was a good bet he wasn't asking with his fists only because his buddy was already in a hospital bed. "I swear to God, I owe you one because you saved Meg. But if you think I'm gonna—"

"She already knows I'm in the hospital because it's Meg, all right? Christ Jesus, Boom, settle down." Tax tested his fingers—they moved when he told them to. If he tucked his chin he could see the lumps that were his feet under sheet and blanket, and they twitched. Another burst of relief, like tequila exploding behind his breastbone, and he wiggled his toes again.

The lumps under the blanket repeated their twitches. It was definite, all his parts were getting the message. He wasn't paralyzed, and with some recovery he'd be ready to tango again.

"Oh." Boom straightened, absorbing the news. "So, you . . . huh. Huh."

"She was being chased by mobsters and dirty cops, I didn't think it was the right time to ask her out on a date, okay?" *Give me some credit here, buddy.* "Figured I'd take her somewhere nice for dinner and an explanation once all this was tied off, and I'll even step in to do those six months' worth of dance lessons you owe her, which *you're* gonna owe *me* a big ol' fuckin' favor for." Tax ran down the list of possible objections Boom could possibly offer, decided he could head off the big one. "And before you ask, I'm serious. I'm gonna marry her, if I can get her to agree."

It was a relief to finally say it out loud.

"Oh." Boom didn't quite deflate, but it was close. "I see."

"Do I have to ask your permission or something?" It was official, he was flat on his back, shot by a ricochet—Klemp was going to razz him *unmercifully* about this—and, Tax found, almost enjoying himself. "I'd like to tell her myself, if you don't mind."

"Sure, sure." Mischief shone in Boom's dark eyes, but he quickly sobered. "That's actually good. I won't have to worry about Tammy the Greek getting ideas about loose ends or making a point, then."

"Who? Oh yeah." The big cheese who had sent that little freckled sociopath into the mix; Tax's mind wasn't at full speed yet, but it was close. "Pretty sure he's got other problems right now." *Or I'll give him a few, once I'm back on my feet.*

Mobsters were easy. Getting Meg to sit down long enough to listen to his case was going to be the difficult part, and he needed to be upright and conscious for it.

"Might be worth taking care of him, if the feds don't." Boom tipped his head one way, then the other, a quick familiar stretch while contemplating mayhem. "But either way . . . sure. You've got my permission. Just don't hurt her, or I'll drop you in a mineshaft."

If you can catch me. "Duly noted. How soon can I get out of here?"

"You're the medic, asshole. You tell me."

Transitory Celebrity

MEG'S CAR WAS a lost cause, but she had insurance and Sam didn't mind helping with the police reports or being a taxi for a while. Getting her phone back was a similarly mixed blessing. Fortunately Sam's badge kept most of the reporters away, but there were a lot of people calling for 'consultations' who were plainly what Rob Barton would have called *lookie-loos*, the type of folk who slowed down to stare at traffic accidents.

It was beautiful weather, and the caskets were highly polished—Gerry's mahogany and gold, Ella's white and silver. Ell's tall, Rolex-wearing fiancé Ben was a nice guy, though he looked a little stunned and visibly flinched when his gaze wandered across Meg.

It was becoming depressingly familiar. At least round-hipped, red-headed Aunt Stace kept Meg at her elbow, which reduced the family gossip and speculative stares to a minimum; the service was Catholic, the graveside address by Father Joseph mercifully brief, and the wake was at Lana Flanagan's sprawling stucco Lone Mountain home.

Stace handed her a tumbler, two fingers of amber whiskey in smoked glass. "I've had a look at the will."

Oh, God. Meg was longing to get out of pantyhose, and this black dress was the same one she'd worn to Rob's far-less-crowded service. This would function as Barton's wake, too; there was a small picture of him in a wooden frame right next to larger ones of Ella and a much younger Gerry resting amid masses of flowers on the mantel over the cold, switched-off gas insert fireplace.

"Gerry believed in being prepared," she said, and was glad of the air-conditioning. Still, her cheeks felt hot.

Preston's photo was markedly absent from the mantel. Though a Flanagan by marriage, Stacey was now the only Roark left, and her feelings on her nephew were abundantly clear. She'd claimed his body and had him cremated, or so Sam said.

Stace's son Levi moved through the mourners, making sure the drinks were topped up and engaging in soft conversation over handshakes with movers and shakers; visibly pregnant Siobhan was in the kitchen with

Lana, ensuring the cold cuts and other catered bits were up to snuff.

It was odd to be part of the event instead of running it.

"That he did," Aunt Stace agreed, and her coral-lipsticked mouth pursed. The diamonds in her solitaire earrings winked slyly. "I'm the executor since Rob . . . well, there'll be a meeting with the lawyers next week. Thursday, I think? But I might as well tell you now, he left you some property out in Napa and a bit else. It's structured so the inheritance tax will pay itself, Rob liked to have things set up that way. You won't have to worry."

Meg looked guiltily away from the photos. Wide bay windows overlooked the patio and manicured, violently green lawn; the sunlight dimmed as clouds moved in. Spring storms often didn't bring rain, though the lightning was always spectacular. The green and wildflowers were short-term as well. Very soon the desert would be dry taupe again; by then Eddie would be married and Arthur gone back home. "Oh."

"Meg?" It was Levi, his eyebrows peaked into angles. A blonde with a spectacular chest job smiled next to him, but her hazel eyes looked like hard, painted gumballs. "This is Astrid, Siobhan's friend. She's getting married next August. Didn't have a chance to introduce you before."

"How do you do." Meg hoped her smile wasn't too watery. "And congratulations."

"Pleased to meet you," Astrid said, lifting her mimosa. "Siobhan says you're a wedding planner? There's so much to take care of."

"There is." Meg's current clients were very understanding; only one had canceled, shifting to a planner who hadn't been on the news. Vegas loved a good scandal, and Meg could certainly parlay this into a bigger client list . . . if she wanted to be that tacky.

Stace was also making it clear Meg's transitory celebrity didn't put her in that category, though. She immediately, smoothly took over. "Astrid, darling, can you see if Siobhan's all right? And Levi, there's Commissioner Peckingham, he looks like he needs a refill." Then she shooed them away, smiling brightly, and when she turned back to Meg, she grimaced. It was an expression very much like Gerry's *Lord bless these fools, for I do not*, and Meg downed half her whiskey in one shot, tossing it as far back as possible.

Sam would pick her up soon. She only had to endure a little longer. Eddie said Arthur was out of danger, resting comfortably. That was a victory, and so was the swelling on Sam's face going down. She was on paid admin leave, and from what Meg could tell was seriously considering Fitzhugh's job offer.

"She has a good heart," Stace said. "Was in Siobhan's sorority, has a marketing degree; the girl will do all right for herself and if you don't charge her extra I'll be disappointed, since her family can certainly afford it. Anyway, I wanted to tell you about the will so you're not surprised, and so you don't take what I'm about to say wrong." She sucked in a breath, her round, florid face under its cap of auburn curls turning set and thoughtful.

She had Gerry's nose and Ella's eyes, but the rest of her was all curves and pillows. People often mistook that for weakness.

"You're about to warn me to get out of town?" It wasn't a difficult guess.

"What? No." It was one of the few times she'd ever seen Stacey Flanagan look surprised. "Of course not, honey. This is your *home*. You were good to Gerry, and he considered you family so that's good enough for me."

Oh. Meg's eyes prickled. "That . . . thank you. That means a lot."

"It had better," Stace said grimly. "*That boy* was never right, but even if it was his idea, Franke didn't have to help. He had my brother gunned down in his own home, and that's gonna cost both him *and* that little Greek bastard. Wherever the Feds put them, it won't be a hole deep enough, so don't you worry about that. But what I mean to say is, please stay out of this sort of thing in the future. The business isn't for people like you, Meg."

Believe me, if I could have avoided this, I would. A river of prickles slipped down Meg's back. "I understand," she said, and took the other half of her whiskey down. Her eyes watered, but she didn't cough.

"Good." Stace nodded briskly. "Oh, and that boy you always hung around with, what's his name? Boomhauer, Bronson, Edgar or something?"

"Eddie."

"Yes, Eddie. He grew up well. Please thank him for his service when you see him, will you?" Stace caught someone's eye across the room and smiled, inclining her head. It was a misty, maternal expression, almost managing to cover the sharp gleam of intelligence moving through her gaze. "But he should stay out of anything else to do with this as well. Do you understand?"

"Yes, Aunt Stace." Meg's feet ached; at least when she was scrambling for her life she'd been wearing sneakers instead of heels.

"Good girl. And look, you're dry. That won't do, go get another drink—but don't let Siobhan rope you into helping today. You've done more than enough." The same small, impatient little shooing motion she'd given Astrid and Levi, very much like her brother's *step lively now.*

The biggest surprise wasn't that Stace might be taking over Gerry's mantle. It was that the tears finally came when Meg was in the guest bathroom off the utility room, her sobs muffled by running water in the sink and her phone buzzing with the text saying Sam was on her way, did Meg want her to pick up anything from the grocery store?

But it was the text before, Eddie saying Arthur had been discharged from the hospital and not to worry, that had finally broken the dam, making her weep like a child.

Places, Gentlemen

THE WAITING ROOM felt a lot smaller with half a dozen guys crowded into it. "Shit." Boom stared into the mirror; he poked at the bowtie with a careful fingertip. "I'm a gorilla. In a suit."

"Stop messing with it." Grey looked almost as nervous as the Squad's demo man; he'd had a haircut but kept fussing with his silver cufflinks as if he was going to do a trick with them. "And you, fucking sit down." That last bit was flung in Tax's direction.

Tax didn't move, peering through the slightly ajar door at a carpeted hallway.

"Still can't believe you got yourself shot." Curly-headed, perpetually cheerful Klemp shrugged into his suit jacket carefully; Beck had given him strict instructions not to wrinkle anything. They'd flown in yesterday evening, the last to arrive; even Jackson and Desmarais had beaten Mr. Punctual. "Right after telling *me* not to."

"At least he wasn't brained with a milk crate." Their CO, sprawled in a chair that looked too spindly for his muscular frame, actually unbent enough to smile. Apparently the missus and his adopted kid had loosened Dez up immensely, but he'd still demanded full reports, from chowder to cashews and over drinks, the night *he* got in.

Tax had been looking forward to dropping a few choice words about Klemp's own brush with the law up in Oregon. "Yeah, well, I wasn't held at gunpoint by my girl's soon-to-be ex-husband, either. In broad public daylight, I might add."

"Oh, fuck me, man." Klemp rolled his eyes. "Can't keep your mouth shut, can you."

"This is another story I'm very interested in exploring." Lithe, pale-eyed Jackson was in an easily defensible corner, capping a very service-able hip flask they'd all just taken a shot from. Tax's gums still tingled; whatever the Squad's wildcard put in that little container could clean engines or start fires; even so, a little bit wouldn't affect the post-surgery antibiotics. "Am I the only one who's not shacking up around here?"

"I don't have any plans," Grey objected, immediately. "*Stop* messing with your tie, Boom, if we don't pass inspection I'll be the one Meg docks for it."

"She's nice," Klemp said. "So when are you getting hitched, Tax?"

"Goddammit, let me be the one to ask her, at least." It would be better if he could get a few minutes alone with her, but Meg Callahan was a busy lady. And he wasn't sure, but he thought she might be. . . .

Well, she might be avoiding him, either because he reminded her of violent bullshit no woman should ever have to face or—what he was hoping—she had the mistaken idea he was taken or uninterested.

He couldn't wait to dispel all doubt.

"I haven't breathed a word." Boom took a deep breath. "What time is it?"

Desmarais turned his hand palm-up to glance at his watch's face. "Ninety seconds later than the last time you asked, ya jackass." He took pity on a poor soldier almost immediately, though. "We're on target, Boom. Mellow down easy."

"Look at that," Jackson crooned, attempting to be helpful in his own inimitable way. "That's one handsome motherfucker in the mirror, bro. Why, I'll bet the old man will even mist up." His particular contribution to the festivities was getting their trainer Sparky Lee Jones on a flight—all the way from his cabin in backwoods Virginia—to see one of 'his boys' tie the knot.

Sparky was probably miserable in his own suit. Tax was under orders not to lift anything over five pounds, but his incision was doing fine, his blood was staying inside him where it belonged, and he'd even had time to make a few arrangements for after this shindig.

"Fuck you," was Boom's prompt, affectionate reply. "Man, I'd rather be dropping into a hot zone than wearing this getup."

"Don't let Miss Callahan hear that." Klemp's grin widened, if that were possible. "I gotta say, though, she booked us a damn nice hotel."

Of course she did. It was the kind of detail Meg excelled at, Tax knew. And this venue was also nice, on the pricier side of quality instead of glitz. Even if she hadn't had him to look over the rate cards, she'd driven a great bargain for her beloved Eddie, and she was no doubt attending to some last-minute details or disaster.

Or maybe not, because a door opened down the hall and his personal fairy appeared. The tips of her hair were now blue instead of pink, her linen skirt matched her eyes and hit just above the knee, her jacket was the same color and wasn't ashamed to hug the curves underneath it, her heels were high and sharp enough to qualify as weapons, and the leftover bruises were mere shadows under her makeup. She strode down the hall like a nine-tailed fox on a mission, hips moving gently, silver bracelets on her left wrist winking, and Tax's heart threatened to bang clean past his ribs.

"Incoming," he said, quietly, and by the time she gave the door two polite taps, every member of the Ghost Squad was upright and ready for inspection.

"Eddie?" Her gaze settled on her best friend, and she smiled. "Oh, goodness. Look at you."

"Not supposed to see the bride before . . . wait." Boom shook his head. "Two grooms. Unless Carl wanted to be the bride?"

"We went over this." Meg folded her arms with only the slightest of betraying winces; she wasn't fully healed yet. She'd gone back to the silver nose ring instead of the plain gold stud, though, and a faint breath of her musk-vanilla perfume was a good, hopeful sign. "It's time. His dad's about to walk him down the aisle, Bill has both your themes cue'd up. The rest of you know your places."

"Yes ma'am." Dez towered over her, and looked like Ferdinand the bull being dressed down by a china shop attendant. "Present, accounted for, and ready to roll, ma'am."

"It's Meg, not ma'am, but that's okay." She wasn't fazed in the least. A quick, sipping glance at Tax—he tensed, waiting for some indication she wanted him to respond.

None was apparent.

She examined Boom from top to toe, and sucked in her bottom lip, biting gently. Her eyes seemed to get bigger, if that were possible, and Tax realized the swelling shine was tears.

Oh, fuck. Was she in pain? He should've cornered her before now, gotten a report, something.

But she loosened her arms, reached out, and brushed an invisible speck from Boom's broad shoulder. "You look great," she continued, softly, and sniffed a little. Then, crisply, "Go take your places, gentlemen. I've got it from here."

A chorus of *yes ma'am*s and they trooped out, leaving their buddy in her capable hands. Tax had to strangle the urge to look back, but this was Boom's big day and she was already handling everything with aplomb.

He knew this was important, but he couldn't wait for it to be over.

CARL WALKED down the aisle on his short, round, blond father's arm to some kind of bagpipe music, the older fellow looking proud enough to burst and wearing a cummerbund that matched his son's kilt; Carl's mom had a scarf in the same plaid. The photographer, a punk kid with very good equipment and an air of weary professionalism, pointed and clicked with abandon.

Boom appeared on Meg's arm, strolling slowly as a female vocalist sang about not being afraid because she'd waited for a thousand years. Tax noted the lyrics to look up the song later. The Squad was in the first row along with Sparky, who did indeed look miserably pinched in his suit and dabbed at his eyes once or twice. Also present front-and-center were Carl's mother and sister Colleen—both dwarfed by Boom's buddies—along with Herb, the sister's accountant hubby. Colleen sobbed unashamedly into a big white hankie, Herb patting her shoulder, and her tiny towheaded son discharged the office of ringbearer with the grim seriousness of a deeply disappointed general.

Sam Morigny—who had turned out to be clean after all—was in dress blues, no makeup over her yellowing, fading bruises. She was also smiling broadly, for once.

The happy couple had no shortage of acquaintances close enough to show up for free chow, and Carl's family was apparently huge. The officiant, a greying blonde in a simple white dress with some sort of red flowery tiara, administered the vows in a clear soft contralto, and when she said *you may now kiss your husband,* a cheer went up, damn near shaking the rafters. The Squad gave a good old-fashioned *oorah,* Sparky adding his own in a surprisingly resonant baritone, and Meg wiped furiously at her cheeks, her mouth trembling and her big blue eyes shining.

Tax ached to go up the altar steps and grab her, but he was stuck in his place and then there was ushering everyone into the reception hall to deal with. The couple's first dance was a song Tax had actually heard before, a guy who liked to wear a fedora onstage half-chanting *I'm yours, I'm yours,* and Meg was everywhere—hugging Carl's father, conferring with some of the catering staff, giving a quiet word to the DJ right before Boom swept her into a careful dancing-school one-two-three waltz while Carl and his mom cut a rug in the same dignified fashion in the opposite direction, dabbing with seltzer water at some spilled wine on the very pretty yellow sundress Dez's new missus wore, exchanging quiet words with Sam, staring in wonder as a full, rhinestone-studded mariachi band spilled into the hall—yes, Meg Callahan was *everywhere,* until she wasn't.

Just as Tax got up the nerve to ask her for a dance, she vanished.

Built On Less

THERE WAS A certain point in any successful wedding reception, past which a planner couldn't do anything else. Whoever was going to get drunk was already there, the DJ was in it to win it and outlast every single dancer, the bar was humming, and you just had to consign the entire affair to God because your own job was done.

When that happened, her favorite thing to do was to find a quiet, out-of-the-way corner, and the Starlight Chapel had a great one. It wasn't a corner at all; the spring storms had receded into the mountains again. Really, they couldn't have asked for better weather, which was a blessing because she liked to sit on the roof in the evenings, when everything was settled and the heat of the day draining away.

The Strip glimmered in the distance, Vegas a bright carpet under a cool breeze. Meg settled on a spare chair snagged from the only event hall not in use this evening and turned it to just the right angle, sinking down with a sigh. The staff here knew her, so there was a complimentary bottle of champagne in a bucket of ice, nice and handy. She poured herself a healthy dose in a likewise pilfered flute—so long as she returned everything, there were zero problems—and checked her phone.

The calls from reporters were tapering off. There was a message from Aunt Stace, confirming the lawyer's appointment tomorrow to sign final papers. Meg was still a little stunned—Gerry reaching out from the grave to comfort her, with Rob's quiet help.

Oh, hell. Her eyes burned. Everyone cried at weddings, it was a law. Even the most experienced planner generally misted up.

But Meg was sobbing at the drop of a hat nowadays. Sam suggested therapy, which wasn't a bad idea. How on earth could she begin to explain any of this to a dispassionate professional, though?

Eddie swore he'd taken care of notifying Arthur's girlfriend. Meg had forced herself not to look at her rescuer—tall and broad-shouldered, he cleaned up *extremely* well—during the festivities, achingly aware of proximity, but she was going to have to find some time to thank him for saving her life very soon and that promised to be excruciating.

For a single evening, though, she could sit and have some time to herself.

She worked her feet free of the very nice blue stilettos with a soft groan, and propped her bare heels on a low, conveniently placed HVAC hood. The relief was enough to set off her waterworks again.

She was so busy staring at the sunset's fantastic crimson and purple dregs she didn't notice him until the other chair settled next to hers. Her heart thumped, she nearly swore, and champagne slopped inside the glass.

"Sorry." Arthur hunched slightly, looking sheepish. His hair was slightly mussed and his jacket undone; he set down a small white and green travel cooler. "Didn't mean to scare you."

Oh, Lord. It looked like she was going to get this out of the way sooner rather than later. "It's okay," she managed, free hand pressed to her chest as she set the flute down on gritty roof-surface. "I'm a little jumpy, since . . . everything. You know? Are you sure you should be carrying things?"

"I do know, and don't worry, I'm fine." He settled in the chair, apparently set on making himself comfortable, and leaned over to open the cooler. "Great ceremony, by the way. You pulled out all the stops."

"Well, I had help. It takes a village." Clichés were awful, but how else did you start a conversation like this? "Though I don't have a clue where that mariachi band came from. So . . . what happened? Did your girlfriend show up?" That was the last little loose thread before Meg could truly relax.

Wondering about this mysterious woman was occupying far more of her time than she liked. Better to make the cut quickly, rip the bandage off in one motion. Eddie was a great believer in the just-tear-it-off theory; Meg always worried at the corners of things.

It was never too late to change.

"Huh? Oh, yeah. Yes, she did indeed." Arthur produced a small white carton. "Here."

"What's this?" She accepted it, and popped the lid. "Strawberry shortcake?"

"Your favorite, right? It's the only dessert you won't share." There was a crackle of ice as he dug again, and held up a condensation-frosted bottle. "And Paulucci vinho verde. Carl swears it's what you like."

What the hell? It was the best wine in the world so far as Meg was concerned, but how had he *or* Carl figured that out? "Um. I have champagne, but sure, thank you. Arthur—"

"Hang on a minute." He set the bottle on the hood near her feet;

its cork was half removed, and a pair of actual white wine glasses appeared right next to it in quick succession. "I've got something else."

"We need to talk," she managed. "I never thanked you for—"

"We do," he agreed, calmly, digging in his suit jacket's breast pocket. Out came his phone, and a pair of earbuds. "Here, take one of these. Right or left doesn't matter, I think. Oh, and here's a fork for the shortcake. You haven't eaten since before the ceremony."

She usually didn't, too keyed-up on event days to absorb more than a smoothie. "This is all very nice," Meg said, desperately. "But I really think we ought to—"

"The girl I have my eye on walked my buddy down the aisle. I'm still her assistant, by the way. I'm not giving up the job even if she hires someone else." Arthur tucked a single wireless bud into his right ear, and frowned at his phone. "Still don't know what your favorite color is, though. Eddie couldn't help me there, said he never really thought about it. Typical, you know?"

Did he sound nervous? It boggled the mind.

What. The hell. "Arthur." She stuck the fork into whipped cream; the dessert looked fresh. How, in the name of everything holy, had he managed this? It was . . . well, it was very nearly romantic. "You almost got killed. And it was my fault."

"Put this in." He set his phone in his lap and leaned over, plucking the remaining earbud from her numb fingers and snugging it in her ear. His touch was gentle, and this close she could smell the same harsh soap and a touch of aftershave. "It's the playlist you made. I want you to tell me about it."

"For fuck's sake." There went the damn tears again. Meg grabbed his hand, and the edge of his body heat caressed her shoulder. "Will you listen to me?"

"All day, bunny." His smile was slow, electric, and he drew her hand away, closing it in both of his. "Long as you like. Tell me everything."

God give me strength. It was something Gerry might have said. "You don't have to do this just because Eddie asked you to look after me. That was an . . . an intense situation, and you got hurt and I can't thank you enough but . . ." She stared at him. "Why are you *smiling*? Nothing about this is funny."

"Nope," he agreed, but the grin didn't leave. It looked good on him. He was a little pale, a little gaunt, and very, *very* handsome. "Serious as a heart attack. I like the blue in your hair, by the way. Almost as pretty as your eyes."

I cannot believe this. It was ridiculous; things like this didn't happen to orphans no matter how well they grew up. The Tinkerbell fairy dust was for other people; she was just the person who dispensed it, made sure the caterers were on time and the balloons the right color. "Arthur . . ."

"Shhh," he said. "Listen." He freed a hand long enough to poke at his phone, and a familiar riff was piped right into her left ear. "Too loud?"

She shook her head. "It's Stealers Wheel. A great band—you know they were Scottish? Jeff Healey did a cover of this one, but I like the original. Everyone thinks it's Bob Dylan, but it's not."

It was her turn to sound nervous, apparently.

He nodded, and settled back in the chair, still holding her hand. "Why'd you put it on the list?"

"I . . . I don't know. I wasn't thinking really clearly then." Meg stared at the carton in her lap. "I'm probably not now, either."

"Don't worry, bunny. I'm sober enough for both of us, at least until the antibiotics are done." He squeezed her fingers, gently. "And I don't expect you to make any snap decisions. I'm just letting you know I'm serious. Figure we can take a road trip back to Cali and you can meet my mother."

"Got it all planned, do you?" Meg could feel her eyebrows raising. It was a novel sensation, meeting someone else who took care of contingencies, and she liked it when it wasn't accompanied by agonizing terror. "What if I say no?"

"Are you saying no?"

This isn't fair. But . . . she liked him, a lot. And he'd come into the Corral's basement, as well. He'd saved her, over and over again.

Plenty of marriages were built on less. Meg braced herself.

"A road trip sounds nice. We can play Twenty Questions and get to know each other." She grabbed the fork, spearing a strawberry. "There's a vineyard in Napa I have to look at anyway."

Gerry would have liked this guy. Rob would have been taking notes, intent on investigating him. Ella would want all the details, every single one, exhaustively, with ice cream and a movie musical.

Were they watching? Did they know?

"Good." Arthur's shoulders softened. So did the rest of him, and she realized he'd been holding himself tense and stiff, maybe afraid she *would* say no. "I'm driving. You'll be in charge of the music."

Meg chewed slowly, thinking it over. But really, there was never any doubt.

"Deal," she said, wondering what else she'd put on this particular playlist. "I've still got a couple more events before I can get away, though."

"One step at a time, bunny." He propped his feet next to hers, carefully avoiding the bottle and glasses. "I'm not going anywhere."

Meg sampled another strawberry. The next song came up—Taylor Dayne, a great set of pipes plus longing lyrics about being a lover's shelter—and together, they watched the sunset fade into night.

Safe at last.

finis

Biography

LILITH SAINTCROW lives in Vancouver, Washington, with her children, dogs, cat, a library for wayward texts, and assorted other strays.

Made in United States
Orlando, FL
07 October 2024